# THE FOREST
# OF HANDS
# & TEETH

# THE FOREST OF HANDS & TEETH

## CARRIE RYAN

GOLLANCZ

LONDON

The right of Carrie Ryan to be identified as the
author of this work has been asserted by her in accordance
with the Copyright, Designs and Patents Act 1988.

First published in Great Britain in 2009 by Gollancz
An imprint of the Orion Publishing Group
Orion House, 5 Upper Saint Martin's Lane, London WC2H 9EA
An Hachette UK Company

A CIP catalogue record for this book is available
from the British Library

ISBN 978 0 575 09084 2 (Cased)
ISBN 978 0 575 09085 9 (Export Trade Paperback)

1 3 5 7 9 10 8 6 4 2

Printed in Great Britain by CPI Mackays, Chatham ME5 8TD

The Orion Publishing Group's policy is to use papers that
are natural, renewable and recyclable products and made from
wood grown in sustainable forests. The logging and manufacturing
processes are expected to conform to the environmental
regulations of the country of origin.

www.orionbooks.co.uk

*to jp*
*for giving me the world*

# I

My mother used to tell me about the ocean. She said there was a place where there was nothing but water as far as you could see and that it was always moving, rushing toward you and then away. She once showed me a picture that she said was my great-great-great-grandmother standing in the ocean as a child. It has been years since, and the picture was lost to fire long ago, but I remember it, faded and worn. A little girl surrounded by nothingness.

In my mother's stories, passed down from her many-greats-grandmother, the ocean sounded like the wind through the trees and men used to ride the water. Once, when I was older and our village was suffering through a drought, I asked my mother why, if so much water existed, were there years when our own streams ran almost dry? She told me that the ocean was not for drinking—that the water was filled with salt.

That is when I stopped believing her about the ocean.

How could there be so much salt in the universe and how could God allow so much water to become useless?

But there are times when I stand at the edge of the Forest of Hands and Teeth and look out at the wilderness that stretches on forever and wonder what it would be like if it were all water. I close my eyes and listen to the wind in the trees and imagine a world of nothing but water closing over my head.

It would be a world without the Unconsecrated, a world without the Forest of Hands and Teeth.

Often, my mother stands next to me holding her hand up over her eyes to block the sun and looking out past the fences and into the trees and brush, waiting to see if her husband will come home to her.

She is the only one who believes that he has not turned—that he might come home the same man he was when he left. I gave up on my father months ago and buried the pain of losing him as deeply as possible so that I could continue with my daily life. Now I sometimes fear coming to the edge of the Forest and looking past the fence. I am afraid I will see him there with the others: tattered clothes, sagging skin, the horrible pleading moan and the fingers scraped raw from pulling at the metal fences.

That no one has seen him gives my mother hope. At night she prays to God that he has found some sort of enclave similar to our village. That somewhere in the dense Forest he has found safety. But no one else has any hope. The Sisters tell us that ours is the only village left in the world.

My brother Jed has taken to volunteering extra shifts for the Guardian patrols that monitor the fence line. I know that, like me, he thinks our father is lost to the Unconsecrated and that he hopes to find him during the patrol of the perimeter and kill him before our mother sees what her husband has become.

People in our village have gone mad from seeing their loved ones as Unconsecrated. It was a woman—a mother—horrified at the sight of her son infected during a patrol, who set herself on fire and burned half of our town. That was the fire that destroyed my family's heirlooms when I was a child, that obliterated our only ties to who we were as a people before the Return, though most were so corroded by then that they left only wisps of memories.

Jed and I watch our mother closely now and we never allow her to approach the fence line unaccompanied. At times Jed's wife Beth used to join us on these vigils until she was sent to bed rest with her first child. Now it is just us.

And then one day Beth's brother catches up with me while I am dunking our laundry in the stream that branches off the big river. For as long as I can remember Harold has been a friend of mine, one of the few in the village my age. He trades me a handful of wildflowers for my sopping sheets and we sit and watch the water flow over the rocks as he twists the sheets in complicated patterns to dry them out.

"How is your mother?" he asks me, because he is nothing if not polite.

I duck my head and wash my hands in the water. I know I should be getting back to her, that I have already taken too much time for myself today and that she is probably pacing, waiting for me. Jed is off on a long-term patrol of the perimeter, checking the strength of the fences, and my mother likes to spend her afternoons near the Forest looking for my father. I need to be there to comfort her just in case. To hold her back from the fences if she finds him. "She's still holding out hope," I say.

Harry clucks his tongue in sympathy. We both know there is little hope.

His hands seek out and cover mine under the water. I have known this was coming for months. I have seen the way he looks at me now, how his eyes have changed. How tension has crept into our friendship. We are no longer children and haven't been for years.

"Mary, I . . ." He pauses for a second. "I was hoping that you would go with me to the Harvest Celebration next weekend."

I look down at our hands in the water. I can feel my fingertips wrinkling in the cold and his skin feels soft and fleshy. I consider his offer. The Harvest Celebration is the time in the fall when those of marrying age declare themselves to one another. It is the beginning of the courtship, the time during the short winter days when the couple determines whether they will make a suitable match. Almost always the courtship will end in spring with Brethlaw—the weeklong celebration of wedding vows and christenings. It's very rare that a courtship fails. Marriage in our village is not about love—it is about commitment.

Every year I wonder at the couples pairing up around me. At how my former childhood friends suddenly find partners, bond, prepare for the next step. Pledge themselves to one another and begin their courtships. I always assumed the same would happen to me when my time approached. That because of the sickness that wiped out so many of my peers when I was a child, it would be even more important that those of us of marrying age find a mate. So important that there wouldn't be enough girls to spare for a life with the Sisterhood.

I even hoped that perhaps I would be lucky enough to find more than just a mate, to eventually find love like my mother and father.

And yet, even though I have been one of the few eligible during the past two years, I've been left aside.

I have spent the last weeks dealing with my father's absence beyond the fences. Dealing with my mother's despair and desolation. With my own grief and mourning. Until this moment it hasn't occurred to me that I might be the last one asked to the Harvest Celebration. Or that I might be left unclaimed.

A part of me can't help but think of Harry's younger brother Travis. It is his attention I have been trying to catch throughout the summer, his friendship I have wanted to turn into something more. But he has never responded to my subtle and awkward flirtations.

As if he can read my mind Harry says, "Travis is taking Cassandra," and I can't help but feel hollow and petty and angry that my best friend has accomplished what I could not. That she has Travis's attention and I don't.

I don't know what to say. I think of the way the sun shifts over Travis's face when he smiles and I look into Harry's eyes and try to find the same shifts. They are brothers, after all, born barely a year apart. But there is nothing except the feel of his flesh on mine under the water.

Rather than answer I smile a little, relieved that at last someone has spoken for me while a part of me wonders if our lifelong friendship could ever grow to be something more during the dark winter courtship months.

Harry grins and he drops his head toward me and all I can think about is how I had never wanted Harry to be my first kiss, and then before his lips can land on mine we hear it.

The siren. It is so old and so rarely used these days that it starts out with a creak and a wheeze and then it is full-blown.

Harry's eyes meet mine, his face now a breath away.

"Was there supposed to be a drill today?" I ask.

He shakes his head, his eyes are as wide as mine must be. His father is the head of the Guardians and he would know of any drills. I stand, ready to start sprinting back toward the village. Every inch of my skin tingles, my heart curling into a painful fist. All I can think is, Mother.

Harry grabs my arm and pulls me back. "We should stay here," he says. "It's safer. What if the fences are breached? We need to find a platform." I can see the terror closing in on the irises of his eyes. His fingers dig into my wrist, almost clawing at me but I keep pulling away, pushing at his hands and body until I am free.

I scrabble up the hill toward the center of our village, ignoring the winding path and choosing instead to grab at branches and vines to help me up the steep slope. As I crest the ridge I look back to see Harry still down by the water's edge, his hands up in front of his face as if he cannot bear to see what is happening above. I see his mouth move, as if he's calling out to me, but all I can hear is the siren—the sound of it burns into my ears and echoes around me.

All my life I have trained by that siren. Before I could walk I knew the siren meant death. It meant somehow the fences had been breached and the Unconsecrated were shuffling among us. It meant grab weapons, move to the platforms and pull up the ladders—even if it necessitated leaving the living behind.

Growing up, my mother used to tell me about how in the beginning, when her own great-great-great-grandmother was a child, that siren would wail almost constantly as the village was bombarded with the Unconsecrated. But then the fences had been fortified, the Guardians had formed and time had passed with the Unconsecrated dwindling to the point that I couldn't remember a time in the past few years when that siren had wailed and it had not been a drill. I know that in my life there have been breaches but I also know that I am very good at blocking out the memories that serve me no purpose. I can fear the Unconsecrated well enough without them.

The closer I get to the edge of the village the more slowly I move. Already I can see that the platforms cradled in the trees are full; some have even pulled their ladders up. All around me is chaos. Mothers dragging children, the implements of everyday life scattered in the dirt and grass.

And then the sirens cut out, there is silence and everyone freezes. A baby resumes its wailing, a cloud passes over the sun. And I see a small group of Guardians dragging someone toward the Cathedral.

"Mother," I whisper, everything inside of me falling at once. Because somehow I just know. I know that I shouldn't have lingered at the stream with Harry, that I shouldn't have let him hold my hand while my mother was waiting for me to accompany her to the fence.

My back is ramrod straight as I walk toward the entrance to the Cathedral, an old stone building built well before the Return. Its thick wooden door is open and my neighbors step aside as they see me draw near but no one will look me in the eyes. At the edge of the crowd I hear someone murmur, "She was too close to the fence, she allowed one to grab her."

Inside it feels as though the stone walls drain the heat of

the day and the hairs on my arms stand on end. The light is dim and I see the Sisters surrounding a woman who is keening and moaning but not Unconsecrated. My mother knew to never get too close to the fences—to the Unconsecrated. Too many in our village have been lost that way. It had to have been my father she saw at the edge of the fence line and I close my eyes as the once-dampened pain of losing him slashes through my body again.

I should have been with her.

I want to curl in on myself, to hide from everything that has happened. But instead I go to my mother and kneel, putting my head in her lap and picking up one of her hands and placing it in my hair.

If I could boil my life down to its essence it would be this: my head in my mother's lap, her hands in my hair as we sit in front of the fire and she tells me stories handed down by the women of our family about life before the Return.

Now my mother's hands are sticky and I know they are covered with her blood. I shut my eyes so that I do not have to see it, so that I don't have to know the extent of the damage.

My mother is calmer, her hands instinctively tugging at my hair, letting it free from its bandana. She is rocking and saying something so low under her breath that I cannot understand her.

The Sisters let us be for now. They huddle in the corner with the most elite of the Guardians—the Guild—and I know they are determining my mother's fate. If she was merely scratched they will monitor her even though she couldn't be infected that way. But if she was bitten and thus infected by an Unconsecrated, there are only two options. Kill her now or imprison her until she turns and then push her through the

8

fence. In the end, if my mother is still sane, they will pose the question and let her be the judge.

Die a quick death and save her soul or go exist amongst the Unconsecrated.

We learned in our lessons that originally, right after the Return, those attacked were not allowed this choice. They were put to death almost immediately. That was back before the tide turned, back when it looked as if it would be the living who lost the battle.

But then an Infected—a widow—had come to the Sisters and begged to be allowed to join her husband in the Forest. She pleaded for the right to fulfill her marriage vows to the man she had chosen and loved. The living had already established this place—had made us safe and secure as any could be in the world of the Unconsecrated. And the widow made an excellent point: the only true thing that separates the living from the Unconsecrated is choice, free will. She wanted the choice to be with her husband. The Sisters debated against the Guardians but it is the Sisterhood's word that is always final. They decided that one more Unconsecrated would not endanger our community. And so the widow was escorted to the fence where three Guardians held her until she succumbed to the infection, and then pushed her through the gate just before she died and Returned Unconsecrated.

I can't fathom leaving an old woman to face such a fate. But such is the way of choice, I imagine.

# II

"You will stay with us now," the Sisters tell me, "until your brother arrives." Jed has still not returned from his rotation on the fence line. The Sisters have sent a messenger to bring him back but we won't begin to expect him for at least a day. Our mother will probably be gone by the time he returns and he won't have the chance to talk her out of her choice.

My mother has chosen to join the Unconsecrated. And I am quite sure that my brother will blame me for her choice. He'll ask me why I allowed her to make this decision for herself, why I did not stand in for her and tell the Guardians to kill her.

I am not sure I will know what to tell him.

It is a complicated process, giving a living human over to the Forest of Hands and Teeth. The Guardians found out years ago that the transfer cannot be done too early because a live human cast into the Forest is nothing but food for the

Unconsecrated who will tear at their flesh and eat until there is nothing left.

But at the same time it's too dangerous to have the Infected in the village. The Guardians will not run the risk of having someone Return amongst the living and there is no certainty about when the Infected will die and Return. Everything depends on the severity of the bite: with a small, simple bite, it may take days for the infection to spread and kill, while a gruesome attack can cause someone to Return within heartbeats.

And so the Guardians have devised a complicated system of gates and pulleys that keep the infected in a sort of purgatory between the living and the Unconsecrated. This is where my mother is now and I sit nearby, listening to her pop her jaw and clack her teeth like a cat lusting after a bird as the infection roars through her body. She is too sick to talk now, too ravaged to even understand.

A rope is tied securely around her left ankle and she picks absently at its frayed ends. We are all waiting for the inevitable but know that, judging from her wound, it will take at least a day. The turn doesn't always come quickly to the Infected.

I'm there with her on the safe side of the fence. But I am not alone because they are afraid I'm not to be trusted and that the sight of my mother as one of the Unconsecrated will cause me to do something terrible and stupid like throwing open all the gates and causing a breach. A Guardian—one of my brother's friends—has been posted to keep watch over me and my mother. He will be the one to operate the gates and he will be the one to kill me if I stray too close to her after she turns. It is the agreement that I struck with the Sisters in order to be with my mother at this time: I can be near her, but if I'm bitten then I am to be instantly put to death.

I sit with my knees pulled in tight and my arms wrapped around my shins. I can no longer feel my feet, as if blood refuses to spread so far from my heart.

I am waiting for my mother to die.

Time becomes nothing to me but a march toward my mother's Return. I wish it were a solid thing, something I could grab and shake and stop. Instead, it slips away from me, the day continually unfurling. People from the village come to console me but they don't know what to say. My brother's wife, Beth, has sent word that she prays for us, but the Sisters will not allow her to leave her bed for fear of her losing the child.

I have seen Harry standing a distance away, the harsh afternoon sun glaring from his face. I'm glad he doesn't try to approach me, doesn't try to speak to me about this morning when he held my hand under the water and kept me from my mother.

I wonder if he still thinks that we are going to the Harvest Celebration together next week. It won't be canceled, even in light of my mother's death. As the Sisterhood always reminds us: this is the way after the Return—life must continue. It is our cycle to bear.

As the sun sets Cassandra brings me dinner and sits with me. It is a painfully beautiful sunset and the colors reflect off Cass's pale face and hair. The Guardian has kept his distance this evening, knowing that the end must be getting near. I have been alternating between hope that my mother turns quickly and is soon out of her misery and dread that she will turn too quickly and I will have lost her forever.

After a while I say, "Cass, do you believe in the ocean? Do

you think it's still out there?" I'm watching the way the light plays off the tops of the trees in the Forest, the way everything in sight undulates.

"Remind me what your mother used to say about the ocean again?" she asks. Her voice is soft and kind.

"Nothing but water," I remind her. Cass has always indulged my fancies, has always listened as I repeated the stories of life before the Return that have been passed down by the women of my family. Once, her mother forbade her to speak with me because she said I was filling Cass's head with lies and blasphemy. But our village is too small for such an edict to ever take hold.

"I just don't see how there could ever be that much water in the world, Mary," she tells me. She has told me this many times before. Her eyes are bright as she turns from the sunset to look at me. "I cannot imagine a place out there without Unconsecrated." She knots her eyebrows together. "Because why would we be here rather than there?"

A tear gathers in the corner of her eye, the fading sun glinting off it as it bulges and spills down her cheek, the image of my mother in her pen too much for her to bear. I pull Cass close and let her lay her head in my lap, her face turned away from the Forest, and stroke her hair the way my mother used to stroke my own. We watch as the lanterns come on in the village. My mother used to tell me about the times when she was a child when the Sisters would crank up the old generator on Christmas Eve. It's one of the stories I have never shared with my friend and I think about telling Cass this—about how once a year this little village used to outshine the sky.

But she is snuffling now, her weeping over, and I don't want to fill her head with more fancies tonight.

When she leaves she begs me to come with her. But I cannot. I tell her that I must be here when it happens and she raises her hands to her mouth as if the horror is too much and then she turns and runs back to the safety of the village.

I want to run with her, to escape from where I am and forget this day. But I stay, my fingers trembling and the air thick in my throat. I need to face what my mother becomes. I owe her this much after this morning, after leaving her to wander alone.

I return to staring at the fence. Watching the light slide down the sky, casting crisscrossed shadows on the ground at my feet. I blur my eyes, throwing my surroundings out of focus. The fence does not exist when I do this. As if we are all one world.

▼ ▼ ▼

"Mother?" I whisper at daybreak. There was a new moon last night and I spent the hours in the darkness listening to the rustling of dry leaves behind the fence, my mind imagining the worst possible scenarios. Every creak I heard was the fence breaking, every scratching the Unconsecrated finally finding weakness in the metal.

Now the air is gray and moist and I crawl on my hands and knees closer to the pen that holds my mother. She is there, in the middle on the ground and she is so still that for a moment I think she has died and is about to Return. Bile and terror rise in my throat but are trapped. I feel the need to scream but I am utterly silent with my mouth open and my teeth bared.

My legs tangle in my skirts and I claw at the ground and am almost to the fence when I hear the Guardian behind me. I look back at him, pleading with him. "She is still alive," I tell him, because I just know that she is. He looks over his shoulder into the mist and, seeing that we are alone, he nods as if giving me permission and I lace my fingers around the thin rusted metal of the fence, feeling its sharp cold edges bite into my palms.

"The ocean," my mother murmurs. Sharp as a crack she whips her head around and I see that her eyes are wide and unfocused but lucid. She crawls toward me until our hands are linked together through the fence.

"The ocean, Mary, the ocean!" She is speaking so urgently now, her mouth moving rapidly. I am afraid that the Guardian will think she is crazy and has turned and that he will kill me but I can't pull my hands back because my mother's grip is too tight.

"So beautiful, the ocean." She repeats the words over and over again, her eyes becoming bright with unshed tears. "The water, the waves, the sand, the salt!" She is shaking the fence now and it causes undulations to ripple outward to either side, the metal swaying back and forth. I am amazed that she has this strength; she has been dying for so many hours.

"It consumes me," she says, her voice only a whisper. She reaches one finger through the wire and strokes my wrist. "My little girl," she tells me. "Do not forget my little girl." Tears slip out of her eyes and I hear the Guardian shout behind me and then my mother slumps to the ground, her fingers slipping away from mine.

▼    ▼    ▼

In the moment between my mother's death and her Return, I stop believing in God.

▼    ▼    ▼

The Guardian quickly grabs the end of the rope tied to my mother's left ankle as I scoot away from the fence. It is anchored over a system of pulleys lashed to branches high above and he heaves against it, the other end of the rope dragging my mother to the edge of her pen. The Guardian pulls a lever, a gate rises and her lifeless body slides into the Forest of Hands and Teeth. He cuts the rope, reverses the lever and the gates grind shut. For a heartbeat the world is silent around us, the sound of our own breathing muffled by the mist.

His duty complete, my mother's body given fully over to the Unconsecrated, the Guardian places a hand on my shoulder. Whether it is to comfort me or to hold me back does not matter. I imagine that I can feel his pulse through his fingertips. We are both so alive in that moment surrounded by so much death.

I can't decide if I want to watch my mother Return. If I can bear to see it. But I can't help but wonder what that moment is like. Is there a spark or an instant where she will remember me? Where she will remember her old life from before?

My mother used to tell me stories about how, long before the Return, the living used to wonder what happened after death. She said that whole religions were born and evolved around this one simple uncertainty.

Now that we know what happens after death, a new question has risen up to take the place of the old: why?

Suddenly, regret screams through me. I wonder if I should have dressed her in something different. If I should have put her in warmer clothes or better shoes. If I should have pinned a note to the inside of her dress telling her that I love her. I wonder how long it will take for her to find my father and if she will recognize him. An image of the two of them holding hands at the fence line flits across my mind.

She is on her feet before I even know what's happening. She stares at me and for a moment all I can think is Mother and then she opens her mouth and my world shatters with her screams that fall off into moans as her vocal cords give way.

I cannot bear it and I start to move toward her, struggling under the weight of the Guardian's hand, but then I hear my name being called out in warning.

It is Jed. I didn't hear him approach but I can smell him now, the scent of woods and work and the smoke from our house. I don't bother to look at him, I just know that he is behind me and I sag back against him. He's home from his rotation on the fence line just in time to see our mother die and Return.

Later, the Guardian in him will question me and chastise me. Because I allowed my mother to make this choice and because I failed both him and her by dallying near the stream. Because I was too selfish to understand that my mother would go to the Forest without me and because I was not there to stop her.

But for now he is my brother and both our parents are gone and we are all we have left.

# III

The first thing the Sisters do when Jed walks me back to the Cathedral is strip off my clothes and half-drown me in the sacred well. I wait to see if the water will burn off my flesh now that I no longer believe in God but nothing happens as the Sisters chant prayers and scrub my body. Through the water and past the arms of the Sisters, I see Jed being escorted from the Cathedral.

They pull me out of the holy water, my eyes stinging and my long hair like a spiderweb over my face so that I sputter and cough. "You will stay here within the Cathedral walls," the Sisters tell me. "We cannot have you going back to the fence line."

I understand this and I know that no amount of protesting will change their minds. But still, it irritates me that they think I would be so stupid as to go after my mother.

She no longer exists.

A blanket finds its way to my shoulders and I am led along

a hallway I never noticed before, down a set of stairs and into a room with stone walls, a stone floor, a cot and a window that looks out past the graveyard toward the Forest. I want to laugh; if they are so afraid of my doing something drastic after facing my mother's death why do they place me in a room that overlooks the site where she turned? I can clearly see the series of gates through which she was dragged and I can even see a few Unconsecrated pressing against the fence line. Their moans slip lightly through the open window.

"Why can't I go home?" I ask as they close the door behind me.

The oldest, Sister Tabitha, pauses on the threshold. "It is better that you stay here."

"But what about my brother?" I cross my arms over my chest, cupping my elbows in my hands and folding in on myself.

She doesn't answer. Then the door closes and I can hear the lock slide into place. I am alone with the sound of the Unconsecrated.

For a while I watch the sun travel across the sky. I notice that in the heat of the day the Unconsecrated abandon their post at the fence and wander back into the woods, shuffling away to down themselves in a sort of eternal hibernation that is only broken when they sense human flesh nearby.

I watch the fences for a glimpse of my mother that never comes.

▼   ▼   ▼

There is no moon that night and I watch as stars fill the dark emptiness. Clouds creep in heavy and low so that there is nothing more to see outside and so I move to my cot and sit down, not bothering to light the candle placed on a small table by the door.

I want to sleep, I want dreams to pull me from this world and make me forget. To stop the memories from swirling around me. To put an end to this ache that consumes me.

A thin sliver of light infiltrates the bottom sill of the wooden door and I can just see the walls surrounding me. A cricket chirrups somewhere. I wrap the blanket around my shoulders and over my head and pull my knees up to my chest and silently heave for my mother.

▼   ▼   ▼

The next day my eyes burn from lack of sleep. I trace the sun as it creeps across my floor, paying attention to nothing else but the light slipping slowly away from me. Someone brings in food and a jug of water but I don't bother with either. Later, Sister Tabitha comes and says she is there to check on me but I know she's there to judge my mental state. To see if I have broken under the weight of my parents' deaths. The day continues like this: food, Sister Tabitha, water, Sister Tabitha and so on and so on.

A small part of me craves to rebel, to break free of this room. To run and grieve with my brother. But I am too exhausted, my body unwilling to move. Here I'm warm and fed and alone and don't have to answer anyone's accusing questions or stares. I don't have to explain why my mother was alone, why I was not with her.

Instead, I can spend the between time remembering. I lie on the floor with my eyes closed and body limp, trying to feel my mother's hands in my hair as I repeat the stories she used to tell me over and over again in my mind. I refuse to forget any details and I am terrified that I already have. I go over each story again—seemingly impossible stories about oceans and buildings that soared into the heavens and men who touched the moon. I want them to be ingrained in my head, to become a part of me that I cannot lose as I have lost my parents.

My brother doesn't visit and I hear no news of him from the Sisters. I wonder if he thinks of me. I want to be angry at him, to revel in any emotion other than shock and pain, but I understand that this is the way he grieves.

And finally, after a week has passed, Sister Tabitha comes to me and hands me a black tunic to change into and says that I am free to go and that I should thank God for the strength He has given me to move forward with my life.

I nod, unwilling to tell her now that God does not enter into it, and walk slowly back to my family's house where just weeks before we lived together happy and safe. My brother's house now that my mother has passed away and he, as the only son, has inherited. I can't help but ache inside as I approach, knowing my mother is not there. Will never be there. I think about all of the memories trapped in the rough log walls, all of the warmth and laughter and dreams.

I feel as if I can almost see these things leaking out, slipping away into the sunlight. As if the house is cleansing itself of our history. Forgetting my mother and her stories and our childhood. Without thinking, I place a hand against the wall to the right of the door. As with every building in our village there is a line of Scripture there, carved into the wood by the Sisterhood. It is our habit and duty to press a hand against these words every time we cross a threshold, to remind us of God and His words.

I wait for them to calm me, to infuse me with light and grace. But it does not come, does not fill the hollow ache inside me. I wonder if I will ever feel whole again now that I no longer believe in God.

The wood under my fingertips is smooth from generations of villagers pressing their hands in this one spot. This one spot my mother will never touch again.

As if he knew I would be coming today my brother opens the door, causing me to yank my hand from the Scripture verse. Seeing him fills me with memories and fresh pain. He doesn't allow me inside and I wonder if Beth can overhear us talking.

I am surprised at my skittishness around my own brother. Once, he and I were friends and shared everything. But he was always my father's son and I my mother's daughter. Losing our father to the Unconsecrated was too much for him and I have watched him harden over the past months. He has thrown himself into his role as Guardian, rapidly rising several notches in their ranks. I twist my fingers together in front of me as I search his face for the tenderness I once knew but all I find is sharp edges.

"Why did you let her go?" he asks me. He holds a hand over his eyes to block out the sun coming over my shoulder, and his stance reminds me of the way our mother would stand and scan the Forest looking for our father.

I have expected this question and yet I still don't know what he wants to hear. "It was her choice," I tell him.

He spits on the ground near my feet and some of the spit catches in the short black hairs on his chin. "It was not her choice." His voice is strained and even and I know that he would prefer to be yelling but does not want to cause a scene in the village. "She was insane, she was sick."

I can feel his rage and pain wash over me and I want to take his emotions onto myself, to help him carry this burden. But my own feelings are too much, they swirl and overwhelm me such that I am helpless to comfort my brother.

"I couldn't kill her, Jed. I couldn't let them do that." I resist the urge to look down at my hands as I speak.

"What do you think throwing her to the Unconsecrated was, Mary?" He reaches out and grabs my shoulder so hard that his fingers dig in around the bone. "Don't you realize that I will have to kill her now? When I'm out on patrol, what do you think will happen if I see her? Do you think I can let her go on"—he waves his hand past me, past the fields and toward the fence line—"like that? That is not life. That is not natural. It is sick and horrid and evil and I can't believe you would do this to me. That you would make me be the one to kill our mother because you weren't strong enough to do it."

I see now that he wanted me to be the one to kill her so that he wouldn't have to make his own choice.

"I'm sorry, Jed," I say, because I don't know how else to make it right between us. He is a Guardian, one of the few whose only duty is to protect the village, to mend the fence line, to kill the Infected. I don't know how to force him to see that it was her choice and not mine. That in making that choice she must have known that it could come to her own son having to kill her later. I don't know how to make him understand that sometimes love and devotion can overpower a person to the point where she wants to join her spouse in the Forest. Even if it means throwing everything else in life away.

I move forward to give him a hug but he keeps his arm stiff, his hand still on my shoulder so that I cannot come any closer.

"I am the man of the house now, Mary," he tells me.

I try a smile, to remind him that he will always be my brother. "That doesn't mean you can't hug your own sister," I tell him.

He doesn't laugh as I hoped. "I hear you are to join the Sisterhood," he says. His words hit me like a slap. I don't know what I was expecting—anger, pain, regret, but not for him to turn me away. Not for him to cast me out and leave me to the Sisters before I've even had a chance to speak with him. To plead my case. This is why he didn't come to me at the Cathedral—in his mind I already belonged to them, I was already a Sister.

A part of me always knew that it would come to this, that this scene was inevitable in our lives. Walking toward the house today I knew somehow that I would not even be allowed inside to gather my mother's meager belongings. Jed would take it all.

"No one has spoken for you, Mary. No one has asked for you. No one will be courting you this winter." His fingers still bite into my arm.

"But Harry," I say, gesturing uselessly over my shoulder toward the hill that hides the stream where only a week ago Harry asked me to the Harvest Celebration. I struggle to remember if I ever answered him.

Jed begins to shake his head even before I can sort through the confused roar in my mind. I open my mouth but he cuts me off.

"He did not ask for you, Mary."

I stare at him, feeling as if everything that I ever was is draining out of my body and leaving me. In my village an unmarried woman has three choices. She may live with her family; a man may speak for her, court her through the winter and marry her in the spring ceremonies; or she may join the Sisterhood. Our village has been isolated since soon after the Return and while we have grown strong and populous over the years, it is still imperative that every healthy young man and woman wed and breed if possible.

The sickness that cut through my generation only made new children more important. And with so few of us of marrying age the past few seasons it is what I have grown up expecting. That one day this fall someone like Harry would ask for me. Or that one of the other boys my age would take an interest. I have hoped that one day I could claim such a love for a man as my mother, who was willing to go into the Forest of Hands and Teeth after her Unconsecrated husband.

Of course, Jed could choose to take me in and wait to see if someone speaks for me next year, give the rest of the families in town some time to get over the fact that both of my parents are now Unconsecrated. That our family has been touched by unending death. But it's clear that this is a choice he is unwilling to make.

"There is still time," I say. I can hear the hint of desperation in my voice, my need for him to take me in now that we are all that is left.

"You belong with the Sisters," he says, his voice devoid of emotion. "Good luck." The pressure of his fingers on my arms pushes me away from the entrance to his home. Looking into his eyes, I think he actually does wish me luck.

"And Beth?" I ask, seeking any excuse to remain with my brother for a moment longer. Hoping to rekindle the friendship we shared just a few weeks ago, have shared our entire lives.

I watch as muscles ripple along his jaw, as his hand clenches on the doorframe. "She lost the child," he says. He steps back into the house, the darkness inside cloaking his expression. "It was a boy," he adds as he swings the door shut.

I step forward, ready to push my way in. But then I hear the lock click and I pause, my hand reaching at the air. I want to grab him and hold him and mourn with him. I would have been an aunt, I think as I let my hand press against the warmth of the wooden door. I want to yell at Jed that I hurt too and that I am sorry and that I need him.

But then I realize that he has his new family to mourn with. That somehow I'm no longer enough to comfort him. I'm only a reminder of our parents' deaths. I flex my fingers against the door, my nails digging into the wood, realizing just how fully alone I am.

Struggling to keep my throat from burning, I let my hand drop and turn my back on the only home I have ever known. I look out at the familiar houses across the way. The vibrant summer gardens crumbling into dirt patches where three little girls hold hands and spin in circles, chanting out a rhyme. I know I should return to the Cathedral but I also know that once I join the Sisters my life will revolve around studying the Scripture and I will have little time for my own whims and desires. And so instead, I walk away from the cluster of small houses and skirt the edges of the fields, now harvested and prepared for winter, and I begin to climb the hill that hovers at the sunrise edge of our village.

As a child growing up, I learned in my lessons from the Sisters that just before the Return They—who They were is long forgotten—knew what was coming. They knew that something had gone horribly wrong and that it was only a matter of time before the Unconsecrated swarmed every-where.

They still thought They could contain it. And so, even as the Unconsecrated infected the living and the pressure of the Return began to build, They were busy constructing fences. Infinitely long fences. Whether the fences were to keep the Unconsecrated out or the living in we no longer know. But the end result was our village, an enclave of hundreds of sur-vivors in the middle of a vast Forest of Unconsecrated.

There are various theories as to how our village came into existence in the middle of this Forest. The Cathedral and some of the other buildings clearly predate the Return and some people suggest that They carved this place out as a sanc-tuary. Others claim that we are a chosen people and that our ancestors were the best of their time and were sent here to survive. Who we are and why we are here has been lost to his-tory, lost because our ancestors were too busy trying to sur-vive to remember and pass on what they knew. What little remnants we once had—like my mother's picture of my many-greats-grandmother standing in the ocean—were de-stroyed in the fire when I was a child.

We know of nothing beyond our village except the Forest, and nothing beyond the Forest at all.

But at least They were smart enough to leave a stockpile of fencing material behind after They finished creating our little world. And so, after the village established itself, it began to beat back the Forest and expand. Little by little my ancestors hacked away pieces of the Forest and claimed it as their own, pushing the fence line until there was nothing left to build with.

This hill was part of the last big push, the last big enclosure.

Our ancestors felt it was important to have the high ground so that we could keep watch over the Forest. For a while there was a lookout tower at the top of the hill but now it has fallen into disrepair and is never used. But that doesn't stop me from climbing it so that for one last time before I go to the Sisters, I am at the highest point in our gated existence.

I look out at the world below. To my right the fields stretch into the distance, dotted here and there with cows and sheep that have been turned out from the barns clustered at the farthest edge of the fence line. It doesn't matter if they stray toward the Forest—like all animals except humans, they cannot be infected by the Unconsecrated.

To my left is the village itself. From up here the houses are even smaller, the Cathedral a hulking shape that dominates the sunset boundary, its graveyard all that stands between the large stone building and the fences lining the Forest. From here I can see the way the Cathedral has grown awkwardly, wings sprouting off the central sanctuary at strange angles.

At the foot of the hill, on the side opposite the village, is a gate that leads to a path stretching deep into the Forest, a scar that runs through the trees. Though that path, and the mirror path that leads from the Cathedral side of the village, are also lined with fences, they are both forbidden by the Sisters and Guardians.

The paths are useless strips of land covered in brambles, bushes and weeds. The gates blocking them have remained shut my entire life.

No one remembers where the paths go. Some say they are there as escape routes, others say they are there so that we can travel deep into the Forest for wood. We only know that one points to the rising sun and the other to the setting sun. I am sure our ancestors knew where the paths led, but, just like almost everything else about the world before the Return, that knowledge has been lost.

We are our own memory-keepers and we have failed ourselves. It is like that game we played in school as children. Sitting in a circle, one student whispers a phrase into another student's ear and the phrase is passed around until the last student in the circle repeats what she hears, only to find out it is nothing like what it is supposed to be.

That is our life now.

# IV

I t is late afternoon by the time I climb down from the tower and walk back to the Cathedral. The Sisters have been expecting me.

"So you have chosen to become one of us?" the eldest, Sister Tabitha, asks me. She stands facing me in front of the altar, flanked by two middle-aged Sisters.

"I have no other choices," I tell her, because it is the truth.

She inhales sharply and I can see her lips tighten into a single line. She turns abruptly and walks through a door hidden behind a curtain near the pulpit. "Follow," she tells, not asks me, and I do, the other two Sisters trailing behind us.

We wind along a hallway deeper into the Cathedral than I have ever been until we reach a large wooden door banded with metal. Sister Tabitha tugs the door open, picks up a candle from a table inside and leads us down a steep winding stone stairway. The air becomes colder, damper, and when we reach the bottom we are in a cavernous room that contains row upon row of empty shelves.

But we don't stop. We cross the room and pause in a shadowy corner. I tell myself that I have nothing to fear in this strange place. That the Sisterhood has always protected the people of the village. And yet I cannot stop the chill that overtakes my body and seeps into my bones.

Sister Tabitha pulls aside a curtain, revealing a locked door. She pulls a key from a chain around her neck, opens the door and urges me forward. I follow her down another hallway—this one more like a tunnel, with stone walls and a dirt floor and a ceiling held up by thick wooden beams. More racks line the walls and every now and then I see a dusty bottle cradled in the shelves.

"Did you know that long, long ago, centuries before the Return, this building used to belong to a plantation? Used to house a winery?" Sister Tabitha asks as we walk, our steps echoing around us. The flame of her candle flickers and she does not bother to wait for an answer because she knows we never learned about this in school.

"What is now the Forest just outside our village used to be fields of grapes. For as far as the eye can see. Guardians tell us that they still encounter remnants of the vineyard, that they still find grapevines smothering the fences."

The tunnel curves to the left a bit. Every now and again we pass a door embedded in the stone. The wood is warped and scarred, with thick bolts driven into the walls. I pause by one, wanting to ask what lies beyond it, but I am thrust forward by the Sisters trailing behind me. I wonder why this history—the vineyard and this tunnel—has been kept a secret and why Sister Tabitha has chosen this moment to tell me.

"They used to store the wine for fermentation under our Cathedral, but this is not where it was made," Sister Tabitha continues. We finally reach a dead end and a set of wooden steps forced into the dirt and leading upward, and Sister Tabitha stops, turns toward me. I look behind her at a wooden door set in the ceiling at the top of the stairs.

"The wine was made elsewhere," she says, commanding my focus back on her. "They had to stomp on the grapes, which is messy and attracts bugs, and so they had a separate well house for that. They used this tunnel to transport and store their reserves. Eventually, when the soil failed, the winery was abandoned. The old wooden well house fell apart and collapsed. But the winery itself, our Cathedral, remained standing because it was made of stone."

Sister Tabitha climbs the stairs slowly, her body hunching as she nears the door in the ceiling. She uses three keys to unlock it and then comes back down, leaving it closed. "This is where the well house once stood," she tells me, pushing me up the steps so that I almost trip. I crouch, my back against the rough wood door above me, its metal bands digging into my skin. I have known the Sisters to be stern before, doling out physical punishment when necessary during our lessons. But I've never known them like this, rough and distant and frightening.

"Open it, Mary," Sister Tabitha says. Her voice is terrifying with its low pitch and ominous tone and I realize that I have no other choice. I heave my body against the heavy wood until the door flips open, swinging wide and falling to the ground outside with a thump that rumbles around us.

From behind I feel Sister Tabitha pushing against my legs so that I will lose my balance unless I climb through the opening, out of our little tunnel. I straighten and stretch, seeming to rise out of the ground, and then I feel a shove against my back. Suddenly I'm on my hands and knees in the fresh air, pine needles digging into my palms. I hear birds, I feel dry grass under my bare toes and I'm disoriented—confused—until the first moan begins. The sound falls and swells inside me—too close, too loud, too dangerously near.

Instinctively I jump up and then crouch, my hands out in front of me. Ready to defend myself. I spin left and right, my surroundings passing in a blur. Frantically I turn back toward the hole I climbed out of, back to the safety of the underground tunnel, but Sister Tabitha is blocking my way.

"What are you doing to me?" I shout. My voice is harsh and scratchy with fear, my words almost choking me as I gulp for air. I grope along the ground, searching with my fingers for a stick or a weapon or anything as the moans get louder, and then I hear a familiar clank. It is the sound of the Unconsecrated pulling at the fence.

Looking around, I realize that I have come up in a small clearing far away from the village that is protected by a ring of fence twice as tall as I am. The Unconsecrated are beginning to swarm around me. Two steps in any direction and they could reach me through the metal links. Blood hammers through my body, panic clouding my vision, making my hands shake and pound with the rhythm of my heart.

I try to look everywhere at once. And then Sister Tabitha stretches out her hand, a finger slipping out of her black tunic, to point past me toward the trees. I had not seen the gate but it is there—the same complicated set of gates that is used in the village when someone is damned into the Forest. All Sister Tabitha has to do is pull a rope that lies on the ground by her hand. The gate will open, she and the other Sisters will slip back down into their secret passage and I will be alone to face the Unconsecrated.

"What are you doing?" I try to scream but my voice is too weak, too breathy. "Why are you doing this to me?" I hiccup as I try to draw in air. The Unconsecrated are so close. Everywhere I turn they are desperate for me, writhing against the fence.

Tears pour from my eyes, drip from my chin. "Please," I whisper, slipping back to my hands and knees, crawling toward Sister Tabitha, grasping at her black tunic. "Please don't leave me here." I am like a child begging her mother.

"There is always a choice, Mary," Sister Tabitha says to me, standing with her feet braced against the steps, the lower half of her body still concealed belowground. "It is what makes us human, what separates us from them."

I look into her face, try to find a way to make this end. Her cheeks are red from the crisp air and her own fervor. There are lines at the corners of her eyes like relics, as if she once knew how to smile long ago.

My shoulders slump. I am kneeling before Sister Tabitha. I drop my head to my chest, despondent. There is nothing I can do.

She places both her hands on my head. "It is important for you to know this, Mary," she tells me. "You must understand the importance of this choice you are making to become one of us. The Sisterhood is not something to be entered into lightly."

I keep my eyes on the ground, staring at the dully colored fall leaves as I nod. My body shakes and I cannot control my jerking muscles. The Unconsecrated claw desperately at the fence all around me. They can smell me here.

"I must hear you say it, Mary." Her hands slip through my hair and all I can think about is my mother and the choice she made.

"I choose to join the Sisterhood," I tell her, desperate to get out of the clearing.

"Good," Sister Tabitha says as she slides her hands from my head to a spot under my chin. Her grip is firm and almost painful. She tugs at me so that I am looking into her eyes, which are the dark gray green of the sky during a summer thunderstorm. "The next and only time you open your mouth to speak," she says to me, "will be to praise our Lord."

It takes a moment for me to understand her words—that I am safe—and then I frantically nod, the sound of the Unconsecrated crawling under my skin. She steps aside and helps me back down the stairs. Mute, I follow her down the tunnel to the cavernous room, and as we climb the stairs back up into the Cathedral I wonder at the coldness I have seen in Sister Tabitha's eyes. How her gaze seemed to sear into my soul, the chill even now seeping through me where I had only ever known the warmth of the Sisterhood.

We return to the Sanctuary of the Cathedral and the Sisters lead me down the hallway to the same room I occupied only this morning, the room with the view of the Forest and the Unconsecrated. There is now a desk under the window and a wardrobe in the corner with two black tunics hanging inside. A fire has been lit in the small stone hearth to keep the chill of impending winter away, but I cannot feel its warmth.

Before leaving, Sister Tabitha thrusts the Scripture into my hands. "When you have read it five times, you may begin to earn your privileges," she says.

And then I am left alone again to contemplate my choices.

▼   ▼   ▼

The Scripture is a book more than a hand's width thick, its binding worn and cracked and its pages see-through thin with crowded letters. I read at the table under the window when there is sun and when there is no sun I stare into the fire and remember my mother. I try to reconcile what I read in the Scripture with what I know about our life here and finally realize that there is no answer.

My world feels so small now, the four walls of my room the only place I am allowed unsupervised. I miss standing on the hill, wind slipping past me, and staring at the horizon wondering what, if anything, is past the Forest. Some nights, as sleep pushes in around me, my mind wanders along the fence line, to the gate guarding the forbidden path. But even in my dreams I do not step through it.

Weeks pass. As winter settles around us and the days get shorter I spend less time reading and more time thinking. I stare out my window at the stars at night and wonder if the Unconsecrated feel the change in temperature. I wonder if my mother is cold in the Forest.

▼　▼　▼

Midwinter my studies are interrupted one snowy afternoon when shouts and screams echo down the hallway outside my door. I run to the window and look out, wondering if the Unconsecrated have finally breached the fences and are swarming the village. But everything in my line of sight is calm and the siren is silent. I go to the door and press my ear against it, afraid. If something has gone wrong inside the building I might be safer in my little room. I remember then that the Cathedral is also our hospital, the Sisters the keepers of the knowledge of healing.

The shouts turn into urgent voices, muffled so that I can't hear individual words. One man continues to scream, as if in pain, and I turn my back against the door and slide down until I am sitting on the floor.

I put my hands against my ears but I can still hear the pain, the voices and the fear. And then there is silence so heavy that I almost drown in it.

This night I don't sleep but instead lie under the covers listening to the Forest creaking and moaning, to the snow settling on our village and to the Sisters shuffling around, tending to their newest patient.

I think about how we are so focused on the peril presented by the Forest that we forget that the rest of life can be just as dangerous. I think about how fragile we are here—like fish in a glass bowl with darkness pressing in on every side.

# V

The next day I am called to tend to the patient, who has been silent all night.

"We have many duties, Mary," Sister Tabitha says to me as she leads me from my room toward the main Sanctuary and then down a hallway, up a set of narrow stairs and down another long hallway with wooden doors off either side.

"Just as you have learned to dedicate your life to the Lord, you will now learn how to care for His children. But remember," she says, turning around and taking my chin in her cold fingers, "you still have your vow of silence. You have yet to earn your privileges."

I nod. I do not tell her that I finished reading through the Scripture for the fifth time a week ago. I have been too busy enjoying my solitude.

She opens the door and I hear a groan that reminds me of the Unconsecrated. For a moment I'm frozen in the hallway, reliving the moment when my mother turned and her screams gave way to anonymous moans.

Sunlight streams in through a window opposite the doorway and reflects off the wood-paneled walls, a contrast to the dark cramped hall. Everything is brighter here than in my room, lighter. A small bed with white sheets and a slightly tattered quilt is pushed against the wall in the far corner and a young man thrashes, tearing at the bedding. "Water," he begs, and Sister Tabitha turns to me and orders me to go outside and gather some clean snow in a bowl for him to suck on while she fetches new bandages.

When I return my hands are red and raw from gathering the snow. I slowly approach the bed. The patient is calm now, and when he hears my shoes against the wooden floor he turns and I see who it is.

"Travis," I gasp. My voice feels raw in my throat and I look around quickly to make sure that Sister Tabitha has not heard me speak. I have no doubt that she would send me into the Forest if she felt the need.

"Mary," he whispers. "Oh, Mary." He reaches out and grabs my hand and brings it toward his cheek such that I am pulled forward and I end up stumbling and falling onto my knees next to the bed. Some of the snow drifts out of the bowl and falls around the floor but his eyes are closed and he doesn't see the flakes melt into the scarred floorboards.

His cheek burns and I slide my hand up to his forehead, the way my mother used to do when Jed and I were sick as children. I think of all the times I have brushed against Travis accidentally while playing games in the fields or walking to our lessons, and yet somehow his skin feels different now. More grown-up. More like a man and less like a boy.

I pinch some snow out of my bowl and hold my hand in front of his mouth. His tongue slips along my fingers and I feel as if my skin is thawing for the first time in my life.

Suddenly, he doesn't feel like my friend but like something more and I have to force myself to remember that he is not mine to desire. He sighs and I see his body relax back into the mattress.

"Please, Mary, more," he asks, his eyes still closed. I nod and continue to feed him snow, his breath melting into my fingers, his body so hot and dehydrated and thirsty.

"It hurts, Mary," he whispers. "My God, it hurts so terrible."

The urge to comfort him with words wells up in me and I want to know what has happened to him so badly, but I'm afraid to ask and risk Sister Tabitha hearing me speak and sending me away from him, never letting me see him again. I press my forehead against his cheek, my cool skin against his, and we are like that when the door opens behind us and Sister Tabitha strides in, her face tightening into a scowl.

There is silence and then Travis says, "Thank you for the prayer, Mary. It's made me feel better," and this causes Sister Tabitha's frown to soften a bit.

"Prayer is always the best medicine," she says and then she comes to the bed and with a tenderness I never thought possible she pulls the sheet down from Travis's body in order to examine his wounds.

Blood has stained the strips of cloth tied around his left thigh but it's old and brown, which must be a good sign. Sister Tabitha has me hold his hands as she peels back the bandages and I steel myself to see what is underneath.

I have seen such horror and such grotesqueness that it never occurred to me that I would feel light-headed and weak-kneed when I saw Travis's injury. One couldn't grow up surrounded by the Forest and not see the most dreadful sights—the Unconsecrated with their hollow skin ripped and gaping from the wounds that caused the infection, their fingers cracked and broken from clawing at the fences, limbs attached by nothing more than gristle.

Travis grips my hands tightly, as if to comfort me rather than take comfort for himself. Midway down his thigh a garish red gash still oozes watery-looking blood. It is held together with rows of large, lopsided stitches. Sister Tabitha places her hands on each side of the gash and presses, causing Travis to whimper, his eyes rolling back in his head.

"There is no infection yet," she says to me without looking up. "Which gives me hope." She winds fresh strips of cloth back over the raw flesh. "But the break was bad and I do not know if we set it correctly so we will have to wait and see. One thing I do know"—she lifts the sheet back up to his chin and tucks it around him tightly—"is that Travis will be in this bed for the rest of winter at least and lucky to walk again. It is in God's hands now."

"Can . . ." Travis hesitates, swallows, his face pale with sweat standing out on his forehead. "Can Mary come pray for me?" he asks.

Sister Tabitha looks long and hard at Travis and then at me, still holding his hands in mine. She nods once, a sharp movement that is over in a heartbeat. "She may. But for now she must return to her studies. And you should know, Travis, that she is not allowed to speak except in prayer, so please do not tempt her to do more than that."

I look down at the way Travis's fingers curl around my own. I think back to the day months ago when his brother Harry and I held hands under the water and he asked me to the Harvest Celebration that now is long past. I remember how puffy and wrong Harry's skin looked then and how tough and calloused Travis's feels against my own soft skin.

I turn Travis's hand over and look at the lines that crisscross his flesh and I wonder at all I have lost since then.

▼  ▼  ▼

I find myself in Travis's room every morning. I help Sister Tabitha clean his wound, which is still raw and red and has the Sisters concerned. They frown and murmur God's words when they pass by. Everyone is praying for his recovery. I want to know what happened to him but I keep silent as commanded. All I need to understand is that there was a severe break in the bone that punctured the skin and it's not healing the way it should.

More often than not Travis is buried in blankets when I see him, half delirious with heat and fever. Most of the time he doesn't recognize me. Other times he grabs at me and begs for water and to make it stop.

When I can, I kneel by his bed and I take his hands and fold them in mine and I lean close to his ear and whisper to him. I know I should be praying and that the Sisters believe fervently that prayer is the only thing that will save him, but I cannot do it.

I cannot entrust my friend's life to something I am so unsure of and that I am still so angry with for taking my family and leaving me here in this world.

And so instead I tell him of the things I do believe in, the things I know to be true only because of faith. I tell him the stories my mother used to tell me about life before the Return.

I tell him about the ocean.

I know that I'm in love with Travis at these moments. I can feel the way that I ache to make him whole again. How if I could drain out my own life and share it with him to make him better I would not hesitate to do so. And I don't understand how, day after day, I can come into this room and lean my face so close to his that my lips brush his cheeks and ears, and he hasn't gotten better.

When I'm not with Travis but alone in my own room I can't forget that day down by the stream, the day my mother became infected. I remember how Harry told me that Travis had chosen my best friend Cass and not me. Even though Cass hasn't been to the Cathedral to sit with Travis the way I have. Even though she doesn't deserve him the way I do, I remember that Travis is already pledged to another. That it is Cass he would be courting now if not for his broken leg. And knowing this fills me with rage and longing that twine so deeply inside me that I cannot distinguish the two and all I know is that I desire.

This is how I know I can never be a true servant of God, why I will never be able to give myself over to the Sisters. Because I love Travis too much to set him aside.

# VI

I have been telling Travis about the ocean. He has fallen into a fevered sleep, his lips slack, but I continue to whisper into his dreams, trying to compel him to get well. As usual I kneel next to his bed, one hand smoothing back the hair from his forehead, and I am like this when the door opens behind me. Before I see who it is I say a quick "Amen" and pull myself to my feet, my cheeks flushed and my breath coming in soft little pants.

My eyes grow wide as I see who the visitors are: Cass and Harry followed by Sister Tabitha.

"Mary!" Cass calls out. She runs to me and throws her arms around me and I do the same to her, burying my face in her white-blonde hair. Even though it's the dead of winter she still smells like sunshine.

I can already feel the tears stinging my eyes and burning the back of my throat. It is the combination of having missed my best friend, of having missed physical contact and the betrayal of falling in love with Travis. For once I am glad that I'm not allowed to speak because I don't know what I would say to Cass, how I could explain why she has found me kneeling next to Travis, one hand in his hair.

"Oh, Mary, how is he doing?" She takes my place next to Travis, folding his hands into her own just as I have done. Even in his fever-induced sleep he leans his head toward hers.

I'm sure that he can smell the sunshine and that he craves it just as we all do. "Travis," she calls out to him, her voice soft as a breath. "Travis." She takes a hand and brushes it over his forehead and he groans softly. When she trails her hand down his cheek he presses his face against her.

Watching his reaction to her makes me ache so hard I can barely stand to watch. It is the same feeling as when I stood before my brother and he told me I had to go to the Sisterhood because no one had spoken for me. The same hollowness tunneling out from the center of my self.

For a moment I want to pull Cass away from the bed, away from Travis. I want to yell at him and tell him that she is not me and he should be responding to me that way. That I am the one who has been here since the beginning.

But I don't. Because I want to believe there is a reason that Cass hasn't come to visit since Travis was hurt. Because I know that she's delicate and that even this, even seeing him feverish and groaning, is almost too much for her to bear. Even though he is her intended, even though the four of us have grown up together and have been friends for as long as I can remember.

Between the two of us she has always been the weaker one and I have always felt the need to protect her. That she is even here at all is a testament to how much she cares for him, and realizing this makes me feel even more hollow and foolish for ever having thought myself in love with Travis.

She has his hand against her cheek now and is silent as tears stream out of her eyes. "How long has he been like this?" she asks me. "When will he be better? When will he wake up?"

I look to Sister Tabitha because I'm not allowed to speak and she steps forward, between me and Cass, and begins to answer her questions. I am relieved to have the burden of explanation lifted from my shoulders and I move away from the bed, away from Cass and Travis and Sister Tabitha, and give them privacy to speak.

"Hello, Mary," Harry says. I have forgotten that he is even in the room, hovering along the wall by the door, and I nod back at him in greeting. His dark hair is longer than the last time I saw him, and is tucked behind his ears. It makes his cheekbones look sharp and severe. We are standing shoulder to shoulder and I feel my body flush with anger and shame at this boy who rejected me. "Sister Tabitha told us that you wouldn't be able to speak, that you had taken some sort of a vow, but I think Cass just forgot."

I nod again. I don't know what I would say to him even if I could speak. Maybe ask him why he never spoke for me. Why he asked me to the Harvest Celebration on the morning my mother became infected but never said a word to me again until now. Never went to Jed and set his pledge for me. Why he has left me to this fate with the Sisterhood.

Maybe ask him what happened to Travis, what caused such an awful break in his leg and why he hasn't visited until now.

"Your brother is the one who found him," he tells me, as if reading my mind. We are both looking at Cass hovering over

Travis, Sister Tabitha perched on the edge of the bed explaining everything in low and gentle tones. It always surprises me how nurturing Sister Tabitha can be in the face of Travis's wounds.

"He is the one who brought him here," he adds. "Beth was beside herself that she couldn't also come be with her brother. But the Sisters are afraid that any movement will cause her to lose the baby." I swallow rapidly, trying to ease the burning in my throat. Jed was here that night. Was here just a few days ago. So near and yet he didn't come to see me. Didn't bother to tell me his wife was pregnant again.

I can't do anything but nod and try to keep my cheeks from catching fire from all the emotions warring inside me. It takes everything I have to clasp my hands placidly in front of my stomach.

Harry turns to face me but I keep my eyes looking forward. Like his brother, he is taller than I am and so he looks down at me when he speaks. "No one knows what happened, Mary, or where he was." He hesitates. "Jed told us that he found Travis half delirious, dragging himself through the fields. But no one has been able to figure anything out."

He searches my eyes as if I should know something, as if I hold the answers to his silent questions. I do nothing but return his gaze. Finally, he leans toward me ever so slightly. "Mary," he says, his voice a low rumble so that the others in the room don't hear. "I'm sorry," he finishes. "I just . . ." He looks down at the floor and then over my shoulder at his brother and Cass.

He opens his mouth to say more, but just then Travis's body on the bed shudders a bit as Cass lets go of his hand and stands. She is sniffling, her eyes are red and bloodshot and her entire face looks haggard, as if she is exhausted from the emotion of being so close to so much pain.

She is a different woman from the one who came in earlier.

"May I come back and visit with him again?" she asks.

The way that we're standing, it takes little movement for Sister Tabitha to look past Cass and meet my eyes briefly as she answers, "Of course you can. Mary prays for him daily. You may join her then. Perhaps with both of you entreating God, He will show mercy."

I can feel Harry's eyes holding me, willing me to meet his gaze. But I don't want his apologies now. I don't want to explain why I have spent so much time at his brother's side.

Cass turns to me and places her hand on my cheek. "My Mary," she says. "You are too good."

All I can think about is that I can still smell Travis on her hands, and it is almost my undoing.

▼     ▼     ▼

When Cass and Harry have left, Sister Tabitha escorts me back to my room. "You have finished reading the Scripture through five times." It isn't a question and while I have no problem lying to her by omission I cannot lie directly to her face, and so I nod.

"Then your vow of silence is over."

"Yes," I respond, language feeling strange in my mouth after so many weeks of silence. My voice feels loud and harsh to my ears, which have grown accustomed to soft whispers against Travis's cheeks.

"You will advance to the next stage of your studies soon. For now, you will help Cass through this ordeal and continue to pray for Travis."

I nod. Because even though I am allowed to speak now does not mean that I want to do so. The ability to speak comes with the burden of explaining myself to Cass.

▼   ▼   ▼

Because I am weak I don't tell Cass that my vow of silence has been lifted. Instead, I sit in a chair near the window as she kneels next to Travis's bed, her lips moving in prayer. Travis's fever hasn't broken and he is rarely awake, though he often groans in pain and thrashes on the bed. After a few visits like this I can see that she is weary and exhausted and lost, and so I go and kneel next to her and wrap her in my arms. She collapses against me in tears.

On the seventh day Cass doesn't come to sit with Travis and I begin to worry that something has happened to her. But then Harry comes in her place and tells me that it has become too much for her to bear, seeing Travis in so much pain.

He does not stay. He does not ask how I am doing or how Travis is doing. Instead, he stands in the doorway to Travis's room a moment, looking at me as I sit in my chair by the window watching his brother sleep peacefully.

"You love him," he says to me. I try to find accusation in his voice but I cannot.

"You did not speak for me," I respond.

His eyes flare for just a moment and then his gaze shifts away from me as he looks out the window. I want him to tell me why. Instead, he says, "I'm sorry, Mary," and turns and leaves, his eyes skimming over me before he closes the door behind him.

I slide out of my chair and crawl over to Travis, pulling myself up to kneel by the bed. It has been too long since I've been the one in this position. For the past few days it's been Cass here and Travis has slowly been getting better, the redness around his scar receding. But he has yet to fully wake up instead of sliding in and out of restless sleep, his mind seemingly blurred with pain.

I clutch at him and begin to sob. I sob for my lost family, for betraying my best friend, for not having been spoken for and for falling in love with Travis so deeply. I sob because my life is nothing like I imagined it would be. I sob for the way we all live and for the Unconsecrated and the Forest of Hands and Teeth and the Sisters and the Guardians. And for me and for Travis and his broken leg and the thought that he may never recover or if he does he may never walk right again and how tomorrow I start my next stage of studies and I am afraid that I won't be allowed to come see Travis anymore.

I sob because this is not a life. This is not the way life should be and because I don't know how to fix any of it.

My tears soak into the pillow. Travis's cheek and neck and hair are wet now but I cannot stop and I go on until I am heaving, trying to suck air into my lungs as my body convulses.

And then I feel a hand on my head and I look up. It's Travis and he is awake. For a moment I wonder if he's confused as to what I'm doing here instead of Cass. It's Cass who had been keeping vigil by his bed and it's Cass to whom he responds.

But then he whispers, "It will be okay, Mary." He pulls my head down to his chest and he wraps both his arms around me and all I can think is why can't life just stop here and now and leave us be in this moment.

Instead, I hear a shuffle at the door and I look up and it is

Sister Tabitha and she is bringing Travis his supper. She raises an eyebrow at my appearance: disheveled and raw. I stand and step away from the bed and wipe at my face with my sleeve.

Travis is back asleep, his body limp, his arms by his side, and I am left to wonder if I just imagined the whole thing.

Sister Tabitha says nothing as I leave the room and run back down through the maze of the Cathedral to the sanctuary of my own solace. But a few hours later she's there at my door and she tells me that my new studies will take up all my day and so I will no longer have the time to go and pray for Travis.

I spend the night sitting at my desk with the window open, the frigid air blowing over my numb body. I look to the Forest, to the fence line, and I wonder about my mother and father. Is their life any easier now? Is there fear in the Unconsecrated? Is there loss and love and pain and longing? Wouldn't a life without so much agony be easier?

# ▾ VII ▾

Sister Tabitha is correct: with my new studies there is no time to visit Travis during the day. Instead, the Cathedral's needs dominate my time. In the mornings I sweep the snow away from the walks, and I dust the pews and arrange the books for services. I make the sacred candles for the altar, chanting the special prayers for each layer of wax. I cook the meals and clean the dishes. But I'm not allowed outside the Cathedral walls. I can't go to the well or to the stream or to the fields.

And so I don't see anyone from the village unless they come to the Cathedral.

Throughout the next weeks Cass and Harry come to sit with Travis. Sometimes they are together and sometimes alone. It is terrible of me, but I hide when I see Cass approach. I just can't stand to face her knowing that she is the one Travis has chosen and I can't bear to think that even though he said my name that night that he may have meant Cass instead.

When I can stand it no longer I creep out of my bed at

night and wrap my quilt around my shoulders. I slip out of my room and down the hallway back toward the center of the Cathedral. Through the years the village has added wings to the building, halls that twist away from the main Sanctuary at odd angles, some intersecting and some not. My little room is part of the old structure, built of stone rather than wood, dank and dark. Most Sisters choose to live elsewhere in the Cathedral, in the newer rooms facing the village, preferring not to overlook the cemetery and the Forest. Perhaps Sister Tabitha meant my room as a punishment, meant to enforce my isolation. But I haven't protested—I prefer the silence and solitude of my empty hall.

As I near the Sanctuary, the ceiling soars into blackness, the room opening to reveal rows of pews. I press myself against the wall so that the Sisters keeping night vigil cannot see me. I pause to watch them as they kneel with their heads tilted toward each other, candlelight casting shadows around their faces. They are whispering furiously and I assume they are praying until one of them hisses and says in a low tone, "It is the way that it has been and will be and the Sisters will not allow you to presume otherwise. You must not think such things, let alone speak them."

Without thinking, I sneak closer in the darkness, trying to hear more. But then Sister Tabitha sweeps into the Sanctuary and I scurry away. Silently, I slip through a door, down a hall and up the narrow stairs and down another hall until I am pressing my hand against Travis's door. My breath comes in pants, my body tingling that I have escaped Sister Tabitha's notice and found my way to Travis. I slowly turn the knob.

There is a candle on the table by his bed and it flickers as the door opens and the draft from the hallway sweeps through the room. I close the door quickly. He is propped up on pillows and facing me, as if he's been waiting.

It takes a moment to realize that he is awake. He holds out a hand to me. It's shaking ever so slightly. "Mary, come pray for me," he says and I run to the side of the bed and kneel down and bury my head against him.

The stench of sickness is gone and his face is no longer pale and sweaty. He places his fingers under my chin and I know that my skin is slick with tears. "Pray for me, Mary," he says.

"I . . . I can't," I tell him. "I don't know any prayers."

"Tell me the one about the ocean," he says and I laugh. He smiles and slides gingerly back down on the bed and I lean in and begin to whisper into his ear. His hand is tight around mine and I can't help but allow my heart to beat faster than it ever has before.

▼　▼　▼

I've come to Travis's room every night for the past week, repeating for him the stories that my mother used to tell me. I am exhausted but deliriously happy. At night we are in our own universe, we belong only to each other, as if we have thrown off every other obligation.

Tonight my body pulses with awareness as I kneel by his bed, our fingers intertwined. We've been sharing each other's breath for what seems like weeks now even though it's only been a few moments. It's as if there is infinity between our lips and we will never actually touch. Like math, where dividing by half can last for eternity.

My lips almost brush his and I forget about Cass and

Harry and Jed and our village. At night, here in this room, it is only Travis and me and our first kiss.

It is in this moment that I realize something isn't right. Perhaps a shift in the drafts around the room, maybe my ears popping as a door somewhere is opened, but I pull back a bit and meet Travis's eyes. I can see that he also feels the difference.

"Shhhh," I say, placing a finger between our lips, surprised there is space between us for even a finger. I strain to hear more and then there are feet—many feet—coming up the steps and starting down the hall. I rear up in panic and Travis flings back the covers and takes my body and slides me over his and pushes me between him and the wall, pulling the blanket over us both.

I hold my breath and wait.

There are whispers in the hallway as a group of people shuffle past the door. Then the door to our room opens, the hinges groaning faintly, and sweat breaks out all over my body. Travis's heart beats in the moments that mine does not and I know that whoever is at the door must hear our combined percussion. From my position I can't tell what Travis is doing but he breathes deep and even as if he is asleep. I squeeze my eyes shut and berate myself for taking this risk.

I hear the person at the door take a step into the room. "Travis?" she asks, as if testing to see if he is awake. I bite my lip, recognizing Sister Tabitha's voice. Travis doesn't move, doesn't react.

Finally, the door closes with a click, the bolt of the lock sliding into place, the sound muffled by the covers. We wait. Travis pulls the sheets down, crisp clean air flowing back into my lungs, but I do not move from my position.

The walls are thin up in this hallway and we hear people

begin to move around in the room next door. There is a scrape of furniture on the floor and then someone hisses, as if to make the noise stop.

Travis and I stare into each other's eyes. All we can hear is mumbling, the cadence of voices rising and falling, over-lapping and rapid. "Do you think someone is hurt like you were?" I whisper.

He shakes his head. "I would think we'd be able to hear them if they were in pain."

I shrug. Maybe they fainted.

"Why would they lock me in if it was just someone hurt?" he breathes.

Turning my head back, I place my ear against the wall. I hear a sudden and sharp rebuke, uttered in harsh tones— "No, we will not tell them until the time is right. You keep your mouth shut about this"—and then whoever was speak-ing must have moved away from the other side of the wall and the voices fall back to murmurs.

While I'm puzzling over what's going on, I suddenly real-ize that I am lying in bed with Travis, my body squeezed be-tween him and the wall, our combined warmth enveloping us both. His breath shifts ever so slightly, heavier now, laced with longing, as if he has realized the same thing.

Every inch of my skin is instantly awake, the hairs on my body searching for movement, as if they are antennae. Travis is lying on his back and my back is against the wall so that I am facing him.

My hand has been resting on his chest and something in-side me urges me to press my fingers against his skin, to press my body against his. My breath comes out shaking. Everything, all of this, is almost too much to bear.

"I should probably leave in case they come to check on

you again," I say, and he swallows and nods his head. I can hear the way the air enters and leaves his lungs, as if it is an effort for him to breathe.

I begin to slide back across his body. Before I hadn't paid attention because of the adrenaline, the fear of getting caught. But this time everything inside me understands what is going on here in this bed. Mindful of his healing thigh, I slip one leg over his hips, leveraging myself against the wall until I am kneeling, hovering over him with a leg on either side of him.

He closes his eyes and leans his head back into the pillow, his lips slightly parted as though in pain. Startled, I lean down to him to whisper, "Am I hurting you?"

His eyes still closed, he shakes his head back and forth and reaches his hands up and places them on my hips, his hands so large on my skin, holding me in place for a heartbeat, the two of us almost one as we press against each other from hip to chin. My mind swirls with the knowledge that my nearness affects him, that I am not the only one who feels this heat.

There is a thump in the room next door and I quickly finish slithering over Travis and slip to the floor, ready to wedge myself under the bed if necessary.

Keeping my head cocked to the wall to listen for change in the movement in the next room, I scurry to the door and test the knob. Locked. There's no way I will be able to open it.

Travis is now propped up in his bed, leaning back on his elbows. By the moonlight I can see that his face is flushed with heat.

I will have to climb out the window. I cross the room and struggle against the sash until the window is open enough for me to fit through. Cold air invades my thin nightgown, fighting with the residual heat from Travis's bed, and I pull the quilt that I brought with me tight around my shoulders.

Thankfully it's been a heavy winter and there is a substantial snowdrift below to catch my two-story jump. I'm about to make my escape when I hear my name.

Travis is holding his hand out to me and even though I know I'm tempting fate I go back to him. "Will I see you again soon?" he asks. The flame from the candle next to his bed whips around in the draft from the window, sending his face into shadows.

"I don't know," I tell him truthfully. "I'm not sure I can risk it."

He nods. He understands. And then he takes my hand and presses his lips against my palm. It feels like fire entering my bloodstream and laying siege to my body. He kisses my wrist, and I am an inferno. He starts to move up my arm, his breath tantalizing, and I almost give in as he pulls me to him.

But instead I step back, cradling my arm to my chest. "Be well," I tell him because I don't know how to explain what I really want to say. And then I slip out the window and am covered in snow that instantly douses my skin, which just moments before had been aflame.

Afraid of being seen by the people in the room next to Travis's, I sprint through the graveyard toward the fence line and into the shadows near the edge of the Forest. I kick my feet as I go, trying to make it look not quite so obvious that a human has walked away from under Travis's window, but before long my feet begin to freeze, the thin slippers I'm wearing no protection against the snow.

I am as close to the Forest as I dare for nighttime when I begin to circle around so that I can enter the Cathedral through the front door. My mind wanders back to Travis, back to his bed and the feel of his skin. My body shivers from the memories, the desire, the frigid air. And so at first I don't realize that I am following in someone else's footsteps in the snow—not just one person's footsteps, but many.

I pause. There is nothing behind me but the Forest, and my heart begins to pound. What if these are the tracks of the Unconsecrated? What if the fence is breached and there is no one to sound the alarm? Terror bolts through me, but I slip and slide in the snow as I scramble to follow the tracks back to their source.

They stop at the fence. At the gate to the path that leads out of our village and through the Forest of Hands and Teeth. I kneel in the snow and look through the gate. Glistening under the moon I can see one clear set of footprints that lead to this gate. They stretch out, through the broken brambles and back down the path into the Forest for as far as I can see. They are not the shuffling footprints of the Unconsecrated, but the strong and distinct prints of the living, as if someone was walking purposefully down this path toward us.

The path is forbidden to everyone: villagers, Sisters, Guardians. Never have I seen this gate opened, never have I seen someone use this path.

Someone from Outside has come to our village.

Which means that there is an Outside—something beyond the Forest.

Excitement, fear, curiosity, panic well up my throat, making me almost giddy before I swallow hard and pull my mind back to the present moment. Leaning over the snow, I trace the outline of the Outsider's print. It is petite like mine but the steps are wide—either a small boy or a woman.

Someone from Outside has come to our village!

The wind begins to blow now, scattering the freshly fallen

snow and obscuring the footprints. I'm almost skipping as I follow the prints back to the village, up to the front of the Cathedral. I am about to throw open the door in excitement, my entire being bursting with energy, when my mind catches up with my body.

No one sounded the siren; no one rang the village bells. It may be night but something like an Outsider is news to wake the village for. Yet the Sisters have kept the Outsider a secret. They dragged him up to the room next to Travis's and they locked him in there. And I heard one of them say that they wouldn't tell the village until the Sisters were ready to do so.

Suddenly, I understand that I am not supposed to know about the Outsider and I wonder to what lengths the Sisters will go to keep this secret. I think about the tunnel under the Cathedral and the clearing in the woods and wonder what other secrets they might be keeping.

I duck into the shadows thrown by the walls of the Cathedral under the moon. With my hands against its formidable stone face, I creep through the bushes and around the snowdrifts until I am under my window. I reach up, slide it open and slip inside, wet and shaking, my fingers and feet numb.

After stoking the embers in my fireplace I undress and hang my clothes over the chair to dry. I sit on the hearthrug, my blanket pulled over my shoulders, my body still cold inside. As I hear the wind pick up outside I am grateful that my footprints will be erased, but know that this will also mar the Outsider's footprints to the gate.

Someone from Outside has come to our village and as I sit and stare at the flames I know deep in my being that this is what I have been waiting for, what I have wished for even though I never realized it before this moment.

The Outsider is my excuse to leave this village. Now that there's proof, now that our entire village will know that there is more, that we are no longer an island, now is our time to re-connect with the Outside world.

Nothing can contain us any longer. Not when word of the Outsider gets out. And I will be the first through the gate. I will be the one to lead us to the ocean. To the place untouched by the Unconsecrated.

# ▼ VIII ▼

Three days pass and I am desperate. There has been no word of the Outsider, no mention at all. Finally, in frustration I go to see Travis but Sister Tabitha is in the hall outside his door, and she tells me his fever has returned and he has been moved and they are not allowing visitors for fear that he will not be able to fight off any other infections. I will not be allowed in to see him until they are sure he is well.

"We cannot have you and him be the reason that we all fall ill this winter, Mary," she says.

I look past her shoulder and into Travis's empty room. "Where is he?" I ask. I feel I have a right to know.

"He is safe," she answers. "And he is none of your concern." She looks down her nose at me, her eyes narrowing. "Mary." Her voice is firm, authoritative. She pauses and brings a finger up to her lips as if trying to decide what she wants to say next. "Mary, you are inquisitive, and that can be a dangerous trait. What do you think has brought us to this moment? What do you think caused the Return and brought about the Unconsecrated?"

My breath is shallow. Even before I was taken to the clearing in the Forest, I have been afraid of Sister Tabitha, the oldest Sister, the leader of the Sisterhood. "I—I—" I stammer. "I thought we didn't know what caused the Return."

Again, I wonder at the knowledge that the Sisters possess that the rest of us do not. They have, after all, been the one constant since the Return, or so we are told. They have been the driving force behind the village—the ones who created the Guardians and the reason we still exist and are all still alive.

Theirs is the word of God, not to be questioned. They are the ones to teach us in school, who tell us that we are all that is left of the world and that the time of the Return is behind us and unimportant in our new world. They are the ones who teach us not to second-guess their proclamations, not to second-guess our survival after the Return and the new world they have built for us.

Sister Tabitha smiles in a way I imagine a mother would smile to indulge a child and his fancies. "We know enough." She takes my arms and pulls me into Travis's old room with her. Her grip is firm but it does not hurt. She leads me to the window until we are standing in front of it looking out at the fence line and the Forest.

"The exact cause of the Return may be shrouded in mystery, but we do know that they were trying to cheat God. Trying to cheat death. Trying to change His will." She holds her hand out toward the Forest. As always the Unconsecrated pull at the links in the fence. "This is what happens when you go against God's will. This is His retribution. This is our penance."

She speaks with such authority and fervor. Her hand is a closed fist now and she pounds against the windowsill to make her point.

"You must remember, Mary, that you live for God now. We all live for God. It is only through His grace that we survive." She turns toward me with a fierce, almost frantic expression. "Remember where we came from, Mary. Where we all came from. Not the Garden of Eden, but the ashes of the Return. We are the survivors." She grabs my shoulders now, shakes me. "We have to continue to survive. And I will allow nothing to jeopardize this."

Looking into her eyes I know that she will not hesitate to sacrifice me to the Forest if it means saving this village or even just saving her position within it. She is a zealot, she is so filled with the passion. For the first time I truly understand the world I live in. Not the world that is always on the edge, on the verge, living under the constant weight of the Forest. But the world beyond that, ruled over by the Sisterhood and their duty to protect and preserve us.

It is in realizing this that I truly understand our fragility.

Sister Tabitha is expecting me to say something but I don't know what to tell her. I don't know how to respond. She must understand what I now finally know—that I will never truly fit in here. As a Sister, as a wife, as a villager.

The Sisters may have knowledge and power, but Sister Tabitha has made it clear that such things will never be within my reach. To her, I am not to be trusted because I didn't come to the Sisterhood willingly and because I ask too many questions and seek too many answers.

I will never be admitted into the elite, I will never be told their secrets: why they have a tunnel into the Forest and what the rooms off the tunnel are used for. My duties here will never be more than tending the sick, cleaning the Sanctuary, reading the Scripture and praying for our souls.

My life will never be my own.

This is a terrifying revelation and I want nothing more than my mother, to run to her and bury myself in her arms, in her safety.

But now my mother is a part of the world that Sister Tabitha is speaking about. She is part of what we fight against every day.

As if she reads my mind she says, "You must find your place here, Mary. You must give yourself over to God and stop looking for something else." She is leaning over me as she speaks so that I am forced to bend away from her hot breath as she rants on. "You think you want answers to your questions but you do not. And you will not. Because it is our sworn duty as Sisters to ensure that such questions are not asked. You must understand—there are no answers for you."

She traces one long finger down my cheek, her fingernail sharp against my skin. "You will be the end of us if you keep following this path! I can feel it, I can see it in you."

A spark of alarm sets fire inside me. Her words echoing loudly in my head, that I will be the end. It's like a puzzle piece clicking into place, a sudden understanding of why Sister Tabitha has been keeping me so close, why she doesn't even allow me to leave the Cathedral.

"What are you asking me to do?" I whisper. I think of Cass and her blond braids and the way she smells like sunshine and the way she sobbed over Travis when he was hurt. I can't be the end of her, the end of such sweetness and light.

"Stop looking for answers to questions you should not even be asking! Embrace your life here. Why do you think this village has survived while the rest of the world perished? Why do you think we have lived so long without a breach? Why do you think we are safe from the Unconsecrated? It is because we do not tempt God's wrath. We do not tempt the Unconsecrated. We do not take stupid risks, but rather dedicate ourselves to God and each other." Her face is close, her eyes wide and white.

"We have survived because the Sisterhood has done what was necessary. We keep order in the village." She stares out the window at the unending view of the Forest. "Imagine this village without order." She bangs her hand on the sill again. "Imagine people breaking vows and oaths. Stealing from each other. That was the world before the Return. And look at the result." She tosses a hand toward the Forest and then turns, her eyes searing over me.

"That is why you must leave Travis alone. I have watched the way you covet him. But he is not for you."

Everything around me seems to be crumbling, my knees weak and barely able to support my weight. I don't know what to say or how to respond and so I nod, the pain inside me too intense. She is asking me to give up the only thing I have left.

She grips my shoulders, her long bony fingers digging through my tunic. "When you leave this room, you will rededicate yourself to the Sisterhood and to this village. To every person here and our continued survival. You will repent!"

Her body heaves as she gasps for air, her teeth gritted and muscles straining. She takes a step away from me and turns to the window. For a moment in her reflection in the glass I think I see sorrow on her face, in the heaviness of her skin on her skull. "I know I must sound harsh, Mary," she says, her voice suddenly calm again, measured. "That the rules of the Sisterhood are harsh. But what is a village without order? Without rules and people to enforce them?"

She places a palm against the window, fingers splayed, and I see that she is shaking ever so slightly. "The Sisterhood carries a sacred burden. We carry it so that the villagers do not. So that we can forget what came before, can heal, become reborn without the weight of our sins before the Return."

My body burns—all this time we have been kept in the dark and the Sisters have known. "Why do you keep such secrets?" I ask. "Why not trust us?"

She turns to me and for a moment her eyes see through me, as if looking back a long distance into herself. As if remembering. I see a ghost of a smile around her eyes, old laugh lines crinkling again faintly.

I begin to realize that I may be pushing her too far. That I may be pushing her to toss me into the Forest to keep from revealing what I have learned: that the Sisterhood is keeping secrets from us all. I take a step back, but her voice stops me.

"Your mother used to tell you stories about life before the Return," she says. "But did she ever tell you of murder? Of the pain and anguish? The heresy and hypocrisy? Wars, deceit, selfishness? Of people allowing human beings to die of hunger outside in the cold when they had warmth and food? Even during the Return, when we were struggling to keep humanity alive, people turned on each other, attacked each other, stole from each other!

"That is why we are here, how we survived—by cutting

ourselves off. By letting the rest of humanity perish. Here, everyone is fed. Everyone is warm and safe and loved and cared for. *We* do that, Mary. It is the Sisterhood that has brought heaven to this hell. People always want to be trusted, but look where it gets them! I have trusted you and look at how you skulk around this place at night when you think I am not looking. Look at how you bend the rules for your own interest.

"Even if it means harming your friend. You lust after Travis, you tempt him even though you have known he was pledged to Cass. You place your own desires before those of your friend, before those of your community and God." She pauses, seems to compose herself for a moment before continuing.

"You think you want love, Mary. You think it is this beautiful gift that does nothing but fill you and make you whole. But you are wrong. Love can be cruel and ugly. It can become dark and cause the deepest pain. Just look at what it has done to your parents." She places a hand over her chest as if she is clutching at her own heart. "Do you not understand that life in this village is not about love but about commitment?"

I take another step back, my hands over my mouth. My cheeks flush. All this time she has known about me and Travis. "How do you know such things?" I ask. I think of all the nights I have crept through the Cathedral to Travis's room. Of all the times I thought I was alone, that I had escaped the scrutiny of Sister Tabitha. But she was only testing me. Seeing how far I was willing to twist her trust and my own loyalty.

For a moment I don't think she will answer me. "It is not an easy life," she says at last, "being one of the keepers of the knowledge of the Sisterhood. It is far easier to live in ignorance, like you. Do you not see that I am trying to save you? To keep you from pain and anguish? This is why you must repent. Because if you do not, you will take away any choices I have in dealing with you. And you know what your fate will be."

My heart pounds as I think of the tunnel under the Cathedral and the clearing in the Forest and I nod. Sister Tabitha tucks a strand of hair back from my face, her hand resting on my cheek the way my mother used to do. "I am trying to keep you safe, but you must help me. I can see now that it is no longer enough to keep you trapped here in the Cathedral. Maybe I was wrong to keep you from the village. Your solitude is over. You may leave this building. But remember that I will always be watching you."

She keeps her eyes locked on mine and it is impossible for me to look away. And then she turns, her long black tunic sweeping the floor, and leaves me by the window, closing the door behind her so that I am alone with the view of the Forest.

Outside, pure white snow covers the trees and fence, blanketing the Unconsecrated. It is a bright clear day, the sun sparkling off the ice crystals. One of those days when you can't understand why there is such beauty in a world that is nothing but ugly.

It is almost too much to bear.

I wander to the bed and kneel by it the way I used to do when Travis was here. I press my face into his pillow, trying to smell him, trying to remember. It is a test to see if I can really give him up.

I know that I never will. Even to save him. I am too selfish.

Before I know it I am pummeling the pillow, ripping at the sheets, a low growl in my throat. I am about to wreak more destruction when I hear a soft knock.

I freeze.

I hear the knock again. It doesn't come from the door but from the wall. I crawl over the bed and place my ear against it. With one finger I tap back. "Hello?" I ask, my voice low.

Part of me wonders if this is a trap set by Sister Tabitha to tempt me, to test whether I have taken her words to heart.

"Who's there?" I hear from the other side.

"Mary," I respond. "Who are you?"

"My name is Gabrielle," she says. "I came through the gate. Where am I?"

"You're in the Cathedral," I tell her. My heart beats wild. I want to let her know she is safe but I can't be sure anymore. I have so many questions to ask her and I know that Sister Tabitha will be back at any moment and that if she catches me she will hand me over to the Forest.

But there is one thing I must know first. "Are you well? Were you . . ." I struggle with the words: "Bitten? Infected?" I have to know if she made it through to the village without harm. If the path is safe.

My uneven breath is so loud in my ears that I barely hear her response. "No," she says. "No, I'm fine. I'm not Infected."

I let my forehead fall against the wall when she says it, relief washing through me for a reason I can't identify or explain.

I open my mouth. I am about to ask her where she's from, if there is a world outside the Forest and what it's like, if there are other villages out there and are they safe. Has she ever seen the ocean and does she know why we're all here, why this happened and why we're trapped in this place.

But instead I feel tears on my cheeks and I hear a scraping in the hallway. I leap off the bed and gather the sheets I had torn from the mattress earlier in my arms and I run to the door so that when it opens Sister Tabitha won't know I was at the wall, speaking to the girl on the other side.

I duck out of the room quickly and go to the laundry, letting the steam from the boiling vats of water roll over me, making my skin glisten so that no one will know that it is tears on my cheeks rather than sweat.

When I'm done washing the smell of Travis out of the sheets I slip into my heavy coat and gloves and sneak outside into the graveyard, down toward the fence line. In the depths of winter I am guaranteed solitude here; no one from the village dares stray too far from the warmth of their hearths, not even to honor the fallen. Here lie my ancestors, all except my father and mother, whose deaths are not marked with a tombstone because they are Unconsecrated.

I glance back over my shoulder at the Cathedral, wondering if I will see Gabrielle at the window in the creeping darkness.

She is there, standing by the curtains. I stop and look up at her and our eyes meet. My breath hitches—it is like looking at a reflection in the water. The same age, same dark hair, same questions in our eyes. She looks like she might be taller, willowier than me. And she's wearing a vest made of an unnatural red so bright and strange that it almost hurts my eyes. She raises a hand and places it against the window, her palm flat against the glass. I raise my own hand and begin to walk toward her but then I see her turn and look over her shoulder and then the curtains fall shut and she is gone.

I scamper away and duck behind a gravestone angel, afraid of getting caught staring up at the Outsider's room when clearly her presence here is meant to be a secret. When I am sure the shadows of twilight will mask my movement, I walk to the gate guarding the pathway to Outside. I notice that the snow is smooth and undisturbed. There's no evidence that an Outsider was brought through this fence a few nights ago. Nothing to give away that an Outsider is among us.

I circle around the dwelling houses, flapping my arms against my sides to keep warm, and wend my way to the village hill. I climb into the watchtower, the boards slick with ice. When I'm at the highest point in our village I look out at the Forest. I strain to see if I can find the edge of it, find where the rest of the world begins.

But all I can see is darkness.

My entire life has been about the world outside the fence line, has been about the Forest. Of course I have wondered if there's anything past the Forest, if anything else survived the Return or if my mother's stories were true and an entire world existed before the Return. We have never even known if there is a fence on the other side of the trees—if there is an end to it at all. Are we merely the yolk of an egg, the Forest the white of the egg, another fence the shell? Or does the Forest run forever, hemmed in by nothing but Unconsecrated? A part of me has imagined that there could be nothing else in our world but Forest.

Forest and the Unconsecrated.

I have wondered too about the ocean, about the Outside before. But it had never occurred to me to go and find out. To leave this village and the only life I have ever known. We are told growing up that there is nothing past the fences worth living for. That the world ended with the Return and we are the last bastion.

But of course we are not. Gabrielle is proof of this. Even though the ground is covered with snow and I am standing on a tower on a hill being swept by the wind, I'm not cold. I am too excited to be cold. There is proof of life outside our fences. And I cannot help but wonder how this will change our lives.

There is a world out there, out beyond us. And now we are part of this world. It is terrifying and wonderful.

# IX

I drum my fingers against the desk under the window in my room. I am impatient. I can't stop my foot from tapping against the floor. I keep my eyes on the fence line, looking for any sign of my mother. Doing this is the only thing that has kept my mind off the Outsider—Gabrielle—and from conjuring ways to sneak up to find her.

After our recent confrontation I know that Sister Tabitha keeps watch over me and yet I can't stay still, can't stop my curiosity. In an attempt to avoid her detection I have slipped out the window and gone to stand underneath Gabrielle's room, hoping that I will figure out a way to climb the two stories and get inside. But the window is always dark, the curtains tightly drawn.

Since that first day when she stood by the window in her strange red vest I haven't seen her again and I begin to worry if she is well. But I know she is still here in the Cathedral. I can see it in the way the Sisters whisper among themselves and eye those of us who are uninitiated into the inner sanctum. The air is tense here, like a cord pulled taut.

I have grown reckless in my attempts to speak with Gabrielle and I know that I'm tempting Sister Tabitha's wrath if she finds out. But I can't help it. It is like a fever. Now that I'm no longer allowed to see Travis, Gabrielle is all I can think about.

I've decided that it is worth Sister Tabitha and the Unconsecrated if I can at last find out what is past the Forest.

A knock at the door startles me from my thoughts. It's a young Sister sent to bring me to see Sister Tabitha. She leads me back toward the Sanctuary in the heart of the Cathedral and through to another wing that is off-limits except to the most elite Sisters.

I wonder if this is it. If these steps will be the last that I will take. If I am finally paying for my curiosity and stubbornness and impetuousness. I wonder if I will beg for Sister Tabitha's forgiveness when she leads me through the tunnel back toward the old well house and abandons me in the Forest.

But Sister Tabitha is not alone when I enter her office, sharp sunlight stabbing my eyes as it pours through three large windows that overlook the village. Harry is there with her, his arms straight by his sides, hands clenched into fists. Travis is dead, I suddenly think. I was told he had turned for the worse and here is his brother looking solemn and sad and I almost sink to my knees.

"I have news," Sister Tabitha tells me and I nod because my vocal cords are being eaten away with acid tears.

"Harry has spoken for you, Mary," she tells me.

I whip my head around to face Harry. I can feel my eyebrows draw together with shock and anger. I cannot believe this could be the truth. Why would he speak for me now when he hadn't done so before, when it would have mattered and when I could have said yes and meant it? Back when I didn't know love and could have been happy with admiration and acceptance?

"But the Sisterhood," I stammer. This cannot be happening.

"I have given him my blessing. So has your brother, Jed," Sister Tabitha says. "You are needed more out there as a wife and mother than in here as a Sister." Her sharp eyes bore into me. "We both know you are ill-suited for the Sisterhood."

The world swirls around me and I have nothing to cling to in order to make it right. All I can think about is Travis and how it felt to press against his body that night. How can I ever be with his brother after that?

"You will marry at Brethlaw in the spring," she continues. "With Travis and Cassandra," she adds as if she doesn't know that she is breaking my heart.

"My duties to God . . . ," I begin to ask, even though I don't believe in God.

"Will be served by doing His will and making sure our village thrives through another generation," she finishes.

She means having children with Harry. My stomach clenches at the thought of it. I think of his hand holding mine under the water the day that my mother was infected. I think about the way his flesh looked, puffy and white and wrong.

I open my mouth, ready to reject his courtship. But then I realize that doing so will tie my fate to the Sisterhood forever, will condemn me to a life inside these walls in service to God and Sister Tabitha.

My mind whirls, trying to determine which is the better

choice, which the better fate: life as wife to Harry or life as a Sister. Neither one bringing me closer to Travis.

"Would you two like a moment alone together to speak?" she asks us.

I glance at Harry, not caring that pain and rage and desolation radiate from my body. He looks at me, his expression soft, his hands no longer fisted. It seems as if he's leaning forward, about to take a step closer to me. I feel my muscles tense and shake in response.

I am surprised that I don't growl like a wounded animal cornered by dogs. He starts to raise a hand—whether to beckon me or fend me off I don't know or care. Already I feel myself pulling away from him, putting physical space between us without taking a step.

His eyes become harder, deeper, and he shakes his head. "No," he says. And then he leaves and I'm escorted back to my room where I collapse and sob. I pull at my hair and pound my fists against my thighs and throw myself onto the ground in front of the dying fire.

Once upon a time life with Harry might have been acceptable. Once upon a time my mother's stories were only fancies and my world was sunny and warm and full of love and friends. But there was never excitement. There was no such thing as life beyond the village. Before I may have had a crush on Travis, but it was a simple childish longing that could have easily been erased by the contentment of being asked to marry Harry.

But all that has changed now. Both Mother and Father are Unconsecrated, Travis is broken, Cass is absent, Jed no longer cares enough to even speak to me when he comes to the Cathedral for worship.

And there is life outside the Forest.

I can hear the Unconsecrated moaning. The sound carries over the old dingy snow and through the window. I think again about how uncomplicated their life is, how much easier. I wonder why we all fight against it, why we have struggled against them for so long rather than just accepting our fate.

No longer caring about the consequences, I slip out of my room and march down the hall and up the steps toward where the Outsider is being kept. I am about to shove someone out of my way when I realize who it is: Cassandra.

She is coming out of Travis's old room.

"Cass?" I ask. "What are you doing here?" I reach out for a hug and she obliges but her arms are weak and limp around me. It has been weeks since we have seen each other, months since we have spent time together as friends the way we used to before my mother became Unconsecrated. For the first time I realize just how far we have drifted apart and how much I have missed her friendship, missed having someone to confide my fear and pain and confusion in.

She lets me go first and pulls the door behind her until she hears the click, cutting off the only source of light in the narrow hallway. "I am here for Travis," she tells me.

My breath catches in my throat, thoughts of the Outsider suddenly eclipsed. "He's well? He's back upstairs?"

She nods and tugs on her long blond braid and bites her lip with her top teeth. "Travis is mine now, Mary. Just like Harry is yours."

"I . . ." I want to tell her that she's wrong and that Travis loves me and will always be mine. But of course that's not true. Travis was never mine. Even during those long nights praying together I knew Travis belonged to someone else. He was always Cass's. Just as I am now Harry's.

She lets go of her braid and places a hand on my arm and I have to force myself not to wince. "You must let him go, Mary," she tells me, her fingers digging into my skin. "He would follow you anywhere and he cannot. He just cannot."

"But . . ."

"You know, I fell in love with Harry. Just in the last few weeks, when Travis's pain was too much for me." She looks past my shoulder, as if she is somewhere other than in a hallway deep in the Cathedral. "We spent so much time together. He held my hand. I was certain he was going to ask for me." She is back to tugging at her braid. "I was so certain that he loved me." Her gaze lands on me, narrow and sharp. "But then he asked for you instead."

Too many thoughts swirl in my head. "I thought you were being courted by Travis. I thought he asked you to the Harvest Celebration." I think back to all the times Cass visited Travis, all the times she knelt by his bed and comforted him and I took her dedication as love and possession. "How could Harry ask for you if you were already pledged?"

She cocks her head to the side as if she is seeing me for the first time in ages. "Sister Tabitha gave me the option of ending the courtship," she tells me. "They weren't sure that he would survive the infection and even if he did they assumed he would be crippled and therefore not a suitable husband able to physically care for a wife. I came to visit him out of loyalty and friendship. Just like you."

Of course Cass would visit Travis in his time of need, courtship or not—all of us have known each other our whole lives, have grown up together almost as if we were our own family.

"Then what happened?" I ask her.

Her eyes harden. "Harry asked for you instead of me."

"But why?" My voice is shallow, desperate.

A muscle ripples along her jaw. Slowly, she shrugs, tilting her head toward her shoulder as she does.

"It doesn't have to be this way," I tell her. I've never seen Cass like this—so serious and resolute and somber.

"It does," she says.

"But if you love Harry and I . . ." I stop but we both know what I am about to say.

"You love Travis," she finishes for me. I can only stand in silence, my hands hanging by my sides. I let my head drop. Not for the first time today my legs feel weak and I am empty inside. How can everything have gone so wrong so quickly?

"I'm sorry," I finally whisper.

"I know you didn't mean it," she says, placing a hand on my arm. "Just as I didn't mean to fall for Harry." I can't look into her eyes, I can't let her see my hesitation. Because I know that I did mean it. Never did I stop in my desire for Travis, even when I saw Cass with him and how she had cried by his bed. All this time I knew they were pledged. That I was tempting Travis to break his word, to reject my best friend in order to be with me and that he loved me enough to do just that.

I place my hand over hers but she pulls away, her cool flesh slipping from mine. "I just don't understand why we can't change this. If this isn't the way things should be, if this isn't what we want—"

"Harry spoke for you, Mary," she says through her teeth. "He has made his choice. He has chosen you over me. And if he intends for me to marry Travis, then that is what I shall do."

Cass is so fervent in her proclamation that it scares me. She has always been the carefree girl, the happy one who pushes worries and problems to the side.

"But we can still change this, Cass." I lean toward her. "I

will talk to Harry, I will tell him that I do not want to be with him—"

Quick as a snake she reaches out her hand, grabs my shoulder, pulls me to her until our faces are close. In the dimness of the hallway she seems to be nothing but shadows, her eyebrows drawn together in a fierce scowl. "You will do no such thing. You will not break his heart like that."

"But this isn't the way things should be. If I want to be with Travis—"

She cuts me off again by shaking my arm, pushing me back against the wall of the hallway. "If you break Harry's heart, I promise that I will never let go of Travis. You will be alone. You will be sent back here to the Sisters." She pauses and as if reading my mind adds, "And don't think that Travis will reject me for you. He would never do that to his own brother. You must realize that anything he may have once felt is gone now that Harry has officially spoken for you. Now that you are to be his brother's wife."

Her words pierce through my body. I have never seen her like this, so bitter and sharp and stormy. "But, Cass, don't you see? You don't love Travis. And he doesn't love you!" I know I am being harsh and cruel but she must face the truth.

She looks at me as if she doesn't understand and then laughs. "Marriage is not about love, Mary," she says, like a teacher talking to a student. "It is about commitment and compromise and caring. None of this has ever been about love."

I shake my head in disbelief. "But you said that you loved Harry and yet you are willing to set him aside. Why?"

Once again she shrugs. "I'm doing what is best for him. And for the village. This is the way it has to be, Mary. This is the way it will be."

I want to shake her, to make her understand. She sounds exactly like Sister Tabitha, as if she doesn't comprehend the choices she's making for all of us. I realize just how strong the Sisters' influence is, how tightly they have bound us in their beliefs.

I open my mouth to continue arguing with Cass, but the look in her eyes, the ferocity, is too unnerving. For the first time my best friend terrifies me.

But she is also right. Even if I reject Harry, Travis would never speak for me in his place. He would never cause his brother such embarrassment or pain. It is as if every door in my life has been slammed shut, every window boarded up until there is only one path for me to take. My choice is either Harry or the Sisterhood.

And so, as my shoulders fall, I relent. "Okay," I tell her.

She nods once. And then says, "You must let Travis go now. Today. Here."

A protest hovers at my lips but her eyes scare me into silence. I wonder if we'll ever be friends again or if this will be the end of us. Of course we'll always be civil—the village is too small to feud—but will we share ourselves fully with each other as we did before?

Suddenly, in this moment I feel as if I have no ground, as if I have lost everything all at once and I need something to hold steady. I see my life in a flash, Cass always by my side, always listening to my stories and laughing with me and sharing our lives. Memories of our friendship fill me and tears prick my eyes. I need Cass now; I cannot lose this last tie to everything I have ever been.

"Promise me," I tell her. "Promise me that we will still be friends, will continue to be there for each other."

She smiles, a hint of the old Cass, the scent of sunbeams floating through the air. "Yes," she says. And all I can think is, if it were only that simple, as I remember how it was always someone else she came to visit at the Cathedral and never me.

I look back down the hallway, past Travis's room to where the Outsider was being kept. Her door is open barely a crack, a sliver of light slipping through. Pushing past Cass, I run to the room but it's bare, no linens on the bed or any other evidence that a guest has recently occupied this space. I should have known. The window has been dark for days.

Cass stands behind me in the doorway, clearly confused. But rather than explain anything to her I walk to the window and tilt my head at an angle until I can see a handprint, the pads of the fingers clearly visible. I step closer and my breath hits the glass and words suddenly appear in the mist it leaves behind.

*Gabrielle*, it says, followed by a series of letters: *XIV*. Other than this echo, there is no evidence that she ever existed. I trace my fingers over the letters, effectively obliterating them.

"What do you see?" Cass asks, coming to stand beside me.

"Do you ever wonder if there is an end to the Forest?" I ask her. I have asked her this before and I already know what her answer will be.

She giggles, fully herself now. "You never do give up your fancies, do you, Mary?" she asks. "You know, like the ocean?"

I smile a little. Still uneasy around my friend. Still afraid of her. "Probably," I tell her. But if there is no end to the Forest, then where did Gabrielle come from?

▼　▼　▼

Even though I am a pledged woman I still live with the Sisters in the Cathedral. Sister Tabitha explains that my brother is unwilling to take me in due to his wife's delicate health during her pregnancy. But a part of me wonders if that is only a pretext and Sister Tabitha is keeping me close in order to watch me. To see if I have given up my quest for answers.

I have not. Over the next week I find excuses to enter every dwelling room in the Cathedral. There is no sign of Gabrielle. It is as if she never existed.

# X

Spring in the village means rain, baptisms and marriages. It means Edenmass, the celebration of having lived another year, of triumph over the Unconsecrated and prayers for the years to come. The centerpiece of Edenmass is the marriages. Marriage in our village is a sacred bond and the three ceremonies that cement husband and wife together are called Brethlaw—a weeklong event beginning with the Troth, leading to the Binding and ending with Vows of Eternal Constancy. It is a culmination of the winter courtships that began at the Harvest Celebration.

The most important and sacred ritual of Brethlaw is the Vows of Eternal Constancy, which forever unites the couple together as husband and wife. The night before the Vows is the Binding ceremony, in which the Sisters tie the bride's right hand to the groom's left hand and the couple spends the night in their new dwelling. They are left alone together and are given a ceremonial blade they can use to cut their Binding. It is an opportunity to air any grievances between them and their last chance to reject each other as spouse.

The days of Edenmass between the Brethlaw ceremonies are a time to christen the children born of marriages from the year before and to celebrate the conception of those yet to come. It is the village's most solemn and joyous time, honoring our survival, our existence, the continuation of our people since the Return. It is a commitment to perseverance and dedication.

As one of only two brides this year, I am dressed in a white tunic that I will wear every day this week. Early spring flowers are woven through my hair. There are four of us getting married and pledging our Troth: me and Harry, Travis and Cass.

We are standing in a row on a dais in front of the Cathedral, its hulking shape throwing shadows over us. We face our intendeds with Sister Tabitha at our side, the entire village in attendance on our other side. The spring sun is especially harsh today, moist heat rising in waves from the ground and thickening the air so that breathing is like swimming.

Sister Tabitha speaks of obligations. Of sins and life and commitment and vows. Of how we signal the constancy of our village. She reminds us of our fragility, of the dangers not just from the Unconsecrated outside the fences, but from the threats within: disease, sterility, miscarriage. She points to the four of us and talks of how sometimes generations fail us in numbers and how it is our duty to grow our ranks, add to the community's larger families.

Her words slip through my mind and I am unable to focus on them. Other thoughts occupy me. It's the first time I've seen Travis since Harry spoke for me. After Travis was released from the Sisters' care. After I was left behind at the Cathedral with no place else to go.

His hair is lighter, blonder, as if he spends his afternoons outside in the sun. He has put on weight so that his skin no longer stretches so tight over his cheekbones. His eyes are brighter, greener, no longer hollow. He looks good. Healthy.

I ache seeing him. And it is everything that I can do to stay still in front of Harry rather than press myself up against Travis, who stands at my back facing Cassandra.

Sister Tabitha continues to speak of our duties to each other and to God but all I can concentrate on is the movement in air caused by Travis as he leans on his cane and imperceptibly shifts his weight, trying to get comfortable.

It's good to see him standing and walking and healthy. Though I hate to see him smile—I am miserable.

As Sister Tabitha brings us into the oaths portion of the ceremony, we all turn to face the altar. Harry is on my left and Travis on my right. If I close my eyes, I can imagine that it is Travis I am pledging myself to, Travis who will take me home at the end of the week to our new life.

We echo Sister Tabitha as she leads us through our Troth. And just as we pledge ourselves to each other, promising to vow eternity at the end of the week, I feel Travis's fingers brush mine. I grab for his hand but there is nothing but air.

I am now Harry's betrothed and he leads me down from the dais and out of the shadow of the Cathedral and into the sunlight. We are surrounded by well-wishers and I can no longer see Travis in the crowd.

I have lost him for good.

▽    ▽    ▽

The week of Brethlaw is a dizzying haze. At every event the four of us are guests of honor, set apart from the rest of the village, put on display. We are shuffled from affair to affair.

Dinners to mark the import of the occasion. Solitary prayer sessions to prepare our souls for their impending commitment.

Other than the Troth, Binding and Vows of Eternal Constancy, the biggest event of Brethlaw is the christening. Each baby is brought before the Sisters and Guardians, is passed around the people of the village. These children belong to all of us, the Sisters say, they are our future.

Four children born of last year's marriages are christened and I can't help but watch as Jed and Beth try to sneak from the edge of the crowd. I wonder if the pain of losing their child this fall is too much to bear.

Finally, in the middle of the week, I find myself alone and I rip the flowers from my hair. I am tired of the villagers, tired of Harry and the Sisters and the Guardians and the well-wishers.

I am tired of the happiness. And so I go to the old lookout tower on the hill, the one place where I'm sure to find solitude.

But when I arrive there's already someone there and I'm about to turn back when I recognize the figure sitting against the tower. It's Travis. I feel a flutter inside me. It has never occurred to me that he would come to this place, that anyone but me ever came to this place.

It's been so long since we have been alone together that I can only stare at him, my eyes hungry. For a moment I consider turning and heading back, of leaving him here and pushing aside temptation. He is not mine, cannot be mine, and it's too painful to be near him and know the finality of our situation.

But before I can move Travis holds a hand out to me and says, "Mary, come pray with me."

His words are my undoing. I run, tripping over my tunic and crawling and scraping at the ground until I am at his side, my hands on his chest, my breath coming out in pants.

"Oh, Mary," he says, thrusting his hand into my hair and cupping my head. He pulls my face to his, across everything that has been separating us. I need him with an urgency that I cannot escape.

He stops my head just as our lips are about to touch, to finally learn home. He is panting and I can only breathe the air from his lungs. We stay like this for what seems like eternity, unable to commit to each other, to bridge everything between us.

"Mary," he whispers. I can feel the movement of his lips.

I am waiting for him to push me away and tell me that we cannot do this. That I am not his to take and that he will not betray his brother. I thrust my head into the crook of his shoulder, pressing my forehead against his neck.

It's a warm day and he's sweating and I press my mouth against his skin, tasting his salt on my lips. I want to melt into him, to forget every barrier between us and it is everything I can do to suck in air and sit here and not press myself harder against him.

He's not mine but Cass's and I know I should turn away, leave this place. But I'm not strong enough to do so. Just this last time I want to revel in his essence, to wrap it around me like a memory.

For a while we sit like this. Me splayed over his lap, clutching at him, feeling everything inside me open. I realize that I am happy. Travis's hand strays back to my hair and I relax against him, releasing the last of my hesitation.

It is a perfect spring day. The birds have come back to our

village, the snow has turned to mud and the sun is bright and soft and warm. A breeze covers us and the sound through the trees reminds me of my mother's stories of the ocean.

"Times like this, it's hard to believe that we aren't the only people in the world. Just the two of us on this hill," Travis tells me. I smile.

He continues, "But then other times I think that we *can't* be the only people in the world. This village, I mean. That there must be more out there, something beyond the Forest."

I try to pull my head back so that I can look Travis in the eyes. It's as if he has spoken my heart, found his way into my dreams. I thought I was alone in my belief in life outside the Forest. With a gentle pressure from his hand he keeps my head against his shoulder and my heart pounds through his words.

"You are not the only one who was raised with stories," he tells me and I hold my breath, waiting for more. "And they just make me think that there has to be more out there. That this can't be it. We can't be it. There must be more to life than this village and its edicts."

His voice is tight, as if he too feels the binds keeping us apart from each other. He places a finger under my chin and raises my gaze to his. "Don't you sense it, Mary? That there's more? That this life here is not enough?"

Tears spring to my eyes and my blood seems to sing. I look toward the fence line as if I could look toward our future. It is far enough away that I can't see individual Unconsecrated, just a mob of them pulling at the chain links. As the wind shifts I can hear their moans carried up the hill.

I am about to tell him about Gabrielle—proof that there is more—when a flash of red darts from the trees and my heart skips a beat, my breath catches. I sit ramrod straight now, every sense attuned to the Forest.

"What's wrong?" Travis asks, also sitting up, a hand on my back.

I think I'm hallucinating but then I see the flash again. An unnatural bright red against the shadows of pine trees. I stand, forgetting the calm, the happiness I just felt, and stumble down the hill, tripping over roots and rocks and not caring. I can barely contain myself as I approach the fence stretching across the base of the hill, pulling back just in time to keep my distance so that I don't risk being bitten and infected.

The red flashes again and then comes near me. She is at the fence now, with the others. And it's clear from looking at her that she is Unconsecrated. Her limbs don't work as if of one body and her skin stretches tight over her frame, as if the bones on her face could punch through at any moment.

But the red of her puffy vest is still vibrant and strange and I know that it's her. It's the Outsider. Gabrielle.

I want to link my own fingers through the fence. Travis hobbles behind me and pulls me back.

"What are you doing?" he demands, his voice a hiss as he sucks in breath. He walks with a cane and a limp and it suddenly occurs to me just how much of a struggle it must have been for him to make it down the hill after me so quickly.

Gabrielle darts around the other Unconsecrated. She's like them but somehow different. Sleeker. Faster. She thrashes against the metal links with a speed and voracity that I have never seen before. I stand with Travis on our side of the fence, not knowing what to feel, what to do.

"Never do that again," Travis says into my ear, his arms wrapping around my shoulders, pulling me against him.

I want nothing more than to let go, to let him envelop me and take me in and protect me. My entire body shakes with each heartbeat, my hands tremble. "She was the one in the room next to you," I say, pointing to Gabrielle. "The Outsider that came to the village that night I was in your room." Heat crawls up my cheeks as I remember the feel of his body under mine.

We watch as the girl in the red vest pulls against the links in the fence, desperate for us. There is something so wrong with her—neither of us has ever seen an Unconsecrated like this.

"She spoke to me through the wall one day," I tell him. "After you were moved and I went looking for you. She told me her name was Gabrielle." My throat burns and I swallow sobs that threaten to break free. I can't believe what has happened to this girl who dared wander the paths of the Forest, who dared enter our village.

Tears slip down my face and I turn toward Travis. "Did she tell you anything?" I whisper. "Did she tell you where she came from? Why she came to the village?"

"Oh, Mary," he says.

And then his lips fall on mine and I am silent.

I remember the wonder of my almost first kiss with him that night so long ago. It was the night that Gabrielle had come through the gate. Back before either of us knew anything about the Outside and cared only about the two of us in that room. How my heart pounded and my body felt on the verge of anything and everything. I have had kisses since then. Friendly kisses. All from Harry. All during our abbreviated courtship. I have never kissed anyone but Harry.

But this kiss with Travis—it's like waking up and being born and realizing what life is and can be. I drown in him, waves pulling me under and spinning me around as if I am nothing. Worthless, but everything.

The sound of the fence shuddering under Gabrielle's assault pulls us apart. He keeps his forehead against mine.

"We should tell someone," I say.

He nods.

"About her," I add.

He smiles. "That too," he says. I can't help but smile as well.

Like the bulbs buried dormant in the ground, I feel as though I am finally unfurling. Warming. Joy blooming inside me, expanding throughout my body. I have pushed aside the horror of finding Gabrielle turned Unconsecrated, pushed it deep down inside myself so that it doesn't rot the joy of this moment.

"I'm faster than you are," I say to him. "I'll run tell the Guardians. They'll want to know." I hesitate. I think about my promises to Cass and Sister Tabitha and Harry and myself. I think about what upholding such promises means, of all that I will be giving up. I have tried to abide by the rules of the village, by the edicts of the Sisterhood, and they have brought nothing but confusion and mystery and lies and pain.

I thought I could let Travis go. I thought I could live with contentment. But that was before he told me he believed in a world outside the fences. Before I realized that he was raised with stories of something greater beyond us, of something more.

Standing here facing Travis, tasting him on my lips, I decide to throw everything else away. I will face the wrath of

Cass and Harry and Sister Tabitha with Travis by my side. "Will you come for me?"

I know I am asking him to betray his brother, to upset the balance of the village, and hurt my best friend. But none of that matters to me anymore. I am willing to throw it all away for him.

He smiles, brushes a finger over my lips like a promise and, with the sound of Gabrielle tearing at the fence fading behind me, I turn back to the village to fetch the Guardians.

# ▼ XI ▼

For the past two days since we spoke on the hill I have waited for Travis to come for me. I pace my small stone room in the Cathedral, straining to hear his voice echo down the hallway, but am met with silence. Any time that I'm finally alone and can break away from the endless chores and festivities, I run to the hill. Hoping to find him there. Hoping he has figured out a way for us to be together.

But every time I find nothing but the wind in the trees. The moans of the Unconsecrated floating up from the Forest. The Guardians have increased their patrols of the fence and I sit and watch as they pace back and forth, peering into the Forest searching for Gabrielle.

Sometimes I see Jed there among them and I want to run to him and tell him everything I know about Gabrielle. Tell him that she came from the Outside. But I keep silent because the Guardians serve the Sisters and I'm afraid Jed would not keep my secret. That Sister Tabitha would find out I knew about Gabrielle and would throw me to the Forest.

Harry, who is apprentice to the Guardians now, tells me that the Fast One, as they are calling her, has disappeared into the Forest. That at times she will come and thrash against the fences and she is so fierce that the Guardians have been unable to kill her.

Her existence has dampened Edenmass. Some villagers worry that the Unconsecrated are changing, adapting, and that the Fast One is evidence of a new breed that will kill us all.

The Guild of Guardians and the Sisters try to calm the swelling panic, telling us that the fast Unconsecrated are not new. At one of our events Sister Tabitha stands, flanked by the two highest-ranking Guardians. The villagers spread out before her, their hands tight on their children, their eyes darting toward the fences. The air is thick with their fear and I can feel my muscles tense with the strain of it all.

"Knowledge of the fast Unconsecrated has passed down through the Sisterhood since the Return," she says, standing straight with her arms by her sides, the long black tunic whipping around her ankles in the afternoon wind. "The Fast Ones are fierce and rare and devastating. They have always existed and God has blessed this village not to be bothered by them." She sneaks a glance at me as she says this, as if I am somehow to blame for the presence of Gabrielle.

"We do not know what causes them to be different, what causes them to be fast. But we do know that they burn themselves out quickly, ripping their bodies apart, and that soon everything will return to normal. The Guardians have doubled their patrols and have pulled men from the fields to assist with the village watches. This threat will end soon, either by the Guardians killing the Fast One or by the Fast One burning out.

"Until such time, our only option is to continue our prayers to God and ask for His forgiveness and blessing."

Sister Tabitha leads us all in prayer and steps from the dais to allow the Edenmass and Brethlaw celebrations to continue. But I can see on everyone's faces that they are unsure and afraid of this new breed of Unconsecrated. The dancing becomes listless. The celebrations end early. People shutter their houses at night, preparing for the worst.

I can't help but wonder what other information they are keeping from us. What secrets the Sisters have locked in their Cathedral. What they know about the creature that was Gabrielle, once a girl like me.

My thoughts constantly turn to the day Sister Tabitha marched me down the underground tunnel and into the clearing in the Forest. Could the same thing have happened to Gabrielle? I want to run to Sister Tabitha and ask her what she has done, ask her how this happened. At first I stay silent because I'm terrified of becoming like Gabrielle and then other worries begin pounding in the back of my head: was there something I could have done to save her? Could I have spoken out? Searched harder? Was I responsible for her fate?

Finally, my curiosity becomes too much and I must know what happened—what caused her to turn into such a fast and powerful creature, unlike any Unconsecrated I have ever known.

In the few days remaining before my Binding to Harry, I begin to slink around the Cathedral as I go about my chores. Stopping outside closed doors, listening in on conversations between the elder Sisters, the ones I assume are the keepers of the secrets.

But I learn nothing of importance. In frustration, time slipping out before me, I begin to explore areas that are off-limits. I test the boundaries of the Sisterhood, of the Cathedral. Knowing that if I am caught I too could be thrown into the Forest to follow in Gabrielle's footsteps.

But I don't care about my recklessness. Because each day that passes is another day that Travis doesn't come for me. That I become more desperate to understand what has happened. That I must know everything: why we are here, who the Sisters are, what caused the Return.

Questions that we have never been allowed to ponder. That we have been forbidden to pursue.

I am ripe with these thoughts rolling through my head. As I kneel at services or attend Brethlaw celebrations, I feel rebellious trying to find a way around the Sisters, contemplating how to sneak past them. How to gain entrance to the forbidden sanctums of the Cathedral.

And yet when my final night alone comes, the night before my Binding ceremony with Harry, I am no closer to the truth. I have found nothing to connect the Sisters to Gabrielle's return. I have found nothing to show their complicity. I sit on the edge of my bed, my dressing gown clutched tight in my fists, and stare out the open window. Looking toward the Forest and wondering if I have it all wrong—if my questions have been for nothing.

Wondering if the Sisters are right and theirs is the only path. Theirs the only truth. Ours, the only village left in the world. Wondering if my mother was wrong and there is no ocean.

I clench my teeth, wanting to cry out with frustration and confusion. How am I supposed to understand it all?

My legs burn with anticipation and I jump from the bed and pace the room. Around me the Cathedral is quietly settling in for the night. My mind wars against itself, commanding me out of my room for one final search then ordering me to stay put. To not tempt fate and the wrath of the Sisters and to wait for Travis to come and claim me as he promised.

But then I think of Gabrielle out there tearing herself against the fences. I wonder if my mother is out there as well. If she somehow knows the answers I seek now that she is on the other side.

I don't bother to light my candle as I slip from the room. I don't bother to listen at doors as I make my way through the Cathedral, sliding along walls until I am sneaking down the dusty steps into the basement. In my mind I am following Sister Tabitha, remembering the day she brought me down here to a place I never knew existed to teach me about choices. I am remembering how I learned for the first time that the Sisterhood has been keeping secrets.

The air grows colder, danker as I reach the bottom of the stairs and slide my bare feet along the uneven stones of the floor. There's no light and I fumble to strike my flint to light my candle. Its weak flame barely illuminates my trembling hand and the light dies off quickly in the thick darkness around me.

With my free hand I feel for the empty shelves that, as Sister Tabitha explained, used to hold wine bottles and barrels for fermentation. I hear a scuttle of sharp nails over old wood and I freeze, a tingle creeping at the edge of my hairline.

When all I can hear is the wisp of my own breath I continue to feel my way through the room until, with the crack of my toe against the wall, I find the corner farthest from the stairs. I sweep aside the heavy curtain hiding the door, crawling behind it as dust coats my mouth and nose. And finally, I feel the rough wooden boards that make up the door leading to the tunnel that will take me to the Forest.

The latch won't move and I'm suddenly not sure what I expected to find down here. Perhaps I hoped that Sister Tabitha had left the door unlocked. Perhaps I hoped it would give way to my sheer force of will.

Instead, I let my head rest against the wood, pressing my ear against it as if I could hear anything on the other side. As if the door itself could whisper its secrets to me. I think about all these walls have seen and I wonder what it was like here when the Return struck. Did they know what was coming? Were they prepared? Did this village even exist before the Return, or was it created as a sanctuary? As a refuge hidden from the world?

But the walls tell me nothing, do not betray their secrets and everything around me is silent—my own breathing muffled by the curtain separating me from the rest of the room. Sleeplessness causes my eyes to burn, my limbs to feel heavy. I want to stay here in the cocoon of this place forever. Not having to face Harry. Not having to wonder if Travis will come for me. Not having to acquiesce to the Sisters, to acknowledge that I'm wrong about them.

I trace my hands along the pitted metal bands holding the wood of the door together, testing for weaknesses I know do not exist. I run my fingers over the hinges, my skin becoming slick with the grease they use in the Cathedral to keep the doors from creaking.

Suddenly, I want nothing more than my bed. To enjoy my one last night alone before I am bound to Harry. My last night to languish and allow Travis to pull me into dreams. I push away from the door, am slipping the curtain back from my shoulders, wiping my fingers along its grubby surface when I realize how to get past. How to gain entrance to the tunnel and the hidden rooms beyond.

I am instantly alert as I sweep the candle up from the floor by my feet. Its flame seems to throb with my heartbeat, the dull shadows it casts around me thrumming at the edges. My fingers shake as I feel along the wooden racks, testing for weakness. Finally, my finger catches the splinters of a split board and I grab it, twisting the wood until it pops and breaks, leaving me with a long narrow slat.

I keep prodding the shelves until I find another, thicker scrap of wood to serve as a makeshift mallet and then trace my way back to the hidden door. I wedge the splinter of wood against the head of the pin holding the two wings of the hinge together and begin tapping the end with the other scrap. I keep the curtain tight around my shoulders, hoping to dull the sound of my hammering.

At first the pin refuses to budge and I have to tap harder, until I'm swinging the mallet against the wedge of wood with all my strength, no longer caring about the echoes I'm creating around me.

I can feel the pin slipping free from the barrel, beginning to wobble, and I pull at it with my fingers, using the hem of my gown to get a better grip on the smooth metal. With a final tug it comes free, dropping to the floor with a satisfying ping. Without hesitating I start working on the other hinge lower on the door.

My nightgown pulls against my back, stuck to my skin with sweat by the time I've wrenched the other pin from its barrel so that the door is no longer connected to the wall by the hinges. I want to whoop and holler with satisfaction but instead wipe my arm across my brow and stretch the kinks from my back as I survey my progress.

While the door is still locked in place by the latch on one side, it's free to move on the other now that I have dismantled both hinges. Taking a deep breath, I jam my fingers through the narrow gap under the door and tug until the door eases open slightly. I scrape at the narrow opening until I have it pulled free enough to squeeze through, the heavy wood tilting now that it no longer has the hinges to balance it in place.

The air is damp, moldy, and my own breath sounds like a windstorm to my ears. I strain to hear in the darkness beyond my weak candlelight, suddenly terrified that there might be someone or something else down here. I have almost convinced myself that I can hear every earth bug moving toward me through the soil until I remember the small table of candles by the tunnel side of the door and I light them all, my body shuddering with relief as the small patch of light surrounding me grows.

My entire body shakes now, whether from fear or the sweat soaking my thin gown I don't know. I wish Travis were by my side, someone to hold my hand, to keep at bay the terror at the edges of my imagination. I have thought of this tunnel and these rooms for so long and yet now that I am here I don't want to press forward.

I'm not sure I want to know the truth anymore. To know what's kept hidden down here.

With the candle held out in front of me I force myself forward, the packed earth of the ground smooth under my bare feet. I pass the racks of wine and remember Sister Tabitha telling me about the history of this building. I follow the curve of the tunnel to the left and stop in front of the first door.

The wood is duller than I remember, the opening smaller. I trace my fingers over the splinters around the edges. I had forgotten about the rusted metal bolts thrust into the stone, keeping the doors locked, and I almost groan with relief and frustration. I tap against the wood and, when I hear nothing in response, knock harder.

I feel like a neighbor come calling and it makes me giggle, the sound bouncing off the stone walls and echoing maniacally around me. The noise is discordant to my ears, causing shivers to trail down my spine.

Trying to steady my breath, I set the candle on the ground, instantly missing the light and warmth. My body pulses with each heartbeat and my hands itch with fear. I take a bolt in each hand, tugging one back and up while pushing the other forward and down.

I hear a click and then a creak as the bolts slide free, the door suddenly swinging open.

A rush of air spills from the open room, dousing the candle at my feet and thrusting me into darkness.

Panic sets in fast and hard and I stumble back until I am pulling at the wall behind me, my feet sliding out from under me. I imagine hands on my ankles and I bite my tongue to keep from screaming. I push up from the floor, stumble and hit the wall, hearing the sound of bottles falling from racks and cracking around me.

Blind, I run. Behind me I hear the rip of fabric, the groan of wood against metal. I trip and fall, wincing as I crash against wooden steps and realize that I've gone the wrong way down the tunnel. The cavernous room under the Cathedral is at the other end and I am now under the Forest. For a heart-beat I consider running back through the tunnel, back to the Cathedral, but the darkness is too much. Too thick.

I climb up the stairs until I am wedged against the wooden door leading aboveground and can go no farther. I pull myself into a ball, tucking my legs against my chest. My breath pounds from my body like a sob. I clamp my hand over my mouth, but it does nothing to muffle the noise, the high-pitched wheeze of my body seeking air.

I try to hold my breath and listen to the stillness around me, between pounding heartbeats that cause my entire body to pulse. I hear the sound of liquid slugging from the broken wine bottles. Nothing else.

A sharp pain pierces my panic and with shaking hands I pull a shard of glass from the side of my right foot. My cheeks are wet with tears. I don't want to be here. I don't want any of this. I no longer care about Gabrielle or the Sisters or Harry or Travis. I don't care about anything in this world.

I imagine pushing open the heavy wooden door above me and slipping into the clearing. I imagine walking slowly toward the fences, my white gown billowing around my ankles as if I were floating. I imagine my mother waiting there on the other side. Her hands outstretched, ready for me.

I let the sobs overtake me then. This was not the way I

imagined my life. Crouched, dirty and terrified in a secret tunnel under the Cathedral the night before my Binding to a man I do not love. As a child I dreamed of love and sunlight and a world beyond the Forest. I dreamed of the ocean, of a place untouched by the Return.

And suddenly I wonder what right we have to believe our childhood dreams will come true. My body aches with this realization. With this truth. It is as if I have cut something important away from myself. The loss is almost overwhelming. Almost enough to make me give up.

It is as if my bones can no longer support my body. As if I am nothing more than blood and tears and fear and regret, slipping into the world around me. I realize I have three choices: find a way through the door above my head and go into the Forest myself, stay here until Sister Tabitha finds me and sends me into the Forest, or finish the job I have started and return to my life.

I push away from the stairs. Force myself to step back down the hallway that is so dark it's like swimming through thick black water. I feel the damp earth under my feet, the smell of the old wine, bitter and sour, sticking to the back of my throat. My body tenses as I pass the newly opened door in the darkness, my breath catches as I imagine hands grabbing me from inside the room and I give into the urge to run until, turning the corner in the tunnel, I see the tiny beacon of light from the rest of the candles next to the door to the basement under the Cathedral. I grab two and retrace my steps, picking my way through the broken glass, the candlelight glistening off the sharp edges.

I hesitate in front of the room, my light not penetrating past the threshold. There is still time for me to turn back. To clean up the broken wine bottles, replace the hinges on the door and return to bed, pretending that this night has been nothing more than a dream.

Instead, I take a deep breath and force myself to step forward.

# · XII ·

The room is tiny, the ceiling low. Against the far wall is a cot, an old faded quilt tucked tightly around it. To my right is a narrow desk, a thick book that could only be the Scripture resting on top of it surrounded by unlit candles. On the other side of the room a large tapestry hangs on the wall, His holiest words woven through it, a thin and well-worn pillow resting beneath it for kneeling and praying. In the center of the room a round braided rug that seems to be made from old Sisterhood tunics covers the floor.

I am stunned by the ordinariness of this room, as if it were any other Sister's quarters in the Cathedral. As if it were a mirror of my own upstairs. I step farther into the room, my footsteps muffled by the rug. I trace a finger down the smooth fabric of the tapestry, wondering how many other hands have touched these words, have sought solace in their presence. The pillow on the floor is dented where two knees would have rested for hours.

I sit on the bed and it creaks slightly beneath me, disturbing the dreamlike silence around me. I pull my feet close and lean back, wondering who was the last person to sleep here. Gabrielle? Travis when he was so ill? A Sister facing some sort of punishment?

Restless, eager for answers, I move to the narrow table and light the candles that surround the Scripture. Though I am facing the thick book with its cracked binding, my gaze is unfocused, my thoughts turned inward. Absently I flip it open, flick through the pages, the sound of them turning like the hush of fall leaves settling to the ground. But I'm not looking at the words written on the page, I'm staring past them, lost in my own world.

Until I realize that the words on the pages look wrong. That the pages themselves are too thick with writing. I bend closer and realize that all the margins, every blank space on every sheet, is filled with cramped writing. The words are so small that I can barely make them out, the ink from the other side of the page casting shadows, making the words essentially indecipherable.

I flip back to the first page and struggle with the cryptic handwriting, blue ink on onionskin-thin yellow pages. *In the beginning,* it said, *we did not understand the extent of it.*

I pull a candle closer but the rest of the writing is lost to me. I flip back through the book, watching as the handwriting changes, as the ink turns black, grows thicker and harder to understand.

And then the writing stops halfway through the Scripture. I run my finger up the page to see what was written last: *As expected, extreme and complete isolation was the cause of her immense strength and speed. God help us all, we will send her to the Forest to see how long she lasts, to better understand her. It is through her sacrifice that we grow stronger. It is through His glory that we survive.*

I do not realize that I am holding my breath until I gasp, choking for air. My body shakes, my mind whirling. I can't seem to swallow enough times to keep the tears from blurring my vision. Shoving myself back from the table and tripping over the rug behind me, I fall back against the door, causing it to slam shut, the sound echoing down the dark hallway.

I am trapped, cut off. Everything inside me screams and I gasp again for air. Panic consumes me and then, out of habit and a sense of security, I run my fingers over the spot next to the door where the Scripture would be, where the Sisters have carved words on the inside and outside of every other doorway in the village. Usually the spot is smooth from so many hands touching it on a daily basis, but here the wood of the threshold is still rough and it pulls me back into the present moment.

I peer closer at the words and realize that it's not Scripture quoted here, but a list of names. And at the bottom is written *Gabrielle,* the carving still deep and fresh.

Suddenly, the wind around me shifts, almost like a pop in the air. As if there is a subtle current that has been introduced into the tiny room. My body tingles with the fear that somehow I am caught. That my fate will be the same as Gabrielle's.

I tug the door and it cracks open. Relief that it didn't lock floods me and I peer into the hallway. It's still pungent from the broken wine bottles. I have no idea how long I've been down here. I'm desperate to read more but I know that doing so will risk being found.

I contemplate taking the Scripture with me but I have no place to hide it. I creep from the little room, closing and securing the door behind me, and clean up the broken bottles the best I can, shoving the largest shards of glass behind the racks lining the walls. Then, with a promise to return, I make my way back to the hidden door and I pinch the wick of each candle on the table, plunging the tunnel into darkness as I slip out. The well-greased pins slide easily back into place in the door hinges leaving no evidence that I have ever been here.

When I escape from the basement I see the dullest shade of pink breaking over the horizon outside the windows. I sneak back to my room and change into my tunic. I light a fire, tossing my dirty nightdress into the rising flames. After tomorrow I will no longer need it anyway.

I stand in front of the open window by my desk, letting the chill spring morning air wash over me, cleanse the scent of must and old wine from my body. I stare past the graveyard at the fences, allowing my eyes to blur until the Forest is nothing but a smudge of fresh green, the Unconsecrated dull specks, the fence nonexistent.

Nothing in life is clear to me anymore. Nothing makes sense and I don't know how to make it right.

Tonight is my Binding with Harry. Today is the last chance for Travis to claim me. The celebrations will start up again this afternoon. But for now my time is my own and I sneak from the Cathedral and skirt around the edge of the waking village until I am back on the hill.

Instead of looking to the Forest, to the edge of my world, today I look down on the village. At the cottages and houses that huddle against the earth starting at the bottom of the hill and spreading toward the Cathedral on the other side of the village. The Cathedral is a hulking shape, its wings spreading out like arms. Behind the Cathedral is the familiar sight of the graveyard and the small drop to the stream where Harry and I held hands the day my mother became infected. Dotted throughout are the platforms set into the trees, stocked and ready for our refuge if there is ever a breach.

The fence surrounds all of it, tall intertwining links forever keeping us safe. I think about how fragile those fences are, how vines like to snake around them during the summer causing endless work for the Guardians who are always on patrol, always repairing and mending.

It astonishes me how something so delicate, like lace metal, keeps us trapped in this world. Unhampered by the Unconsecrated, but also by our dreams. The sun slips across the sky, for a brief moment glinting off the fences protecting the path beyond the gate by the Cathedral.

I spend the morning thinking about how together Travis and I can make it all right. And I continue to pace at the top of the hill, waiting for Travis to come claim me, time slipping around me like water over a rock.

▽    ▽    ▽

When it is time to prepare for the Binding ceremony that night I sit on the bed in the small cottage near the Cathedral that will become Harry's and mine once our union is completed tomorrow. My hands lie limp in my lap as I realize that Travis may never come for me after all.

A knock on the door triggers my heart and it pounds hard in my chest. I stand, hoping it's Travis. Knowing that this is our last chance. That once the Binding begins I will have to give myself to Harry or cancel the ceremony.

And canceling the ceremony means throwing myself on the mercy of the Sisters. Begging them to allow me to rejoin their ranks even if it means being nothing more than their servant. A woman in our village is not given a second chance at marriage.

I smooth my hands over the white fabric that drapes down my legs. My hands shake as I reach for the door. My stomach tenses, my whole body flooding with fear and hope and joy.

The light outside the door is the blinding last gasp of the day, and for a moment I think it's Travis and that my life has finally fallen into place. That I finally understand where I belong in this world.

And then I hear the rustle of skirts as Sister Tabitha steps through the doorway and stalks to the middle of the room. She turns to face me, looks me up and down with her sharp eyes.

"I have come to prepare you for the Binding," she says. "To give you the blessing of the Sisterhood."

I want to crumple right there, to fall into myself until I am nothing more than a heap of emptiness on the floor. My head feels light, my vision blurry. My throat burns to scream and cry. But I refuse to allow Sister Tabitha to see any of this and so I raise my chin, close the door and steady myself by placing a hand against the wall.

We are alone in the little one-room cottage that will house Harry and me, until we have children and need more space. The thought of children with Harry falls like a stone inside my stomach.

In the last few days I had already begun to imagine what Travis's and my children would look like, how their tiny hands would curl around my finger. I had already dreamed an entire life between Travis and me. And now that was the only life that we would ever lead together—the one in my dreams.

Sister Tabitha and I stand facing each other, our backs rigid until she smiles just a little, releasing a breath as if on a laugh.

She shakes her head. "There are things we must accept in this world, Mary. Things that may not make sense to us now, but that we must adhere to. That we must keep sacred if we hope to persevere."

She walks over to the narrow bed and sets a basket down on the white quilt. As she continues to speak she starts to unpack its contents. "Take for example the Unconsecrated. We do not understand them. We only know they hunger. But we know to leave them be. No one in this village even bothers to question their existence anymore, although I am sure our ancestors wasted a lot of time doing so."

She sets down a delicate-looking white braided rope and then pulls the Scripture from the basket. She winds the rope around the book as she continues with her speech.

"It is the same with marriage. Our ancestors knew that in order to survive we had to persevere. They knew to keep strong bloodlines. That creating each new generation was the most important task beyond keeping the village safe and fed."

She brings the bound Scripture to the small table on my side of the room and sets it down. Then she turns to the fireplace and stirs the embers while adding small strips of dry wood until the logs begin to crackle.

The flames eat at the bark, curling it into red-rimmed tendrils but the heat cannot penetrate me, cannot warm me. "There is something you need to know about your mother, Mary," she says, kneeling by the hearth. "You should know that she lost children."

# XIII

I fight to keep my face passive, swallowing my gasp of shock. I can only think of my brother and me when we were young, sitting by my mother and father in front of the fire. I hear the lullaby that my mother used to sing to us at night.

I am at war with myself. At once desperately needing to know more and detesting myself for giving in to Sister Tabitha. For giving her what she wants, which is my obedience to her will. To her superiority.

"When" is all that I say. I swallow, clear my throat. "When did my mother . . ." I can't finish, fearful of bridging this gap between my mother's life and my own.

"Before you," she tells me. "And after you." I can't see her eyes but I wonder if there is sympathy there. If she is sad for the babies that my mother lost and if she feels futile that she couldn't stop it even though she is the healer among us.

For a moment it is as though Sister Tabitha and I are connected through my mother's grief.

She rises and then turns to me. "Many, many times. So much that it seemed you were never supposed to have been born."

Any sympathy I may have had for Sister Tabitha shatters; the sound of my mother's moans the day she turned comes screaming into my ears. It washes over me until I feel nauseated and unable to stay in this room, to be near this woman.

But still I stand my ground, unwilling to let her see the effect she's had on me. She walks back over to the table and lays her hands on the Scripture. Then she comes to stand before me.

Her eyes meet mine as she reaches down and grasps my right hand. She then unwinds the rope from the Scripture and wraps it around my wrist as she goes. Each time she completes a circle she knots the rope in a complicated pattern, forcing me to repeat Vows Of Fidelity. Three times we repeat this, three circles of rope, three knots, three vows.

With each twist, each tether, each word, I feel myself falling farther from Travis and I must bite my lip to keep from weeping.

"You are a Bound woman now, Mary. And you have a duty to your husband, to God and this village. It is time to own up to that duty, Mary. It is time you stopped playing by the fences. There is nothing out there. Your mother found that out the hard way and you would think that you would have learned your lesson from her."

I try to yank my arm back but she keeps a tight hold on my wrist.

"I have done everything that I know how to do for you, Mary. I have taught you of our Lord. But you were not happy.

I procured you a husband. But you are not happy. What will it take, Mary? Will it take the destruction of this village before you will find happiness? Before you will be content with the life you have been given?"

Her eyes are a summer thunderstorm. Sweat pricks my skin and trickles down my back, seeping through the thin material of my gown.

I can feel her breath on my cheek and I try to lean away from her but the wall keeps me from moving.

"Pray to God, Mary." She continues, "Pray that He will bring you mercy and that He will give you a child, a way to love outside yourself." She shakes her head as she speaks, her voice now a whisper. "It is what your mother did, Mary. How do you think she ended up with you?"

I want to slap her, I want to rail against her body with all the fury and pain and hate inside me, eating away at me. But I can't. Because suddenly, it's not Sister Tabitha I despise, but myself. Never has it occurred to me that my mother had any difficulty conceiving me. Never did I question the ease with which I assumed I had entered her life.

I am struck with the knowledge of my own selfishness. That this woman in front of me knows more about my mother than I ever did or ever will. All of the stories my mother passed down to me flood into my head at once. Never did I wonder why my mother told me these stories. Never did I wonder what these tales meant to her.

Never did I wonder what my mother believed. What sort of life my mother lived at my age. So acutely do I miss her at this moment that I want to crawl into myself with shame and longing.

Sister Tabitha is about to say more when we both hear a

knock at the door. My heart skids. Travis, I think. He has finally come for me. My face is so close to Sister Tabitha's that I can see the sweat as it escapes her skin. For a moment I wonder if she can hear what I'm thinking, if she can feel the way my body tingles in anticipation. She smiles again, barely, and then leans back. Harry enters the room and I want to weep when I see him there, his cheeks pink from the evening air, his hair damp and starting to curl over his ears.

I look past him out the door into the dusk of evening, hoping to catch a glimpse of Travis, hoping he's out there waiting just at the edge. My eyes search every shadow but there's nothing—the world is empty. And then with a click the door falls shut.

In his arms Harry carries a squirming black dog that doesn't look older than a year, its body just growing into its paws. The dog tumbles to the floor and runs in a few circles and then comes and wiggles over my feet, its tail sweeping items off a low table nearby. "A wedding present for you, Mary," he says, dipping his face a bit as if embarrassed.

I want to smile. I want to thank him. But in my mind I'm still looking past the door, waiting for Travis.

Harry holds out his left arm. Sister Tabitha takes it and, leaving a length of slack between us, wraps the other end of the rope around his wrist three times, completing the same series of complicated knots and vows that she had performed with me.

Keeping her hand around the middle of the rope that joins us, Sister Tabitha recites an old prayer from the Scripture. When she's done she says, "You are now Bound," and then she walks to the bed and pulls a long blade from the basket she had brought with her earlier. She sets it on the table, next to the Scripture. "This is your last chance to renounce each other. Your last chance to sever the ties between you. Tomorrow you take your final Vows of Eternal Constancy." And then she slips from the cottage, leaving us alone.

Harry turns toward me and I keep my eyes on the awkward-looking dog, who has curled up by the fire and is gnawing on a thin log he pulled from a pile stacked next to the hearth. Harry reaches out and plucks something from my cheek and holds it out for me to see, but I can't tell what it is.

"Eyelash," he says. "Make a wish, blow on it for luck."

The earnestness of his expression reminds me of when we were children. Of how we used to run through the fields just after a harvest when the air was full of sun and the smell of life. In that moment I remember one afternoon when all the children of the village were playing, chasing each other through the maze that our parents had cut through the corn.

Getting lost and tangled together in the late-afternoon sun as if there were nothing else in the world that mattered besides twisting along a path that led to nowhere but the middle of a field. When finding the end of the path was not quite as important as the journey to getting there.

That one afternoon, when I couldn't have been older than eight, I grabbed Harry's hand and I pulled him into the maze with me. How we laughed as we tripped our way down the many paths, going in circles, discovering dead ends. And how it began to rain, not enough to drive us out of the maze, but enough that we could quench our thirst by sticking out our tongues.

How we found a cove off the path that was easy to miss, just a narrow little entrance that opened up into a small round clearing filled with nothing but soft clover, as if this spot had never been planted or never sprouted.

A spot where the rain didn't fall and the sun still shone.

I remember how Harry and I grabbed each other's hands and spun in circles until we were dizzy with laughter and twirling and how we fell to the ground, our fingertips just touching.

Just then the most amazing rainbow burst through the rain and covered our little cove of clover. Everything around us was color and light and I remember how Harry turned his head toward me and how I turned toward him and how he said, "For luck, Mary. For us. Forever."

The passion in his eyes at that age, still a boy, is the same that I have seen in Travis. The same I see in Harry now. I realize that I've been so angry at Harry for my own fate, as if he has been my enemy and not the friend I have always known. I can see now that his life is as constricted as mine. That we are both tumbling against the same rules and that perhaps it's unfair for me to blame him for where we find ourselves now.

And I crumble. "I want to leave here," I tell him. My voice is nothing but a whisper.

He is silent and so I continue. Now that I've said this, I can't help but say more, can't help but speak the words that have been gathering in my head like dark clouds before the storm, building pressure and growing, and rolling over themselves in chaos.

"There's a world out there. Beyond the fence—there's another side. An end. I know it. There was a girl. Her name was Gabrielle and she came from the other side. She was an Outsider and she was here and now she's Unconsecrated and I know it was the Sisters who sacrificed her. She's the Fast One, the one in the strange red vest and she's the proof and they killed her because they didn't want us to know. They have never wanted us to know."

My tirade leaves me panting, and I'm terrified at having let this idea out into the world, of having spoken my true desires. These are not proper thoughts—no one I know has ever expressed a desire to leave our village. To trade utopia for what may lie beyond.

"Will that make you happy, Mary?" he asks. His voice is soft, without censure or judgment.

I finally look him in the eyes. He reaches out and slips his hand into mine, the white rope dangling between us.

For a flash of a moment I hate Harry for not being Travis. And hate Travis more for never coming for me. For leaving me to this night. But most of all I hate myself for loving Harry's brother with everything that I have so that there is nothing left over for him.

And for being too much of a coward to cut him free. To use the knife to sever our bonds.

He leans forward and I realize that he smells like Travis. I have to close my eyes as he brushes his lips over my forehead. The heat from the fire almost suffocates me. His mouth moves to my ear. "Will leaving here make you happy, Mary?"

He's so tender, so eager to make me happy in ways that no one else has. Tears start to crowd in my eyes and my body begins to respond to this man as if it were his brother whispering into my ear. As if my body can't tell the difference between the two, between their whispers and the feel of their breath on my flesh.

I squeeze my eyes and nod my head. Terrified that he'll cast me out for such a desire—that he'll refuse me and I will be left to the Sisters.

"We will find a way for you to be happy, Mary. I promise you I will find a way for us."

I nod again, unable to open my mouth and speak for fear of letting out the sobs I'm trying to trap inside.

"I just want you to be happy, my Mary," he echoes, reaching out and tucking a strand of hair behind my ear and then leaning in to kiss the path his fingers just took. I open my eyes and look at my new dog, at the way he twitches by the fire as he sleeps his young dog dreams, likely chasing something he will never catch. The only difference between him and me being that tomorrow he will forget that he ever wanted something beyond his grasp and I will always remember.

Harry continues to trail kisses down my neck until I am forced to close my eyes, a gasp slipping through my lips like pleasure.

Eyes still closed, I raise a hand and trace the curve of his shoulder blades. I wonder if Travis's back holds these same curves. If my hand would fit against his skin the way it fits over Harry's. So many times have I relived Travis whispering in my ear, imagined Travis kissing along my jaw. Tonight I try to draw on those same memories, afraid that I've forgotten them, feeling traitorous at my own confusion.

But the visions refuse to come and I can recall nothing of Travis. It is only Harry in the firelight, his skin warm and smelling of fresh-turned soil. And I cannot help but hear Sister Tabitha's words repeat themselves around the room. About this being the life I have been given.

Not the life I have chosen.

# XIV

When the siren wails the next morning I am in bed. The dog Harry brought me last night as a wedding gift, whom I have named Argos, begins to bark madly, trying to decide whether to attack the noise or hide in the corner.

I feel a sharp tug on my wrist and suddenly I'm half sprawled on the floor.

"Mary, get up," Harry shouts. He's pulled me from the bed and I stare at the rope stretched taut between us. With his free hand Harry is reaching for something on the table, and yet all I can do is stare at that rope. My mind is a haze of images from the night before: Harry kissing me, Sister Tabitha admonishing me to be a good wife and bring children to our village, Argos and his puppy dreams.

"Mary, you have to help me here!" He is yanking on the rope and I feel it bite into my wrist. I can see how his hands are shaking. He steps to my side, grabs my shoulders and pulls me to the table. He picks up the ceremonial blade left by Sister Tabitha and slides it under the Binding rope.

And then the pressure on my wrist releases. Free, Harry starts to ransack our cottage, gathering clothes and food and stuffing them into a bag.

I pick up the other end of the rope, let it slip through my fingers. The fibers are still warm where the knots around Harry's wrist used to be.

Time feels as if it has slowed, stretching taut like a thread of wool. The siren blocks out every other noise so that I can see people running past the window by the door, throwing glances over their shoulders, fog swirling around their feet so that it appears as if they are gliding, but it's all almost silent, their moves lost in the one long solid note of the alarm.

The panic I have been bred to feel doesn't come. Instead, I walk to the window, not bothering to cover my body as I watch my friends and neighbors scramble for the platforms. Even now a part of my brain, the part that is buried in my subconscious, urges me to action. Urges me to get dressed and to run. Run with the rest of them before it's too late. Before the platforms are full and all the ladders have been pulled away.

Behind me Harry is shouting orders but his words mingle with the siren, all a jumble in my head. A small part of me wonders if this siren will delay the ceremony, if there will still be time for Travis to come for me. I wonder if there really is a breach or if it's something like my mother, someone getting too close to the fence. Someone taking a risk, losing their mind, getting Infected.

Argos scratches at the floor frantically trying to dig his way out. His nails scrabble and slide uselessly on the wood and I can sense his rising panic. He lifts his head as if to howl, his teeth bared, his eyes pleading for me to do something.

Finally, I am just reaching for my skirt when I see it. A flash of bright red out of the corner of my eye as it streaks past the window. I know that color. I know how unnatural it is. I know that speed.

The Unconsecrated are here, among us. This is no drill.

Gabrielle is here.

I fumble with the buttons on my skirt and I go to the door as I pull a shirt over my head. I pause with my fingers just touching the latch. What if it's too late? My heart pounds as indecision streams through my blood. What if the platforms are already full?

I look back at Argos who is trying to determine whether to follow me, whether he trusts me to protect him. Harry is oblivious as he races around the cottage flinging open cupboards, searching for weapons.

Outside the window I see two children running through the fog, holding hands. They're brother and sister. I know them—have known them since the boy, Jacob, was born six years ago. Jacob trips and falls, grabbing at his now-bloody knee. The sister pauses, noticing that her hand is empty where it just recently held the hand of her older brother. She looks back over her shoulder at Jacob on the ground, his arm stretched out to her for help. She shakes her head, her fingers in her mouth and her eyes wide, her blond curls bouncing with the gesture.

Suddenly, her body stiffens with an age-old terror. I see a wetness appear on the front of her skirt and she stumbles back, her eyes shifting between her brother and something beyond. Jacob turns his head and then flops onto his back, using the heels of his hands to drag himself across the packed dirt. My view is blocked by the frame of the window and I have to press my face awkwardly against the glass to see what I already know is there. It's a pack of Unconsecrated shambling toward the boy. They always come in packs.

The sister takes two steps toward her brother, grabs his arm and tugs, but she's too small and weak to drag him. The Unconsecrated approach and the boy struggles against his sister, batting her little hands away, pushing her toward the platforms.

All of this takes place in the space between heartbeats and I back away from the window before my heart beats again, before I see Jacob's fate which I know all too clearly. Like the little girl I shake my head in disbelief.

This is panic. And panic means the people on the platforms will pull up the ladders early. Will do anything to save themselves first.

The hair on Argos's back spikes, his head is low and I see his body vibrate with a growl. All dogs in our village instinctually fear the Unconsecrated and have been trained to scent them. His entire being is focused on the door to our cottage, he is warning us of what exists beyond.

Something crashes into me. I'm pushed away from the window. Harry shoves the ceremonial knife into my hand and grabs my chin, his fingers digging against my jaw as he searches my eyes.

His chest heaves, sweat trickles down his temples. And then he throws open the door, dashes outside and is back before I have a chance to recover. Before I have a chance to scream or hold him back. While I am still rubbing where his thumb dug into my skin. In his arms is Jacob, who had been left for the Unconsecrated by both his sister and me. Harry drops the boy onto the bed and returns to his work gathering supplies.

He tosses a bundle to me and I clutch it to my chest with one hand, the ceremonial blade in the other. He grabs two water bladders from a hook by the door and then pauses, looking at me. I'm still standing where he pushed me against the wall.

He reaches a hand out toward me and I take it. His fingers trail along the white Binding rope on my wrist and I see a hint of a smile touch his lips. He opens his mouth to say something but I'm deaf with the continuing siren.

I feel the cottage shudder as something crashes into the door. Harry turns from me and grabs Jacob. Slings him over his shoulder. At the door Harry pauses, placing his hand against the wood, touching the Scripture carved into the frame. I want to close my eyes, to block out what is happening. To pretend as if this day has never begun—will never begin.

I try to get a feel for the blade in my hand, for my only weapon. From a young age everyone in my village is taught how to fight for a day such as this. The wood on the handle is smooth and slippery from the dampness of my palm. It feels awkward and unwieldy, and the bag of food throws me off balance.

And then, before I have a chance to rearrange myself, to prepare, Harry throws open the door and we are running.

Even encumbered with the boy, the water, an ax and his own bag of food, he's faster than I am, his steps surer than mine, my terror blurring my eyesight. Argos tangles himself around my legs, not knowing any other refuge, and I stumble.

Our cottage is set back behind the Cathedral, just on the edge of the main living area of the village. Platforms are scarce here and I run for the closest, thrown off by the bulky bag I carry pressed to my chest. My fingers are about to close over the rungs of a ladder when it slips from my grasp, the mist of the morning making the wood slick. I pause and look at the people above—only half full. The man who pulls the ladder up to the platform just shrugs at me. Not even an apology. Not that I could have heard it with the siren continually pulsing in my senses.

Beside him on the platform men pull at bows, letting loose arrows toward targets somewhere behind me. I can feel the compression of an arrow splitting the air as it cuts next to my head. I don't know if the arrow was meant for me or for something behind me and I refuse to look over my shoulder to find out. Reality is too much to bear at this moment and so I shove it aside.

Frantic, I glance around for another platform and scramble toward it. Argos is still at my side and he bites at my skirt to get me to stop and I stumble and fall to my knees. I look up and see Travis at the ladder, not ten lengths from where I kneel. He's waiting for his turn to climb, Cass at his side.

I can't stop myself from shouting out his name.

It's useless, of course. The siren is too loud, our combined panic deafening us. I yell again, closing my eyes with the effort of pushing every bit of breath in my body into this one word. The siren cuts off just as the sound leaves my mouth and the world is silent except for me and the echo of Travis's name leaving my lips.

It's as if I've frozen the world for this moment. He looks up and our eyes connect. Two heartbeats, and then three—we are almost one person. There amongst the nothingness we exist for a brief moment in our own calm and I can almost imagine the feel of his lips against my wrists.

And then there's a tug on my sleeve as men begin to shout

out orders and the moans of the Unconsecrated press in around us, crashing into the silence. I swing out wildly with my bag but it's Harry again and he deflects my blows.

He grabs my arm and pulls me away from the circle of houses, away from the too-full platforms and Travis and toward the Cathedral. I hear people screaming. Panic, pain, terror. The sound becomes a harmony with the moans, with the shouts of battle.

Something pulls at my hair and I stumble, fall to one knee. I roll to the side as slick gray arms lunge for me. I'm on my back, Argos barking madly as an Unconsecrated woman falls toward me. I thrash at the grass around me with my hands until I feel the smooth wood of my knife. I swing up and around and bury the blade in the Unconsecrated woman's shoulder.

It's the first time I have used a weapon against an Unconsecrated, and I gag as I feel the smooth metal slice through the flesh and dig into bone. The woman keeps coming at me, her arm almost severed, her filthy blond hair falling in clumps across her face. I try to pull at the blade to dislodge it but can't seem to gain enough leverage.

She continues to fall on top of me. Her mouth is hanging open and I can see the gaps from where she is missing teeth. I hold up my hands to try to keep her away and she claws at me. Her mouth is so close to my flesh that I can feel the stench of death seeping through me. I kick at her, whip my arms at her, but to no avail. I close my eyes and wait.

# XV

The pain does not come. I open one eye to find her progress toward me stopped. The end of the long handle of the blade is buried in the dirt by my head and barely keeps her teeth from my flesh. She continues to flail and snap, her fingertips scratching my cheeks.

I fall back, lie flat with her hovering above me and begin to push myself along the ground, sliding out from under her. Hands grab at my shoulder and I begin to struggle again but it's Harry and he pulls me free.

With one clean stroke he decapitates the Unconsecrated woman and her head tumbles to the ground. I reach for my weapon but it is buried too deep, stuck in the bone. Harry tugs on my arm and I have to leave it behind, making my hands feel too empty, too vulnerable.

My body quivers, my legs wobble and I can already feel the burn of tears stinging in my throat as we start moving again. The air feels heavy with the smell of blood, its tang sticking to the back of my mouth as if I taste it rather than smell it. My chest convulses with each breath as if I can't get enough.

Around me my friends and neighbors fall to the Unconsecrated. Some have already died and Returned, their throats mauled, their limbs torn. They continue to pour from the mist enveloping us all.

They're everywhere. Those on the platforms struggle to fight them, to protect the living left on the ground, but the Unconsecrated flow in a never-ending wave, multiplying as they come. The fog confuses everything, making it difficult to discern living from dead.

Harry stands to the left of me, Jacob thrown over his shoulder again. He points past me and I turn. To my right is the Cathedral, its stone walls thick and solid. While the Unconsecrated press in behind us, they have yet to make it to the shelter of the Cathedral. Already Sisters and Guardians stand at the second-story windows letting loose a constant flow of arrows.

I can hear the sound of hammers as those inside fortify the large windows on the ground floor. We are still a distance away when I see two Sisters come around the side of the building. Together they fling closed the thick shutters bounding each window and make their way toward the large front door, where another Sister stands beckoning them with her hands.

There seems to be a problem with the last shutter. As we draw closer I can see that they are furiously working to get it secure. Finally, one Sister pushes the other to the door and stays outside alone and I realize it is Sister Tabitha.

She struggles against the heavy wood with all her weight,

leaning away from it. Finally, it budges and I watch her stumble backward as the shutter slams shut. She pulls a thick length of metal and settles it into the brackets on either side of the window, reinforcing it. Her task complete, she hustles back to the front door and I see her knuckles rap against the wood.

Harry and I sprint toward her, running for the temporary sanctuary of the Cathedral. I try to yell to her to wait for us, but I am too out of breath and the words fall limp from my mouth.

But somehow she seems to know and as the door opens she turns. She watches as Harry and Jacob and Argos and I draw closer even while hands try to tug her into the safety of the Cathedral.

Still she stands in the doorway. Hesitating.

It's not as though the world around me slows as much as every detail becomes bright and vivid. For a moment I feel as if I'm outside myself, floating and watching. I no longer feel the sear of my lungs or the strain of my legs, the tenderness in my knee from having fallen earlier.

Sister Tabitha almost smiles, and I can see that her knuckles gripping the edge of the door are white. My every step seems to take longer and longer. We are close enough now that I can see the Sisters behind her begging her to come inside, yelling for her to close the door. Shouting for the fortification.

But still she waits. Barring the door open, holding them off. She takes a step forward, reaches up a hand as if she can pull us toward her faster.

She does not see the streak of red.

And yet she must sense that something is terribly wrong

for suddenly I stop running. She must hear the crack of feet sprinting over dry ground to her right. She must see the look of horror on my face.

Gabrielle is upon her before she can turn her head. Crashes against her before she can register any expression. Sister Tabitha tries to pull back, tries to escape into the Cathedral as Gabrielle tangles in her long black tunic. I watch as the other Sisters' hands shove her out the door. I can hear her cries of pain that turn into screams and gurgles. I hear the panicked shouts of the Sisters inside as they try to close the door, try to thrust Sister Tabitha outside, away from them.

Gabrielle's attention shifts to them and she pushes around Sister Tabitha to gain entrance. She almost makes it, is almost into the Sanctuary. But then Sister Tabitha wraps her arms around Gabrielle's thin body and pulls her away from the opening, even as Gabrielle twists and sinks her teeth into Sister Tabitha's throat.

The door to the Cathedral slams shut and still Sister Tabitha and Gabrielle wrestle on the ground. Fog spins and twirls around their struggling bodies.

I can feel the whimpers choking me and I clamp a hand over my mouth, knowing not to draw attention to myself lest the thing that was Gabrielle seek out a new victim so soon. The Unconsecrated never hesitate to leave a fresh kill in order to bring down another living victim. It's in their nature to kill and infect above all else.

The world around me seems to speed up and I suddenly feel dizzy, everything spinning. The platform ladders have all been pulled up or pushed aside. The Cathedral is closed. There's nowhere left.

Except for the path, I realize. Except for the gate Gabrielle came through when she first entered the village so many weeks ago. Back before, when she was healthy.

I turn and sprint, Harry behind me. I hear the sound of too many feet in pursuit. I'm sure Gabrielle is chasing us. As we draw near the gate the siren begins to wail again, alerting the villagers to what I already know—the platforms are full, those left on the ground must seek other refuge.

The fence bulges where the Unconsecrated who haven't found their way in push against it, the smell of fresh blood in the air driving them insane with hunger. My fingers feel clumsy as I fumble with the latch on the gate and then Harry is behind me, pressing against me, his breath hot and fast in my ear.

Finally, the latch gives and he pushes us through with such force that I stumble and fall down on the path, my palms stinging. I turn back just as Argos slips through. The gate crashes shut and Gabrielle slams against it, her mouth open, blood trailing from her chin.

I close my eyes, hold my breath, let the siren pulse through my body, for once grateful that the sound is so overwhelming that it takes over and blocks my other senses. I do not want to see right now. Or hear or feel or smell.

But my body screams for air and the stench of death filters through me. I get to my feet and walk back to the gate we came through, pushing Harry's hand off my shoulder as he tries to stop me. An arm's length away, I stop. I stand and face Gabrielle.

I look death in the eye.

Her fingers are all broken; some have bone pushing through the flesh. Her arms are ragged and yet she flings herself at me with a passion that will not end until her body is too spent to stand and still she will crawl onward.

The siren halts its wail again and the sound is replaced by the rattle of the fence as Gabrielle lunges against it again and again, her broken teeth clacking as her jaws snap in anticipation. But her eyes are still clear—that clarity of the newly Unconsecrated. And she stares at me as if I am her only salvation.

I realize I am standing on the path that she traveled to our village and it's now she who is trapped on the other side of the gate. I want to ask her who she is, where she came from and what she wants from me. Why we are connected in this place.

But then she raises her head as if she is sniffing the air, something catching her attention from the corner of her eye, and she darts off back toward the village. Back into the fog and my friends and neighbors. Back to her sustenance.

Harry comes to grab me, to urge me down the path. Argos spins around us both, barking and growling at the Unconsecrated that pulse against the fences on either side of us. But I refuse to move, to go any farther. Instead, I lace my fingers through the mesh of the gate where Gabrielle just stood and look through the early morning haze back toward our home.

"It was her," I whisper. My body is beginning to go numb, as if it can't take any more and it's shutting down.

Harry tugs at my arm, tries to pull me away from staring at the carnage swirling in the mist. "What are you talking about, Mary?"

"The one I was telling you about last night." I start to beat at the gate, wanting to feel as many emotions as possible to prove that I am still alive. "Gabrielle. The girl who came down the path. She was the one who caused this. She was the reason . . ."

"Mary, what are you talking about?" His voice is sharp around the edges, as if he will shatter at any moment.

I feel as if I'm ripping apart inside, everything fragmenting at once. "Don't you see? They did this to her! The Sisters, they caused this and—"

Harry pries my fingers from the fence and pulls me against his body. "That doesn't matter anymore."

I struggle against him, not wanting comfort as fury and terror mix in the pit of my stomach. "But what if the Guardians had something to do with—"

"I said it does not matter, Mary!" His voice rumbles through my chest, vibrating my entire body. "What is done is done and now is not the time to speak of it!"

I bow my head. I know I shouldn't press him and yet I can't help it. "But it proves—"

"No!" he shouts. His nostrils flare and he takes a deep breath, closes his eyes, shakes his head. When he speaks again his words are carefully measured, barely contained. "It proves nothing. Only that the fences have been breached and that our village is under attack and that we are not there to help them."

Looking back at the village, I see figures moving but I can't tell if they are living or Unconsecrated. I can't tell if it is a skirmish, a battle or a war. I think I see that flash of red again but I can't be sure that it isn't my mind playing tricks on me. Telling me what I want to see.

But then there is someone coming toward us out of the fog. Two people approaching. I take a step back, wondering if it's more Unconsecrated. Wondering how I have now found myself on the side of the Forest fearing what is in my village.

Their features begin to crystallize and I recognize the limp of Travis.

# XVI

The path just on the other side of the gate is wide enough for the four of us to stand in a row—me and Harry, Travis and Cass—our shoulders sometimes touching as we watch the fog lift and understand fully the chaos that's taking place in our village.

The oddest thing about an Unconsecrated invasion is that no dead litter the ground; they all rise and join ranks with the enemy or are devoured. Again and again we see friends and neighbors felled, only to return and fell more friends and neighbors in time.

I stand between Harry and Travis. Cass is on the other side of Harry. Behind us Jacob lies wrapped up tightly like a roly-poly, his arms around his knees. I can hear his body jerk as he struggles to contain his sobs. Occasionally Argos goes to Jacob's side, whimpers and licks his face. But Jacob doesn't notice and Argos returns to place his muzzle in my hand and whine.

Next to me I feel Travis shift and the skin of his knuckles skims my hand. I twitch my fingers in response, and we link our pinkies. He pulls my hand into his and I sway with relief. With this simple gesture that he is safe. That we are still okay. I tamp down the thoughts that had crept through my dreams the night before: that Travis never came for me. That he never cared for me. That he did not want me.

His thumb glides over the pulse in my wrist and then I feel his body stiffen. His fingers trace along the rope still tied to me, frayed and dingy now. It's the rope that bound Harry and me together the night before.

Travis's hand slips away from mine. I feel its absence the way it must feel to lose a limb. Desperate, the ghost of its presence still taunting me.

I want to turn to him, to talk to him. But I can't force the words from my mouth with Harry standing so close. With our village dying before us.

"Do you think we should go help them?" Harry asks.

Out of the corner of my eye I can see his hand clenching and unclenching from the ax he brought from our cottage. His voice is flooded with the same hopelessness we all feel.

None of us moves. Instead, we simply stand and stare. Unable to fully comprehend what is happening. That the world we have always known is crumbling.

That such a thing would occur must have been inevitable and yet none of us ever believed it would happen. Never really thought it could happen. Of course we have known breaches and have lived always with the threat of the Unconsecrated. But it's been generations since the Return. We were surviving. Our village is a testament to life constantly surrounded by the threat of death.

And now that is gone. Everyone we have ever known, the only place we have ever been, every possession: gone.

Soon enough the dead shuffle through the village and one by one they approach the gate. As if we are the last of the living for them to hunger after. While the day wears on we stand and watch the Unconsecrated gather on the other side, watch as they push against the fencing. Listen to the shouts of the survivors as they try in vain to beat them back, as they fight from the platforms to recapture the village.

I begin to recognize those clawing at the gates. Some of them are—were—my neighbors. Were my friends and classmates. Some were their parents. Fresh blood still stains their clothes, in some cases drips from their mouths.

I wonder about those left on the platforms, fighting against these newly turned Unconsecrated. I wonder if they realize that by pulling the ladders up in their panic, they have only added to the chaos, only added more victims for the Unconsecrated to turn. Only created more enemies—hundreds of them.

After a while it becomes too much for Cass to bear and she breaks away from our group, goes to Jacob, who has been lying comatose on the ground, and pulls him into her lap. I can hear her singing lullabies, humming where she forgets the words.

In some small way it's a comfort to hear her voice. To be reminded that there can be normalcy. Even as everything else in our world slips away.

"I worry about the latch on the gate holding," Harry says as the sun begins to slip away at the end of the day. "It wasn't meant to keep back the Unconsecrated. Only to guard this path."

I shudder as I look at the metal latch that is all that protects us from the ravenous horde. I look at the fence on either
side of us, at how it's wide here but narrows as it leads away
from the village. Its links are red with rust and vines twine
through them. Because the path is off-limits, the fences have
never been cared for and I wonder how many Unconsecrated
pushing against it would bring it down.

"We should go down the path some," Travis says. "Far
enough that they lose interest and turn back toward the village. Stop pressing against the gate. Maybe . . ." He trails off
and then seems to find his voice again. "Maybe during the
night they can fight them off. Regain control of the village."
No one responds and it is as if he is compelled to add, "We
should at least give them the night; see what it looks like in
the morning."

Harry nods, his hand still gripping the ax, his shoulders
tense.

I say nothing. I can't trust my emotions, the tingle that
vibrates up my arms and legs. I turn to look down the trail,
the others still concentrating on the gate and Cass's attention fully on Jacob. I take a few steps, at once scared and
thrilled.

The path here is overgrown and brambles tug at my skirt
so that I have to fight against them with every step.

Behind me I can hear Travis and Harry arguing about
food and weapons. About whether the village would be able
to repel the breach or if the path is our only hope.

I am silent as I walk away from the village. Far enough
away so that I am not a draw to the Unconsecrated at the gate.
As the path begins to narrow I stretch my arms out wide and
almost scrape the links of the fence with my fingertips. Here

the Forest is clear of Unconsecrated and for a moment I imagine I can hear a bird chirp in the distance.

Finally, I make my own decision: I will give them the night to see if the village repels the breach. But then I will go down this path. Alone if I have to.

▼   ▼   ▼

Sometime during the night it begins to rain. Taking Travis's advice, we've moved our little group down the path, and here it is too narrow for us to huddle together against the cold and the wet. Travis and Harry sit next to each other, Harry closest to the gate since he is the only one with a weapon.

I sit at the other end of the line, Argos with his head on my knee as I tug at his ears and press my hand against his smooth fur. Cass is between us with Jacob curled tightly in her lap. Her hair is scraggly, pulling from its braid to create a halo around her face in the darkness. Jacob drifted into limp-limbed sleep some time ago but Cass continues to rock and hum, as much for her own comfort as his.

Travis and Harry continue to murmur together, Travis's light head tilted toward Harry's dark one as they whisper, trying to determine what to do next. The rain throws off the Unconsecrated's ability to sense us—the air heavy with water, our scent dulled. Some have wandered away from the fence on either side, slipping back into the Forest. It's a welcome reprieve from the crushing sound of their moans, even though if the wind changes I can still hear the last gasps of the battle in the village just down the path.

The Unconsecrated are a determined foe that never sleeps. I know that the villagers must take advantage of the rain for their attack—the scent of human flesh deadened in the water-soaked air making it harder for the Unconsecrated to find them.

Every now and then Harry or Travis will raise his voice and the Unconsecrated will stir out in the Forest. Each time Cass hisses for them to be quiet and once, when one of the Unconsecrated curls his fingers through the fence behind her, rust flakes drifting to the ground, she begins to whimper.

I want to place my arm around her but the space here is too narrow, our bodies too awkwardly arranged with Jacob in her lap.

"There is an end to the Forest, Cass," I tell her, trying to comfort her. "There's an Outside—there's more out there."

"So what?" she says, her voice quivering.

"Don't you want to know what's on the other side?" I ask her. "To see the ocean? To know that there is more? To find a place that isn't touched by all this?" I wave my arms at a thin Unconsecrated man scraping at the fence but the night is so dark I doubt she can see me.

"The ocean has always been your dream, Mary, not mine." She pauses for a moment and suddenly I feel a hand on my cheek. I flinch, not expecting it, but she keeps her chilled flesh against me. The rain has caused her fingertips to wrinkle.

"It's the only way for us to make it," I say. "For Jacob to have a chance at a life."

"Our place is in the village. Jacob's place is with his parents," she says.

I want to shake her but instead keep my fingers in the fur of Argos's back.

"Don't you see? Everything has changed," I say. "Jacob's

parents may not have even survived. Nothing will be the same."

She moves her hand from my cheek to cover my mouth. "I don't want to hear such things," she says, her voice even and serious. "Don't you see that believing the village is gone means that everyone we have ever known is dead? I won't give up that easily on them. And neither should you."

Her hand slips from my face. I can hear as she resettles the boy in her lap, hear him groan and then fall back into dreamless sleep. The rain barely dribbles now. Another Unconsecrated has joined the first at the fence next to us, summoned by the moans. It's too dark to see anything but I can hear them scrabbling against the metal. Hear their desperation.

I wonder who those hands belonged to. Which of those hands once stroked the head of a sick child, once touched the lips of a loved one, once clasped together in prayer. I wonder if any of those hands belong to my mother.

"Going down that path would kill us all, Mary," Cass says. "You're selfish to want to sacrifice all of us for your own whims."

Her words echo, crashing through my body. For a moment I imagine going back to the village to help beat back the breach. Of returning to the cottage with Harry and continuing our lives, finishing the ceremony, bearing his children instead of Travis's.

Trying to be content.

"Cass," I whisper. Water slips down my face and into my mouth. "We're already dead. We're surrounded by it every day. And we shuffle along in our lives just like they shuffle along in theirs. It's inevitable that it invade our lives someday the way it invaded our village this morning. We aren't part of any cycle of life, Cass."

She doesn't respond. Once I would have told Cass everything about Gabrielle. I would have shared my fears that the Sisters brought this destruction down on us all. I would have told Cass that I had proof of a world beyond the Forest.

But instead I stay silent. I peer out into the darkness, down the path that leads away from the village. Where Gabrielle came from. I place my hand against the damp ground, wondering if maybe Gabrielle paused here before entering the village. I wonder what made her choose to come down the path and if she started out alone or whether she had companions that died or left her along the way.

I want to tell Cass about Gabrielle so that she can feel the same hope I do. But I'm afraid that Cass will only speak aloud the dark fears that seep through my thoughts: that Gabrielle's story is not one of hope and that none of us can expect a happy ending.

I tug at the knots of the Binding rope on my wrist, twisting them, fraying the ends, trying to loosen them. But they hold tight.

I want to know why Travis and Cass don't still wear their Binding ropes. If they ever wore them. It is the rule of Brethlaw that once the bride and groom are bound with the rope they are not to undo the Bindings until after the final vow ceremony is complete. Until they are bound in the eyes of God—bound spiritually so that the physical bonds are no longer necessary.

I know that it's reasonable to believe that, like Harry and me, Cass and Travis cut the rope so that they could escape from the breach more easily. But the thought, the mere idea that they may have never been bound eats away at me. That they may have refused the ceremony with Sister Tabitha, or that one of them may have cut the rope during the night, simmers in my veins.

I pull my knees up to my chest and place my forehead against the wet fabric of my skirt, squeezing my eyes shut. It feels as if my heart is about to explode as I wonder if Travis and Cass were ever Bound. As I wonder if I have ruined any chance for Travis and me to be together because I didn't wait for him until the end.

Because I chose to Bind myself to Harry. Because I gave up on Travis. On love.

I want to weep and laugh at the same time but instead I clench my teeth.

I try not to let the idea of the outside world tingle through my veins. But I cannot help it. On the edge of sleep, when my thoughts are no longer my own but controlled of their own volition, the sound of the ocean comes to me: the rustling of leaves of a hundred thousand trees that surround me, pulsing with the wind as the waves crash over my head. Pulling me under. Tossing my body as if it has no need of bones.

Every night I drown and every morning I wake up struggling to breathe.

# ▼ XVII ▼

I wake to chaos. Voices shouting, Cass screaming, Argos barking. I thrash my legs, try to stand, and stumble a few steps until I'm brought up short by the fence. Cold fingers slip against my skin and I shriek and fall back until I'm huddled in the middle of the narrow path.

Cass holds Jacob behind her as she points toward the village. "They're coming," she says, and in the murky fog I can see Harry standing with his legs spread, his ax held tight in his hands. Travis stands behind him, a thick branch his weapon. Argos crouches low and growls, ready to attack. The fences lining the path tower over them both, the predawn light slanting through the links casting crisscross shadows over all of us.

We can hear the shuffling of feet growing close. I reach out and take Cass's hand and she squeezes mine so tight in return that I can feel the bones grinding against one another.

"We should go farther away where it is safe," I say as I tug her. "So long as it isn't the Fast One, we can outpace them."

But before we can get too far I hear Harry shout and then he's running, the ax slipping from his fingers. Travis limps along after him and then, from around the corner, I see two figures coming toward us—a man and a woman.

Harry takes the woman in his arms and that's when I realize it's my brother and his wife. I run back down the path toward them, stopping a few arm's lengths from where Harry and Travis surround their sister, blocking me from my brother.

Jed steps aside and faces me. "Hello, Jed," I say, approaching him as if I were the prodigal child, not him. I see him glance at the dingy white braided rope still dangling from my wrist and then his eyes search my face. For a moment I'm afraid he will say nothing but then he opens his arms and I am finally hugging my brother who has been gone from my life for so long. I can't help but think about the bond of friendship we used to have and how much I have missed him.

I step back and Jed slips a protective arm around his wife. She pulls a damp and grungy shawl tighter around her shoulders and leans her head against my brother, her frizzy brown hair falling loose from its bandana.

"The village is gone," he says. We huddle as close together as possible on the narrow path. Beth at one end, leaning against my brother, then Harry and Travis and then Cass, Jacob and I at the other end. The fences hem us in on either side, making me feel slightly trapped, forcing me to breathe deeply to keep calm.

"Too many have turned," Jed continues. "It's no longer safe on the ground." He pulls Beth against him, using his hand to guide her head down to his shoulder. "We took the chance in the rain to come after you. This path was our only hope."

Beth shudders at his words and it seems to pass from her bones to mine.

"But how can that be?" Harry asks. "The Guardians are trained for this."

Jed's jaw clenches. "The Guardians train to repair fences, to repel a breach of slow and unwieldy Unconsecrated. It was the Fast One," he tells us. "The one with the strange red clothing. She was too much. She came too quickly, killed too many. Then the dead turned and even though they were slow, they were too many. It was too much for the Guardians. For all of us."

"But aren't they still fighting?" Harry asks. I can feel the frustration rolling from his shoulders. His hands clench as if searching for the ax to wield.

Jed just drops his head to his chest, brushes a soft kiss on his wife's forehead as tears drip down her face.

I feel the breath leave my body; my stomach burns with the knowledge that this is truly it. That our village is no more. It's as if everyone has had large weights dropped onto them. Their shoulders sag. Their legs buckle.

A hundred faces flicker across my mind: teachers, friends, Sisters, Guardians, neighbors. They are all Unconsecrated. Beth, Harry and Travis's parents: gone. Cass will never be hugged by her mother again. Jacob will never play with his sister.

I think about how it felt to lose first my father and then my mother. Of the crushing pain. And I can tell from the faces around me that such reality is beginning to settle in, become comprehensible to the others.

Jacob doesn't seem to understand, his expression puzzled as he glances from face to face.

Around us the Unconsecrated continue to moan, continue to paw at the fences. Harry clears his throat, grasps Jed by the arm. "Are you sure?"

"It's gone" is all that Jed says. "There is no going back."

I can see how Harry's jaw tightens and I remember that look so well from our childhood when he used to watch the older boys tussle and play at being Guardians. I know he wonders if his presence in the village would have made a difference—if he is a coward for escaping through the gate.

"The path is our only option, then," Travis says. He glances at all of us, and I can't help but think that his gaze lingers on mine more than the others.

The rest of us are silent and then Harry speaks. "We have some food that Mary and I brought from the village. And two bladders of water. We took them when we heard the sirens yesterday morning."

"But will it be enough?" Cass asks. She has pressed Jacob's head against her chest and covered his ears so that he doesn't hear our conversation.

"There are food and weapons on the path," Jed says. His voice is calm and even.

Harry is the first to respond. "How? Why would . . . ? I don't understand," he finally says.

Jed takes a deep breath. "The Sisterhood. Since the beginning, since after the Return, they have instructed the Guardians to shore up the path. To keep supplies out here in the event of a breach. It wasn't unforeseen that this could happen. That we would be forced from the village. The Guardians prepared for such an event."

"But I'm a Guardian and I knew nothing about this."

"You're an apprentice to the Guardians," Jed says.

Harry's cheeks flash red. "My father was the chief of the Guardians and he said nothing of this!" Harry is shouting now, agitating the Unconsecrated that press against the fence on either side and causing their moans to intensify.

He looks over at me, his chest heaving. "You were a member of the Sisterhood, did you know about this?" There is fire in his eyes and I take a step back.

"The Sisters kept secrets," I tell him. "And it appears as though the Guardians did as well." I cannot look them in the eyes as I say this. We all keep secrets.

Harry thrusts his hands into his dark hair, his cheekbones appearing even sharper in the morning light. "They forbid us from this path, and yet they keep supplies here? Would I have ever been told?"

Jed shrugs. "What does it matter?" he asks.

Harry stays silent for a moment. "Then where does the path lead? If you know about the supplies, why don't you know where it leads?"

"Because even though I was chosen as a Guardian, I was not a member of the Guild. I doubt the Guild would even know. It's the Sisterhood that keeps the knowledge. We just do their bidding." Jed turns to me. "That's where I was the day that Mother was . . . infected. I was out on the paths, checking supplies, making sure the fences still held. That's why I couldn't return before she . . . turned."

I think back to my first day with the Sisters, to the hidden tunnel under the Cathedral that led to the clearing in the middle of the Forest. Of the little room where the Sisters had kept Gabrielle. I wonder again what was behind all the other thick doors and if the rest of them also hid rooms or if some concealed other tunnels that led to other paths. If right now the Sisters and the Guardians locked in the Cathedral had found their own way out of the village and were starting over again.

Leaving the rest of us behind to die.

"The Sisters and the Guardians no longer matter. What's important," Jed says, interrupting my thoughts, "is that we can survive on this path. At least for a little while. But we need to start moving now."

Harry is still scowling. He distributes the few bags of food that we have, bends to pick up his ax and says, "Since I'm the only one with a weapon, I will take the lead." He commands Argos to his side and together they stride down the path, Cass and Jacob close behind him. Travis takes Beth's hand and walks with her, each supporting the other as they make their way carefully down the center of the path to avoid the looming fences. Jed and I trail behind.

We travel in silence the entire morning, picking our way through the brambles and over fallen branches. Finally, Jed stops walking and I do the same. The others continue down the path, curving away from us until we can no longer see them and we are alone. He seems anxious, jittery. He keeps shifting from one foot to the other as if he can't get comfortable.

Finally he speaks, his voice low. "Mary, I . . ." He hesitates and I watch as the muscles along his jaw twitch. Tears begin to spill down his cheeks, his face crumbling. "I don't know what to do," he says.

I have never seen my brother cry and my heart begins to race. I step forward to comfort him but he holds up a hand, keeping me at bay.

"What is it, Jed?" I ask. "What's wrong?"

He turns toward the fence at his side, shakes his head.

"Jed?" I prod.

"She's infected, Beth is . . ." He chokes on his words. He scrapes a hand over his face as if it's the only thing holding his body together.

I stumble back, away from him. All this time she has been among us. All this time and he hasn't told us.

"You must kill her!" I say before I can think better of it. I am about to apologize when he falls to his knees in front of me. He grasps at my shirt, begging, and I am too stunned to speak.

"You don't understand," he says. "You don't know. It's a small bite. It's nothing. Maybe she isn't sick . . . maybe . . ." His voice trails off.

I crouch down in front of him so that we're face to face. "Jed," I say, trying to make my voice soft and soothing. "You are a Guardian. You know what a bite means. You know what infection means."

He nods but I don't think my words have truly penetrated.

I take a deep breath. "You know there is no hope."

"I cannot kill my wife," he pleads with a hoarse voice, helpless, falling back on his heels. He beats at the ground and roars in anguish, causing the downed Unconsecrated nearby to rise, sensing our presence. I hear the moans as they begin the process of scenting us out. The first one hits the fence, not two arm's lengths away, and then another and another.

I listen to them rattle around us and then I say, "You can always let her go. You can turn her loose into the Forest."

Jed starts to laugh, the sound low and bitter. He is on me

before I can move, his fingers around my throat as he pushes me back and back. My legs tangle in my skirt and I fall against the fence, feel its rusty metal links digging through my clothes. "I see, Mary. You take pleasure in this, don't you." His black hair is wild around his face. He bares his teeth. "I get mad at you for allowing our mother to become one of them and so now you can be smug that my wife will become one as well?"

I feel Unconsecrated fingers through my hair and I buck against the fence and try to scream but Jed has cut off any sound I can make. I thrash against him, my eyes rolling back in my head as all I can smell is death and decay and I'm desperate. Suddenly, he seems to realize what he's doing, what he's done, and he drops his hands.

I push away from him, away from the fence, and stumble down the path clutching the pinched skin of my neck. My breath comes in ragged gasps, tears burn my eyes and my body shakes with rage born of the terror I just experienced.

I've taken only a few steps when I hear him. "Mary, please." His voice has lost its wild edge. "Please, I'm sorry. I'm so sorry." He is sobbing now, sounding like the little boy I grew up with. I stop but don't turn back.

"I cannot lose her," he says to me. "If you had ever been in love you would understand."

I spin around. "Don't tell me about love!" I roar. "Don't ever tell me what I know and do not know about love. Your situation is not about love. You are a Guardian. Killing the Unconsecrated is what you are trained to do. You've put us all in danger by keeping her alive. You know the rules."

He rubs a hand over his face. He's sitting in the middle of the path, his knees bent, one arm wrapped around his legs.

"Love is not something our village has ever cared about," he says, looking out into the Forest. "It's always been about the bloodlines, about preserving ourselves and taking care not to intermarry." He tosses his hand at the Unconsecrated scraping at the fence. "It has always been about surviving them."

I think about Harry and the Sisterhood's edict that I marry him and I cross my arms over my chest.

"The Sisterhood has it wrong," he says. "It's not about surviving. It should be about love. When you know love . . . that's what makes this life worth it. When you live with it every day. Wake up with it, hold on to it during the thunder and after a nightmare. When love is your refuge from the death that surrounds us all and when it fills you so tight that you can't express it." He rocks forward and backward as tears stream down his face. Around us the Unconsecrated continue their moaning.

I think about Travis. About the way he said he would come for me. "I have known love," I whisper, as much to myself as to my brother.

He lifts a corner of his lips, almost smiling. "You can't ever have known love." I am about to protest when he holds up a hand to stop me and continues, "Because if you had you wouldn't be telling me to kill my wife as if it were an easy choice. You would realize that you don't let love go like that. And you would realize that you certainly never kill it. Never."

I take a step forward but I'm still wary of this wounded man, afraid that I may say the wrong thing and he will lash out again. I'm torn between fearing him and wanting desperately to comfort him. "Jed, you don't have a choice," I tell him. "She's a risk to all of us."

It's as if he doesn't hear me, doesn't comprehend. "I just wanted another day with her," he pleads. "One day to forget. To pretend there is no infection, no such thing as the Unconsecrated. One day to memorize her."

"But the infection—"

"It's a small bite, Mary," he tells me, his face folding in on itself as he says the words. "She has another two days at least, if not three." His voice turns hollow. "Her infection is spreading slowly. If I have learned one thing as a Guardian it's how the living turn. I know the signs. I know what to look for." He swallows. "She has time left."

I stare out into the Forest. I cannot imagine Beth becoming one of them. Becoming Unconsecrated.

"Please, Mary. Let me have this day and night with my wife. If you know love, then you understand what this means to me."

I nod before I realize what I'm doing. He rushes to me and wraps his arms around me. But I'm still thinking about what he said about love. Even as he runs down the path to rejoin the others, to rejoin his wife.

I cradle my face in my hands, Jed's words grinding in my head. Guilt tears through my veins and I wonder if I ever did truly love Travis since I allowed myself to give up on him. To be bound to Harry. My betrayal sinks heavy in my skin.

# XVIII

I stay true to my promise: I don't tell the others about Beth. But I still watch her. I watch to make sure that Jed never leaves her side. Even without a weapon, I am ready to kill her, whether he is or not.

That evening, just as the sun is setting fire to the treetops, the path finally bulges wider, giving us relief from the constant overwhelming nearness of the fence and the fear that one wrong step will send us clattering against the links and into Unconsecrated fingers. Sitting in the middle of the clearing is a wooden trunk held together with metal bands. It's long and wide and has a large rusty lock hanging from one end. Argos sniffs at it, tail swinging back and forth as he dances around excitedly.

We gather around it and I notice that letters are branded onto the top. I wipe my hand over them, clearing away rotted leaves. *XVIII*.

I think back to the letters that Gabrielle traced into the

window in her room: *XIV*. "What do these letters mean?" I ask Jed.

He shrugs. "Does it matter?"

"Did the Guardians put them here?" I prod.

"No, the chest has always been here. It was the Sisters that told us about it and asked us to keep the supplies fresh."

"What about the key?" Harry asks.

Jed shrugs again. "Somehow I didn't think to bring it with me."

I turn and hide my face against my shoulder, stifling laughter.

Harry swings at the lock with his ax, busting it on the third try. Inside are two water bladders, two bags of food and two more double-sided axes. Jed takes one and Travis the other.

"We should camp here tonight, where there is space," Harry says. We all agree, relieved to be out of the narrow gap between the fences, and the men begin to pull the boards off the trunk to start a fire while Cass and I prepare a meager meal.

We say little that evening as we eat. I watch as flames consume the letters once branded into the wood of the trunk and I think about Gabrielle and how she looked that night when I saw her through the window in the Cathedral. Her long black hair framing skin that was both pale and dark, like the moon as it hangs just over the horizon. Before she became Unconsecrated. When she was just a girl like me, staring through a locked window at the promise of the path through the Forest, the promise of another world.

That night, as I fall into a broken sleep, Argos tucked in my arms, I dream of Cass and Jacob straining through the fence for me. Except they are not Unconsecrated. They're on one side of a locked gate and I'm on the other and the sounds of the Unconsecrated fill my ears but I don't know if they are coming for me or for them.

Cass opens her mouth and screams and I am jolted awake only to find that her screams still echo in my ears. Under my hand I can feel the reverberation of Argos growling and I sit up and turn to where Cass is still screaming and pointing.

My first thought is that Jed was wrong and Beth has turned, but then out of the corner of my eye I see a flash of red and my heart stops beating. I choke on my own breath as I see Gabrielle coming for us. I brace myself for the impact, for the clash of teeth, but then I hear the rattle of the fence as Gabrielle slams into it. Three arrows protrude from her torso and one arm hangs at an odd angle, but that doesn't stop or even slow her down.

Other Unconsecrated stumble behind her, eventually joining her at the fence, all clamoring for us.

Travis throws dirt on the embers of last night's fire while Harry and Jed stand ready with their axes. But the fence holds the Unconsecrated back and we are merely assaulted by the smell of their fetid flesh and the sounds of their desperate moans.

We leave our little campsite without a word, slipping back into single file as the path narrows. We walk quickly, leaving the slow Unconsecrated dragging behind after us, unable to keep up. But Gabrielle is with us at every turn. She is like Argos, running ahead along the fence, pushing against it, testing for weakness, running back to us, trying to get through.

"How did she get out of the village?" I hear Beth wail. "How did she find us?"

Jed draws his wife against him, the path barely wide enough for them to walk side by side. He meets my eyes over her head. "She must have made it back through the breach," he says.

"That means there must be nothing left in the village for her," I hear Harry say. "That means the village must be totally gone. If they couldn't kill her . . ." His voice trails off, allowing the rest of us to draw our own conclusions.

Cass, near the front of the line, stops at these words, and when I approach she slips Jacob's hand into mine and falls in line behind us. I can hear her sobs, hear her body shuddering as she struggles to breathe. I want to stop and hold her, to comfort her, but instead I grasp Jacob's hand tighter.

"Why is that one so different?" he asks me in his small voice tinged with a slight little-boy lisp. He points to Gabrielle in her bright red vest.

I shake my head. I think of Gabrielle being locked in the Cathedral with the Sisters, of the last time I saw her and how I searched and searched but could never find her. I think of the tunnel, the doors set off it, the little room, the handwriting in the Scripture. I cannot help but wonder again what the Sisters did to Gabrielle, how they must have caused this destruction.

▼  ▼  ▼

A bright puffy cloud has just doused the harsh sunlight directly overhead when the path widens again and we come across the gate bisecting the fences. Situated above the lever is a small metal bar with the letters *XIX* inscribed in it. For a brief moment it reminds me of the doorways in my village and how the Sisters inscribe every door with words from the Scripture. I slide my hand over the letters the way I was taught to acknowledge the Scripture verses when I enter a room.

But instead of thinking about God, as we are supposed to, I think about Gabrielle.

I wonder what the relationship is between the letters Gabrielle wrote on the window, those burned into the trunk we found earlier and these, but I can't figure out a pattern. I look over to where Gabrielle pounds at the fence with an insane passion we have never seen in the Unconsecrated before. I wish I could ask her these things, comfort her, tell her to hush and then ask for her help.

Instead, I grasp the burning metal of the lever and am about to pull it when Cass gasps and steps forward from the others.

"What are you doing?" She shouts to be heard over Gabrielle. "You don't know what's out there. What that gate is for. What if there are Unconsecrated on the other side? Mary, you would kill us."

"We don't have a choice," I answer her as I pull the lever and the gate glides open, barely emitting a creak. I'm surprised at how heavy it is and I stand and hold it as the others slowly slip through.

Jed walks with a protective arm around Beth and already I notice how her eyes have sunk into her skull, how her footsteps have become less sure, how her brown hair hangs lank around her face. I try to grab my brother, to tell him that tonight he must take care of her. That she is too dangerous. But he shakes his head before I can speak and tells me that everything is under control.

I wonder, as Harry and Travis walk through the opening, if they see these changes in their sister. If they know what waits for her at the end of this day. The inevitability of it all.

I know that Jed still hasn't told them that Beth is infected, even though with every step we grow closer to her death.

I let the gate close softly once everyone is through. As I set the latch I find another small metal plate on this side of the gate. Etched in it are the letters *XVIII*—the same letters that were burned into the trunk. I struggle to put it all together, to figure out what these letters mean, but I can come to no conclusions. I shake my head and rub my finger along the metal. Its sharp edges cut into the pad of my thumb.

I suck the blood away as I turn to rejoin the others. We don't walk much farther before the path branches and we face a decision. Argos trots down each one, sniffing furiously before coming to sit at my feet, tongue lolling from the side of his mouth.

"We can either separate, scout them out or just choose one," Harry says, his hands on his hips as he peers down the path that branches to the right. There's a small clearing where the three paths meet and Beth has taken the opportunity to curl up on her side in the dirt, her shawl tight around her shoulders and her head resting on Jed's outstretched legs.

Cass sits with Jacob, her hand wrapped around his as she helps him trace his numbers in the dirt.

"It's an easy choice," she says without looking up. "We should take the path that leads us away from her." She points at where Gabrielle throws herself at the fence with the same furor as the first time she found us. She is the reason we've been forced to walk single file down this narrow path, fearful that if we walked side by side she would be able to reach one of us.

"Cass makes a good point," Travis says. "If we take the left branch, there's no way she can follow us."

Everyone in agreement, Jed helps Beth from the ground and we trudge down the path to the left, leaving Gabrielle mauling the fence behind us. The path almost feels empty without her constant presence and a small part of me realizes that I miss her.

We come to two more breaks in the narrow path during the heat of the day, each time randomly choosing which direction to take. Just as the light shifts, causing distances to blur, Harry, who has been walking ahead, suddenly stops.

"It's a dead end," he says.

# XIX

"What?" Cass yells. Her voice has a note of hysteria in it and she steps around Harry to see for herself. She begins to bang against the section of fence that ends the path, and she reminds me of the Unconsecrated, always wanting what is on the other side.

Finally, Travis goes to her and wraps her in his arms. He tells her to shush and he rocks her slowly and Harry steps behind her and lays a hand on her shoulder. Together they try to ease Cass's shuddering sobs. Even Argos trots to her side, leaning against her legs and licking her hand. She clutches at Travis; I can see how her fingers sink into the flesh of his shoulder by the collar of his shirt, and I cannot help but watch with a sense of jealousy, a small pebble like possession in the pit of my stomach.

"Useless," Cass mutters. "Everything. We've lost everything. My father and mother . . . my sister . . ." She struggles to breathe and I see tears in Travis's and Harry's eyes. "Gone," she goes on. "All gone. Dead. And we . . ." She shudders again, her whole body shaking. "We . . . the path, oh God . . ." Her words slip into wails. Travis pulls her closer and runs his hand over her hair to comfort her.

The back of my throat stings and I feel my stomach heaving, but nothing comes up and no one notices. I want to rip Cass from his arms, but instead I step around where Beth has curled up on the ground and take a few steps down the path to get away. I try to take deep breaths but my body still thrums. I know their pain. I understand it, I have lived with that kind of regret. I know I should feel sympathy, I know we are in this as one. But I can't stop the heat, the rage from curling in my stomach.

"We should just stay here for the night," Jed calls out. "I'm not sure Beth can go farther today." I wait for him to tell them why, as he promised. To tell them she is infected. But instead he says, "She's been so desolate after the loss of their parents."

I throw my hands up and start to stomp away but Jed catches up with me before I get out of earshot of the group.

"It's no use," he tells me and whether he means Travis or Harry or Beth or the path I don't know. I only know that I am full of anger at everything that's happened. It feels like lightning shooting through my body, this fury.

I cannot help but laugh, the sound of it raw in my throat. "You want to talk about what is of no use, Jed?" I ask, because I want to lash out and he's the closest. "What about keeping your little secret about Beth?" I say this loudly, meaning for everyone to hear it, and as I intended both Travis and Harry look up at me when I mention their sister's name.

Suddenly, I feel a profound need to hurt Travis as he stands with his arm around Cass, her fingers possessive around his wrist like a Binding rope. For making me want him so fiercely and for not coming to claim me before my last night with Harry. For not coming before everything grew so complicated and ugly.

"Tell them, Jed," I say, my eyes still locked on Travis's questioning gaze. "You promised you would. Tell them how Beth is already dead. Tell them how you refuse to kill her. How you endanger us all."

I don't move as I see Jed's hand coming toward my face, as I feel the burn of it across my cheek. I don't even flinch or raise my hand to squelch the sting.

It's easy to see that Travis still doesn't understand what is going on. Beth, hearing her name, wakes up. Noticing that we are all staring at her, she sits up quickly, the shawl slipping from her shoulder and exposing the festering wound underneath.

Harry shrieks like an injured animal and falls to his knees, crawling to his sister. Travis just stands and stares at me as I feel my body flare with heat. Already I despise myself, shame flooding through me, drowning me. I turn and run back down the path.

But at least I know that Travis now hurts as much as I do.

▼    ▼    ▼

I wander along the various paths, leaving piles of rocks or twigs each time I come to a branch in the path so that I can retrace my steps back. I wish I could find something helpful—something to bring back as an offering to make amends and prove that we are going in the right direction. That we won't wander the Forest until we die of starvation or dehydration.

But I find nothing—just the endless path filled with

brambles and overgrown grass. Dead brown vines trail through the links in the fences with buds that may have once held flowers but now hang limp and desiccated.

Eventually, I find myself back at the first break in the path, and I sit and stare into the woods. It's quiet here, the Unconsecrated not having risen at the sound of my steps.

"Gabrielle?" I ask the silence. At first my voice is tentative but then I grow bolder. "Gabrielle!" I shout. Soon enough I hear the sound of an animal charging through the under-brush, and then her bright red vest breaks from the trees and she throws herself against the fence. It's not her name she responds to, but my existence. She does not come because I call her, but because she craves me. Because she is mindless and hungry and knows nothing else but desire for human flesh.

She seems a little slower, as though her body is tearing itself apart in the effort to sustain so much energy. Still, she thrusts her fingers at me through the links in the fence, her mouth grinding against the metal in case I step too close.

I think about slipping a finger through the fence and into her mouth. Letting her consume me and infect me. Being done with the path and the longing that's too painful to bear.

I think about my mother out there in the Forest some-where and how maybe I could find her if I was Unconsecrated. I have always wondered if there is any spark of recognition be-tween the Unconsecrated—if it is like a feral animal that un-derstands something so deep and true as love.

I reach out and press my finger against the nail of her pinky, the only finger that is not bent and broken from trying to rip through the fence.

"Who are you?" I ask. Her eyes are now scratched and a milky blue and I know that she does not see me.

Tears drip down my cheeks, splatter on my shirt. "Is it easier on the other side?" I ask her, still tracing her pinky with my own fingers. She tries to grab my hand, but hers is too mangled for such dexterity.

She's barely taller than I am, with a similar build. In another time we could have been mistaken for sisters, though her nose, once long and straight, is now crooked with the bone piercing through at the bridge.

"I'm sorry," I tell her.

So badly do I want to believe that she can hear me. That she can understand. But she keeps clawing and as the sun slides down the sky, I continue to cry heavy tears.

I am just turning to leave her, wiping my hand under my nose, when something gleams from the grass where the two paths come together. I squint my eyes and turn my head but I don't see it again, and so I walk over to where the fence splits and kick at the ground.

I hear a tiny little clink and I drop to my knees, using my tear-damp fingers to pry through the grass until I find it. Wired to the bottom links is a small metal bar just like the ones that hung over the levers to the gate. This one is just to the right of the split, less than a hand's length down the path.

Like the other metal bars, this one is inscribed. I rub my fingers over it, dislodging dirt. I can feel the ridge of each letter: *XXIX*.

Out of curiosity I scrabble down the other branch of the path and push away the thick overgrown weeds to find another bar with similar letters: *XXIII*.

I rock back on my heels until I fall with a thud and am sitting. Just like the gates, these paths are marked—they are not random.

Almost afraid that I might be seeing things or making them up, I jump to my feet and run to the next split in the path, my body screaming for air by the time I get there. I slide to my knees and dig through the grass and dirt until I find two more small metal bars, one marking each path. Again with similar letters: *VII, IV*.

I close my eyes and try to figure out the pattern to the letters. Try to figure out what they are telling me. What they have in common. But my heart beats too fast, my blood flows through my body with such speed, such excitement, that I can't concentrate.

My fingers shake as I rub them over the letters again and again and again. I think back to the window where Gabrielle wrote her name and clear in my mind are the letters she wrote underneath: *XIV*. The letters have to be some sort of code, the metal bars some sort of markers.

And yet I still cannot figure it all out. I cannot piece it all together. I grit my teeth in frustration and toss dirt back over the bar I've been examining. Burying it back in the underbrush.

As the sun hovers on the tips of the trees and my skin stings from its slow burn, I walk back to our camp at the dead end, running the letters through my head over and over again.

Every time I come to the same conclusion: there's a connection between the letters and Gabrielle. The letters will lead me to her. Will solve the mystery of who she is and maybe even where she's from.

She was trying to tell me something when she wrote those letters in the mist of her breath on the window. And I have no choice but to accede to her message.

I tap my fingers across my lips as I think. I burst with the need to tell everyone about this discovery. To explain to them that we now have a direction of some sort. A purpose.

I trip down the path, racing past the little piles of stones I set out to mark the way back to the others, pausing only to search for the little bars, the path markers. Each time I rub my fingers over the engraved letters I can't help but laugh.

And I'm still reeling with joy and laughter when I turn the corner in the path and find Cass sitting, Jacob asleep on his side a few feet away, his little body clutching Argos like a memory of life before the breach.

"Beth is dead," she says, not even bothering to look up at me. "They are digging her grave. I didn't want Jacob to see them decapitate her. He has seen too much already."

Grief rolls over me, the joy of my discovery leaching from my bones. I never said good-bye. I was not there.

I did nothing in her final hours but cause her pain.

"I should go help," I say. My voice feels strained, and it hurts as it leaves my throat. Already the tears are climbing from my eyes again, slipping down my cheeks.

She reaches out a hand and grasps my ankle as I try to pass. "No," she says.

I let my legs collapse under me until I am huddled next to her. "I'm sorry," I say. Apologizing again, as if these are the only words I am allowed to speak anymore.

She nods. Her expression is so grave, so serious. It isn't the Cass I have ever known, the one who was nothing but sunshine and light. Who was always carefree and happy. I ache seeing the darkness creep into her spirit, taking hold of her.

I drop my head between my knees, cup my hands over the back of my neck. Suddenly, finding little scraps of metal with letters on them seems useless. It's as if the world has opened its maw. Has brought reality back down upon us, to remind us of how unfair our life is. How useless it is to try to exist when surrounded by nothing but death. Unceasing, determined death.

A cloud dims the sun, throwing the world around us dark and cold. The wind lifts through the trees a bit; the leaves flash their white undersides. The taste of rain coats my tongue and in the distance I can hear the soft low moans of the downed Unconsecrated who rise to find us. Who heard my steps and smell my stench.

I decide not to tell them about the letters. Not to give them that hope. I don't want to see Cass fall apart again, don't want to carry the burden of their expectations.

What if the letters mean nothing? What if the path leads nowhere? What if we figure out the puzzle, what if we suddenly expect an end and we don't find one? It's enough that I know the paths are marked, enough that I know to look for Gabrielle's letters.

I wonder if maybe all paths lead to the Unconsecrated. If it's a fate that none of us can ever escape—as certain as death. I wonder if maybe I was right as a child, that there can be no such place as the ocean, no place too large to be untouched by the Return.

# XX

After Beth is buried Harry and Travis come back down the path to where Cass and I sit in silence, watching Jacob nap with Argos, his bony shoulders rising and falling hypnotically. Harry announces that the plan is to retrace our steps while there is still a trace of light and camp at the last split in the fence, where the path is wider.

I let them go without me. Instead, I slip back toward the dead end and find Jed standing next to a mound of dirt. I can see the weight of his grief in the slump of his shoulders, the way his hands hang so limply by his sides as if there is no life left in them.

"It was the one in red that got her," Jed says, his eyes fixed on the dirt that's even now settling into his dead wife's flesh. "She was too fast. Too much. Beth was . . ." He swallows. Stays silent.

"Beth was pregnant again," he finally says. His voice cracks as he says this and I hesitate before walking to his side, before slipping his arm around my shoulder so that I can bear some of his grief.

For a moment I fear he'll rebuff me. But then he sags against me. I am the only thing holding him standing and I finally feel as if we are brother and sister again. The bonds forged when we were children too tight to break.

"Jed," I say. And then I pause and take a deep breath. Afraid of harming the moment. "What happened to Beth? How did she get infected?"

A pebble slips down the mound of dirt at his feet and he releases me, bending down to pick it up. He rubs it between his finger and thumb. "We were on our way to the Cathedral," he says. "We were going to tell Sister Tabitha that Beth was pregnant so that she could be blessed with the other mothers at the final Vows ceremony."

My cheeks burn at the memory of what was to occur our final day.

He squints into the Forest. "We heard the siren and tucked ourselves into an empty cottage. I was trying to secure it when you ran by with Harry. I watched as you ran to the path and I realized that you had the right idea. That the path was the only way to survive. And I was so afraid for you, Mary.

"But Beth"—he shakes his head as he remembers—"she didn't want to go down the path. She was too terrified. She wanted to go to the platforms. Where she knew it would be safe. Just like we had always been told. She didn't understand what I was saying when I tried to tell her that the path was safe. That I had been down it before with the Guardians, securing it."

He hoists his hand back as if to throw the pebble into the Forest but stops at the last moment. "I'm the one who pulled her along behind me. I'm the one who pulled her to the path when it started raining. I thought that if we waited until it got dark . . . that maybe we would be able to sneak past them all. We weren't but a few lengths from the cottage when the Fast One grabbed her. I thought the rain would help throw them off. Would give us the time we needed to make it. But not the Fast One. With the confusion of everyone screaming and yelling and fighting . . . I couldn't hear her coming. I pried her off Beth. And God help me, I threw her at another living person, hoping to keep Beth safe."

I wrap my arms around my body, imagining what it must have been like for Jed. Imagining being responsible for the person I loved most becoming infected.

"There was nothing we could do then." His voice is soft. Defeated. "The people on the platforms next to the cottage— the people we have known our whole life—they saw Beth get attacked. And they started to shoot arrows at her. They tried to kill her and so we couldn't go back. And the blood from her bite drew the slow Unconsecrated. We barely made it to the gate as it was."

He fights to control his breathing, to contain his sobs, and I want nothing more than to cradle him to me. To wipe away his pain and misery like a mother with a son.

But I do not. I stand at the edge of Beth's grave and stare out into the Forest and wonder how it is that we are never truly prepared for death. How we can be always surrounded by it, reminded of it, knowing that one mistake can lead to infection. And yet when it comes we are not ready. We still have too many regrets.

"I had no choice," he finally says, as if asking me for absolution. "I couldn't let her become one of them. Couldn't bear to think of her in the Forest."

"I know," I tell him, thinking about our mother and the choice she made, the choice I let her make.

"It was the hardest thing I have ever done."

"I know," I say again, at a loss for what else to tell him.

Jed nods, squeezes my shoulder and walks up the path to rejoin the others, who are setting up camp. I stay behind, contemplating my lie to Jed.

Because I do not accept the hand of God; I do not believe in divine intervention or predestination. I cannot believe that our paths are pre-chosen and that our lives have no will. That there is no such thing as choice.

▼   ▼   ▼

The next morning the sun doesn't so much rise as seep around us, the air thick and heavy with moisture that coats our skin with sweat. Even though we must push on this morning, no one has made a move to leave the little clearing where we spent the last night. Cass takes a small sip from one of the water bladders and passes it along. It feels empty in my hands.

It has been three days since the breach. We are angry and terrified and miserable.

"We should go back," Cass says.

Next to me Harry lets out a breath as if he's been holding it. Argos lies next to me, his head on my knee, his ribs protruding like waterbars as I slide my hand down his side. His tail thumps lethargically in the dirt.

"We don't have enough water to keep wandering aimlessly like this," Cass continues. "We can't live without water and we can't hope to keep going and just pray that it rains again."

The day has barely begun and already I feel as though I

could wring enough sweat out of my shirt to fill one of the water bladders.

"Maybe we should scout for water," Travis suggests.

"What we need to do is go back," Cass responds. Her words are tightly coiled, as if she has played out this conversation in her head many times before.

"Cass, dear, I don't think . . . ," Travis says, and I feel my stomach clench at the word *dear*. I turn my head away from the group, staring out at the Unconsecrated that are gathered at the fence, trying to see beyond them into the Forest.

"I don't care what you think," Cass says to him, cutting him off. I have to bite my lip to keep from laughing. I'm not used to this stern Cass. It feels unnatural, strange and for some reason suddenly very funny.

"What I care about is that we are almost out of water." She stands and thrusts the empty bladder in his face, forcing him to lean back on his elbows. "We'll be out of food in a few days. What I care about is not wasting away out here in the Forest because we were too scared to go back to our village," she says. She taps one foot on the ground vigorously, as if she can't control her own body.

"There is nothing to go back to," Jed says, his voice the tone of finality.

"You don't know that," Cass says. Her voice is growing higher-pitched, more desperate. "You can't know that. You only know that things were going badly when you left. You can't say that they didn't get better. That they weren't able to push back against the breach."

Jed says nothing, his expression indicating that he has retreated back into his mind, back into his memories of Beth.

Cass begins to pace around us. "Aren't you able to see

what's going to happen here? The way this will end? We will follow these paths until we're too weak to move and then we will die out here." She waves her hands around as she speaks and she is so caught up in her own fervor that she doesn't see the tears in Jacob's eyes, that she is terrifying him.

"What is the point of wandering around out here like that?" she screams.

"There is something out there," I finally say.

She laughs, her eyes wide and wicked. "What's out there, Mary? Do you mean your ocean?" She places her hands on her knees and bends over until her face is level with mine. "Can we drink the ocean, Mary? Will your precious ocean save us when we're dying here on this path?"

Straightening back up, she announces, "I am going back." She looks around at us before adding, "And I'm taking Jacob with me." She holds her hand out to him but he just whimpers and backs away—afraid of the insanity glinting in her eyes, afraid of the death he witnessed at the village.

Cass goes over to where Jacob sits and grasps his hand, pulls him to his feet, but he will not stand. His whimpers turn to full sobs that shake his little body but Cass won't let him go. Finally he cries out, "Ow, that hurts!" and Harry goes to her and pulls her away.

She whirls on Harry, grasps him by the upper arms. I can see where her fingers dig into the skin.

"Come with me," she tells him, practically begs him. She's panting now, her whole body taut and trembling as if she would combust with the slightest breath. "Jacob can be ours. You and I. We can change all this. We can make it right—make all of it right. The way it should have been." She speaks fast, her words falling into one another as if she will forget them or lose the will to say them at any moment.

None of us moves, none of us breathes as we watch Cass fall apart.

"Just think of it, Harry," she says. Her voice is softer now. "It would be like it was before. When Travis was sick and it was just you and me."

In this moment I'm reminded of Cass as a child. Of her white-yellow hair and her innocent eyes. How she would listen to me recount my mother's stories even though she never cared for them. She never understood about the world before the Return. Her life was always in the here and now. In the bliss of a village permanently protected from the Unconsecrated and anything else that may have once existed past the fences.

"What if we are the only ones left," she says, turning to us all, waving her hand over us. "What if we are all that is left of the world? We can't let ourselves die. We can't be the end of everything."

Harry looks around at us, his eyes wide, his cheeks flushed. His gaze lingers on me last, as if he's sending out a silent plea for help. As if somehow I know what to do.

"The paths are marked," I finally say, looking down at my hands. "Down at the bottom, where they split. There is a bar of metal that's inscribed with letters. There were the same letters on the gate from our village. The same on the trunk we found."

Harry's eyes widen and then he wrenches free of Cass and kneels at the point where the paths split and pushes aside the overgrown grass until he finds the little metal tag. He reads out the letters: "I-V and V-I-I."

I fiddle with the dirty Binding rope still circling my wrist. I don't want to share with them the letters that Gabrielle left on the window for me. It's the last connection between us. The last secret we share. "These letters, they have to mean something," I say instead. "I think that if we follow them we may be able to figure out an order to them. Figure out the pattern and where they lead."

Cass growls low in her throat. "So what," she says. "We followed one of those paths and it led us to a dead end; it led us nowhere. It's like we were told growing up—there is no end to the Forest of Hands and Teeth!"

"What if they lied to us?" Travis asks, his voice calm and measured. He looks at us each in turn. "Clearly they lied to us about the path. The Guardians placed supplies out here even when we were told the path was off-limits. Permanently off-limits. What if there is an end to the Forest?"

"We need to go back," Cass says again. But this time her shoulders slump, her face slack with exhaustion and her voice empty. "Please," she adds. She turns to Harry and says again, "Please." But no one moves to join her and finally she turns and stumbles down the path away from us.

She doesn't get too far before she drops to her knees and begins to sob, great heaving wails that seem to be echoed by the Unconsecrated pushing against the fences surrounding us. Finally, Jed stands and walks to her. At first she holds a hand up as if to push him away but he doesn't allow it.

Instead, he sits next to her and pulls her into his lap and wraps his arms around her shoulders. I remember how he used to hold me like that when we were children and I woke up whimpering from a nightmare. I have to turn my head away from the way Jed rocks Cass, my eyes stinging, longing for those days. When all I worried about were monsters in dreams. When my brother was always there to comfort me.

We sit, each in our own world. "What if she's right," Travis finally asks. "What if we are the last people? The only survivors?"

None of us answers.

# ⬮ XXI ⬮

We spend most of the day backtracking, not making any real headway on the new path we've chosen. We decide to camp early, everyone exhausted. That evening I slip away from the group and go back down the path, back toward our village to where we split from Gabrielle. It's only been a day since I last saw her, since I found the tags labeling the paths, but when I step up to the fence and search the Forest I do not see her, do not glimpse that strange shade of red.

I sit down with my knees tucked to my chest and enjoy the solitude. That too-brief moment when it's quiet before the Unconsecrated scent me and come to pound at the fences for me. It's rare to sit near the fences without the Unconsecrated, to have a small glimpse into what life must have been like before the Return, before the constant moans.

My skin prickles and then I hear the sound of feet shuffling behind me. I crouch and turn, but it's only Travis limping toward me down the path. Neither of us says a word as he sits next to me, his bad leg jutting out straight, his hands massaging the area where the bone once protruded.

I lean my head on his shoulder and he turns to kiss my forehead. It's meant, I'm sure, as a tender gesture. To let me know that he's still here for me. But the feel of his lips pounds in my body, throbbing everywhere. It combines with the silence so that it's only us, no death, no responsibility.

I am past desire. I need Travis with a fierceness I have never known. Except with him.

My skirt swishes as I sit up and pivot on one knee until I'm facing him. His eyes wide, he glances down the path. I grab his chin in my fingers to force his gaze back to me.

The air is musty as I breathe it in and grasp his shoulders, press myself as close as I can and then press more and more and more. There are too many layers of clothing between us and I am angry at all that separates us and that I can't consume all of him at once, his whole being. For a moment I understand the craving of the Unconsecrated, the need for the flesh of a living soul.

His hands slip through my hair and his lips are close, oh so close to mine. Memories and doubts and fears flood through me and I push them all away so that I'm only here and only now.

We breathe each other, gasp for more air, for more of each other. And then his lips brush mine. Gentle, soft, like a leaf falling on water.

He takes my hands and then I feel his hesitation. Feel his fingers running over the Binding rope that still dangles from my wrist.

He lets go of me, his lips leave mine and I feel tears hot on my cheeks. I can't bear to meet his eyes. To know that he wonders.

He pulls away from me, like ripping my own flesh from my body, and stands. His eyes glisten, and then he turns and shuffles back down the path. I want to run after him, to throw him against the fence and demand him to tell me why he did not come for me before the Binding. I want to blame him for these ropes around my wrist.

I want to explain that I never would have done it if I'd known he would come. I want to beg him to forgive me for doubting him, for doubting that he would have claimed me before we had uttered the Vows of Eternal Constancy. I want to believe that he never would have allowed me to marry his brother but that his plans were lost to the breach.

But then I'm distracted by movement in the Forest, a glimpse of red at the edge of my vision. She's no longer running, no longer even walking or standing, but crawling now. Dragging her broken body across the ground toward me, her fingers clawing at the dirt. Gabrielle's progress is slow, unbearably so. Such that it's almost sad to see her reduced to this. Her body has used up its stores of energy and has begun collapsing in on itself.

As long as we have ever known, the Unconsecrated don't die, don't perish, unless decapitated or burned to ash. They do not rot, do not decay, only slowly pull themselves apart, a process made slower when they down themselves like hibernating animals. And it's strange to see Gabrielle like this, so helpless. Her arms stretch toward me, almost begging. Her moans now soft and high like a baby's last gasping cry for comfort.

But her eyes are the same. Her need the same.

I ache for her nonetheless. At what her dreams have now become. I try to remember her standing in the Cathedral window and I wonder if her life ever held complications such as mine. I wonder if she ever felt torn between duty and love. I wonder if her existence is simpler now that it's only about one need, one desire.

I think about Travis and Harry and this endless path and I realize that sometimes death comes before you expect it. That while we are rarely prepared for our friends, family and loved ones to die, we are never prepared for our own deaths. Never prepared to reconcile our own regrets.

I storm down the path, tears blinding me. When I rejoin the others I go straight to Harry and hold out my arm, the Binding rope dingy and dangling. "Cut it," I tell him. "With the ax."

He takes my hand in his, lifts the rope away from the delicate white skin of the inside of my wrist. The blade of the ax is cold and sharp and slices easily through the thin rope.

He still grasps my forearm in his hand while the tatters of the delicate Bindings float to the ground. I feel him tug at me slightly but I resist. He then raises my wrist to his mouth and kisses the raw skin chafed by the rope. Harry's eyes are not on me but on his brother as he lets me go, a small possessive smile on his face.

▼    ▼    ▼

There seems to be no end. In the mornings we lick dew from the leaves. We try to find shade in the heat of the day, sleep to conserve energy. But still we are slowly dying. Our steps have become shallow and lethargic. Travis's limp is more pronounced, as if he doesn't have energy except to simply drag his leg behind him. Argos trails along after us, no longer bounding ahead to explore but panting with the effort of existence.

One afternoon, two days after burying Beth and five days

after the breach, a storm rolls around us and we are almost giddy with excitement. But it only drizzles, enough to dampen our clothes and tongues but not nearly enough to refill our water bladders.

We are barely living. With each step we mirror the Unconsecrated that pace along beside us on the other side of the fence. Some days I wonder what the difference between us really is.

As the days wear on I feel the weight of responsibility on my shoulders. Travis's question echoes in my mind: are we the only survivors? And if so, have I killed us by insisting we continue through the Forest? If we had returned to the village could we have made a difference in the fight against the Unconsecrated? Should we have turned back? Taken a different branch in the path?

Am I responsible for the final fall of mankind?

▼ ▼ ▼

Ten days after the breach, as the morning sun burns away the fog, we come to another break in the path. This time, rather than two diverging paths, we come to a square clearing with a different gate on every side. Cass collapses, pulling Jacob to her and offering him the last of her rations—the food that she herself has not been eating but saving for him.

She closes her eyes and rests her sharp cheek on his head as he slips the small bit of dried meat past his lips.

I have lost count of the number of forks in the path we have traveled through. At first I tried to keep it all in my head like a map. Tried to remember which paths were marked with which letters. I would spend our days walking trying to puzzle it all together, trying to find the pattern.

But then I began to forget, the mental images I had pre-served of each path and each metal bar began to grow hazy and fade so that sometimes I was sure that the letters were re-peating themselves. That we would end up crossing paths we'd already come across, just like a true maze.

I am ready to give up. To admit defeat. To tell them about Gabrielle's letters and beg for forgiveness that I've brought us to this place when Harry reads off the letters from the bars attached to the gates as he has done at every branch we've come to.

"X-X-X-I," he says, before dragging himself to the next. "X-I-X," he says. "And finally, X-I-V."

My head snaps up. My heart pounds in my chest as if I have come up for air after too long underwater. I scramble to where Harry leans against the last gate, looking down the path with his face pressed against the rusty links.

I run my hand over the metal bar and then trace my fin-gers over the letters: *XIV*. In my mind I'm tracing my fingers over a pane of glass in the Cathedral, following the path that Gabrielle laid out for me: *XIV*.

These are her letters. This is her path.

"We should rest before going farther," Harry says, but al-ready I'm tugging on the lever, pulling open the gate. I hear them protesting behind me but my ears rush with blood. I cannot wait for them. I can't rest.

I trip down the path, my legs still weak but my mind pushing them forward. I can hear the others behind me, hear Cass yelling that she doesn't want to keep going. To leave her alone.

But I do not wait.

The afternoon sun is slipping through the sky when I'm

forced to my knees, my breath heavy in my chest—my body protesting, spent and exhausted. The others finally catch up, panting.

"It has to be here," I tell them.

And that is when I see the village through the trees.

# ▾ XXII ▾

There are no people. No smoke rising from the houses. The elaborate platforms in the trees are empty, the ladders lying in the dirt, their rungs covered in weeds. The world here is silent. Still. Barren.

For as long as we've walked along the path the moans of the Unconsecrated have been constant. When the sound is that unceasing the mind must find a place to store the incessant reminder of death. And so the moans become nothing more than a hum, a background rhythm to life.

Perhaps that's why none of us notices when the tenor of that hum changes, intensifies, harmonizes. When it echoes around us and pushes in on us until we are surrounded by the noise.

Instead, we each go our own way, mesmerized by this new and yet empty place. "Food!" Jacob says, his voice tinged with ecstasy. He pulls away from Cass's starved hands and runs toward the nearest building. Cass calls weakly, her voice scratchy from dehydration, and stumbles after him.

No one stops her; the rest of us continue farther into the village. Even though it's empty this place seems more settled than our own village. Here the streets are wide and laid out in a grid. The buildings are larger and more solid. There's a street dedicated to commerce: signs announcing the wares inside hang over each opening, shifting in the breeze.

We walk down what looks to be the main street and Harry and Jed veer off toward a building ringed with weapons, leaving Travis and me alone to stare with wonder at our new surroundings.

I look up and notice that, like our village, this place has platforms in the trees as a refuge from breaches in the fence. But unlike our village, these platforms have structures built in: houses, pathways between platforms, ropes and pulleys. It's as though an echo of the village on the ground exists in the trees. Like a reflection in a pail of water.

I stand there, my head tipped back in wonder as sunlight shifts through the buds on the trees and dapples my face. Fills me with peace. I close my eyes and listen to the sound of air sifting through the branches, knocking knotted ropes against tree trunks and causing a door on a nearby house to bump against a wall ever so subtly.

Even with my senses trained on the world around me, I don't notice the crescendo of the moans.

Until I hear someone yell. Until I hear my brother shout, "Run!" Until I feel Travis's hand grasp my arm, the sound of breaking glass by my head.

They stumble from doorways out into the sun. The downed Unconsecrated that have waited so long in this village for living flesh to arrive push aside crumbling fences break through dusty windows. Anything to get at us.

I move to the closest platform but Travis pulls me back. "The ladder," he says, his fingers pushed deep into my arm. "My leg. I can't."

For a moment I don't understand and then he tugs me away from this street and draws me back toward the gate and the path. Back to the known world that's safe and free from the Unconsecrated. Back to where we came from.

I jerk my arm from his, unable to return to that path. To give up on this village and my search for the end of the Forest and the ocean. I know that once we go back to the path we will be trapped, the Unconsecrated barring the gate for days and weeks to come. We will never be able to get back in.

"We'll never make it," I say to Travis. And I'm right. Already we're too far into the village, and the Unconsecrated between us and the fence are too many to dodge.

I urge Argos from where he cowers at my feet, ears pinned to his head, the low thrum of a growl reverberating against my legs. He looks at me for a moment, his hesitation clear. And then I nudge him with my knee and he's off, his training taking over as he runs from building to building. Backing away and growling when he smells the death of Unconsecrated.

This time it's me pulling Travis along, his gait halting because of the stiffness of his bad leg. He slows me down but I am unwilling to leave him.

I hear the panicked shouts of Jed and Harry but I don't take the time to locate them. I can only assume that they are also seeking refuge, hopefully in the empty world up in the trees.

At every doorway Argos barks and turns back. The Unconsecrated pour from the structures, from every hidden place in the village, and I begin to fear that we may never find a safe haven. That this place is nothing more than a hive of hibernating Unconsecrated.

We move out from the center of the village, away from shops and toward the houses. Unconsecrated drag themselves from the surrounding fields, a mass of them scenting and trailing behind us.

Travis stumbles and his hand slips from mine. I turn and see a small boy coming toward us. His clothes are tattered and his arms hang loose by his sides. I'm mesmerized by his eyes—a fathomless milky blue against pale white skin and a shock of red hair. Freckles splatter across his nose and over his cheeks and the tips of his ears.

He looks almost alive, as if he's just woken from a nap to find his world abandoned and shifted. Before I realize it, I have extended my hand as if to welcome him to me. To tell him that everything is okay, that he's only awoken into a nightmare and that this will pass into sweeter dreams.

He's almost in my arms, his head turning toward my hand, his mouth opening to expose teeth when a boot-clad foot flashes in front of my eyes, connects with the boy's head and sends him spinning back.

It's Travis and he clutches his bad leg. He grabs me and pulls me away from the boy, saving his ire until we're safe.

I can't resist looking back over my shoulder at the boy, who is now struggling to stand. Spots of blood mix with the freckles on his face, and his nose is now concave, pushed back into his head from the kick.

But still he comes for me. His eyes locked on to me.

Argos nips at my heels, his teeth insistent on the flesh of my calves. He uses his body to push me, to herd Travis and me toward a large thick three-story house that dominates the end of the street.

The Unconsecrated are now within touching distance and as we close in on the door to the house we have to push them aside, their mouths gaping open as they grope for us. They lean toward us and I smell their death and then we are inside and Travis pushes at the door until it clicks shut.

The stillness of the house spurs me to action and I run to the windows, throwing closed the shutters, using the thick boards propped against the walls to reinforce them. When we have the first floor safe and secure I run upstairs and am faced with a long hallway lined with closed doors on each side.

Argos's nails click against the wood of the floor as he sniffs at the cracks under each door. The air up here is close and heavy with must. At the last door Argos begins to tremble, a low and long growl shaking his frame.

I press a hand against the door, place my ear against the wood. I can hear a soft thump over and over again. Like the sound of a cat locked in a cupboard—it echoes my pounding heart. Even though I know I should wait for Travis, I swallow the fear in my throat and ease the door open a crack, ready to push back against Unconsecrated hands.

But there is nothing. Just the continued thump that is louder now that there is no barrier between us.

I allow the door to swing the rest of the way open and I'm surprised by the brightness of the room. A large window allows sunlight to slant across a faded rug. Against one wall is a small bed with a patchwork quilt done in blues and yellows.

Above that, hanging on the wall, is a painting of a tree with lush green leaves.

I turn to look behind the door and then I see the origin of the thumping. Tucked into the corner is a white crib with a white lace skirt. I don't want to know more, but still I'm compelled to walk closer, to look over the edge.

There is a child—a baby—who long since kicked off her blankets. Her skin is ashen and her mouth open in a perpetual yet silent scream. She isn't old enough to roll over, to sit up, to climb. So she lies there kicking her fat legs against the footboard of the crib, eternally calling for her mother. For food.

For flesh.

Her eyes are crinkled shut and yet I know that she is Unconsecrated. I can tell by the fact that no blood pumps through her body, the soft spot at the top of her head no longer pulsing. By the fact that her skin sags. By her smell.

And because no child could have survived in this village for this long were it living. She thrusts one bare foot in the air and I see the bite marks, the ring of wounds that circle her ankle and that have led her to this place.

I stand and stare at her. I have never seen an Unconsecrated infant. I should feel compassion. I should feel something inside me tugging me toward this helpless child, some sort of dormant maternal instinct. I should want to change her soiled clothing, to care for her.

My legs begin to quiver from exhaustion, the world around me tilting so that I have to clutch at the rails of the crib to keep standing. Argos paces in the doorway, whining, his scruff raised and teeth bared. The room reeks of death, engulfing my senses, invading my head—he doesn't like me being so close to the danger of the Unconsecrated.

And still the child with its silent, openmouthed wail, its kicking fervor. Its blatant need.

I am so tired of the need. The need for survival and food and safety and comfort. All I want is silence and sleep. Peace.

I think of the choice my mother made to join my father in the Forest. I used to believe that she became infected by mistake, in a wild burst of passion at seeing my father along the fence line. Now I'm not so sure. Now I wonder if she simply gave up, if the struggle of life and hope finally overwhelmed her.

And this realization sparks deep inside my body, heat raging through me until I feel as though my fingertips are on fire. Fury pulses through me. At my mother, at myself, at our very existence that has always been constrained by the Unconsecrated.

I take a deep breath and then pull a blanket from the basket by the crib and lay it on the floor. Gently I pick up the baby, supporting her head, and for the briefest moment she turns her face to me as if she were healthy, as if I were her mother, and I feel tears begin to slip down my cheeks.

This child could be my brother's. It could be my mother's. It could be Travis's and mine. Someone was her father. Someone once held her as I do now.

I kneel next to the blanket and place her in the middle, my tears creating dark circles as they fall on the fabric. I am humming as I carefully fold the corners tight, swaddle the infant and hug her to me, trying to give her comfort.

Once, back in the village, I imagined my children with Travis. They would have my dark hair and his green eyes and they would be strong and healthy. They would be nothing like this child and yet the feel of her, heavy in my arms, is just as I imagined.

I run my finger down her forehead and over the bridge of her nose. Cass taught me this with her younger sister, this trick to make an infant sleep. But this child will never sleep, will never dream, will never love.

I am shaking as I hear Travis limp down the hallway. "The others made it to the platforms and are safe," he's saying as he enters the room. He stops when he sees me, sees what's in my arms. His face constricts in horror as the reality of the situation sinks in.

"Mary," he says, holding a hand out, beckoning me into the hallway. His tone is taut though he tries to sound gentle and soothing. I can feel his hesitation, almost hear him screaming for me to come to my senses.

But I cradle the child to me and hum and rock her and she wails her silent scream.

"Mary," he says again, this time a plea. He steps toward me to take her from my arms.

But before he does I walk to the window, pressing her soft weight against me. I tuck her in the crook of my arm as I use my free hand to push open the sash. I let the cool fresh air roll over me, wash the stench of death from the room. I lean out, let the sun burn at my skin, scorch my tears.

And then I let the newborn drop.

It falls into the mass of Unconsecrated below and I don't see or hear it hit the ground. I hope that its delicate head didn't survive the two-story drop and that it's finally, fully dead. But I also know that even if the creature survived that it won't be a threat to us any longer.

A deep shiver presses through my body.

Travis comes up behind me and places his arms around my shoulders, his hands shaking.

I raise my fingers and place them against his cheek, feeling the strong pulse of his heart thrumming under his skin. The warmth. "We're safe now," I tell him.

"Tell me a story, Mary," he murmurs against my ear, his breath tender and moist and alive. He pulls me to the small bed against the far wall.

"I'm not sure I remember any." I'm still crying and he sits and pulls me down next to him.

"Tell me about the ocean," he prods. His hand covers mine and he pulls my fingers to his mouth. His lips close over the flesh of my thumb. I remember the first night he came to the Cathedral and how I fed him snow and the feel of his searing mouth against my frigid fingers. I remember the feeling of my body thawing for the first time. Of truly feeling alive. I allow myself to let go of the tension and fear and pain of the past few days as I slump against his strong body.

I allow myself to fill with hope again.

"I'm afraid it might not exist." My voice cracks.

He slides to the other side of the bed and pulls me down next to him until I'm cradled against him, his breath hot on the back of my neck, his lips trembling against my skin. His arms hold me tight, my hands grasped in his, his thumb caressing the inside of my wrist.

I allow myself to forget about the world that we live in. I forget about our village and this new village and the Sisterhood and the path and the Forest. I don't think of the Unconsecrated or of my brother, of being bound to Harry or of my best friend.

We are alone in a house that could have existed before the Return and could exist after. It exists in a time that is normal and not burdened by death and survival and fear.

For just this moment I want to think about life and us and nothing else.

# XXIII

It appears as though the founders of this village truly understood the nature of the threat that existed outside the fences. Whereas the platforms in our village were small and stocked with meager supplies, the platforms here are almost a village in and of themselves. Houses almost as large as the one I grew up in are nestled in the crooks of thick branches and rope bridges connect the platforms. Even though we can't communicate across the distance from our house to the platforms except for waves, it's clear that the rest of our group are happy and healthy in their tree houses.

Similarly, even though our little sanctuary is surrounded by unrelenting Unconsecrated, we seem to be safe inside, thick shutters reinforced by bars covering each window downstairs. While the Unconsecrated never cease to push themselves against the walls and doors, we are tucked away inside and safe until their persistence overwhelms the strength of our fortifications.

It feels as if this house was built for such a siege and it makes me wonder how and why our own village was so ill-prepared. Makes me wonder why this village differs so much from my own. Why their houses are so much bigger and more sophisticated.

Downstairs is taken up with one immense room that serves as the kitchen, dining and living area. A large wood-stove sits in the middle of the room and taking up most of one wall is a cooking fireplace that is almost big enough for me to stand up in.

There is a dining room with a long table bounded by benches—enough seating to feed a large family and plenty of neighbors. Lining one end of the living area is a wall covered with weapons. Some are long spears, some are long-handled axes and some I have never seen before; all have sharpened blades. There are crossbows and trunks filled with arrows. And placed in a position of honor over the fireplace are two gleaming swords with curved blades and intricately carved hilts.

In the back of the house, tucked away behind the stairs, is a tidy room filled with food. Stacked three or four deep along wide shelves are jars and jars of preserved fruits and vegetables. Dried herbs and meat hang from the ceiling, and large barrels with flour and meal line the walls.

This pantry has enough food to keep the two of us alive for years, it seems. It is more food than I have ever seen and I wonder if even the Cathedral had such stores.

Just outside the small pantry door is a tiny courtyard enclosed by a thick brick wall. A few pots ring the perimeter, ready for planting. In the middle is a pump that brings fresh water to the house and garden. There is just enough cleared ground for Argos to sleep his afternoons away in the sun.

It's apparent that the original owners of this house were expecting this, were expecting the inevitable breach that would leave them stranded. An island in the sea of Unconsecrated.

Upstairs are four rooms: three bedrooms and the nursery, the door of which we closed that first day here and haven't opened since. Just like my old shack of a house back in our village, this grand house has a ladder bolted into the wall at the end of the hallway upstairs. I climb it and push against a trapdoor that leads into a large space that spans the length of the house.

Up here there is more food lining the walls and more weapons amassed in neat piles. There are trunks stacked at one end that I don't bother to explore. At the other end of the room is a small white door. I flip the latch and struggle against it and finally it shudders, the vibrations moving up my arms as it jolts open.

Outside is a small porch with thick railings on the left and right and nothing across the front. As I step into the bright sunlight I caress the threshold to the right of the doorway, habit causing me to rub my hand over the Scripture that is always carved there.

But these walls are bare and smooth. Nothing written on the wood, no reminder of God or His words. I think back to all the other doorways I've walked through here and realize that they too have all been bare.

I wonder why the Sisterhood of this village didn't compel the people to inscribe the Scripture and then I realize that there is no kneeling bench in this house. No tapestries on the walls containing His prayers. This house contains nothing of God. The realization startles me—how could a structure in this village be allowed such blasphemy? Such freedom?

And I wonder, for the barest moment, if the Sisters of this village didn't control as tightly. Or perhaps didn't control at all.

I lean against the porch railing, staring down at the throng of Unconsecrated over two stories below. I notice that none of them wears the garb of the Sisterhood, none of them wears a tunic. I glance at the buildings around me: none bears the trappings of God. As far as I can see there's no Cathedral.

My head spins, trying to understand this new village. Trying to figure out if it was a place absent of God or just the Sisterhood. Trying to figure out if it's possible to still believe in God without the Sisterhood.

Dizzy, I sit down, my feet hanging off the edge of the balcony and swinging in the air, making me feel even more groundless. I have never known a life without the Sisterhood, without their constant presence and vigilance. It has never occurred to me that God could be separated from the Sisterhood, that the two had not always been so intimately intertwined that one could exist without the other.

The thought startles me, making my breaths come short and shallow.

Something flickers at the corner of my vision, pulling me from my revelations, and I recognize Harry standing at the edge of his platform in the trees a short distance away. The world around me falls back into focus as I stand up, placing a hand over my eyes to block the sun so that I can take in my surroundings.

I notice a huge tree lying not too far away across the dirt road in front of the house, between Harry's platform and the porch where I am standing. I see that it used to be part of the elaborate system of tree houses and that there are ropes hanging from boards at my feet. They dangle from the edge of the porch where there is no railing down to the ground where the Unconsecrated tread on them.

It looks as if the ropes used to be part of a bridge spanning the gap and I realize that this house, our house, was probably the anchor to the entire system. And now, for some reason either natural or unnatural, we have been cast off, left adrift.

I wonder if there's any way for Travis and me to make it across to the others or for them to find a way to the house—if there's a way to repair the bridge broken by the felled tree. My heart stumbles at the thought, unwilling to give up my solitude with Travis so soon.

Harry waves at me and I wave back. We stand and look at each other for a while before I realize that I am rubbing my wrist where the Binding ropes once chafed me, where scabs still dot my skin.

He's trying to tell me something but I can't understand over the distance and the constant moaning of the Unconsecrated. I shrug my shoulders and put my hand to my ear. He shouts again, his fingers cupping his mouth, and again I shake my head. He waves his hand, giving up, as if what he has to say is not important.

After a while he walks back down the platform, back to his tree house where Cass and Jed and Jacob are waiting. Already I can see a plume of smoke rising from the chimney and I wonder if they too have created their own life. If they have found a way to be happy in this new place the way that Travis and I have.

I slip back inside the attic, my palm brushing against the smooth wall by the door. Habits die hard and absence doesn't stop my fingers from searching.

▼  ▼  ▼

As the days pass Travis and I begin to belong to another world. We live most of our lives together upstairs where the windows are left open to the light and to the air. Once again the moans of the Unconsecrated become integrated into our every day, the constant noise relegated to a hum in the back of our minds.

Only rarely, when I climb to the platform to look at my brother, my betrothed and my best friend, do I wonder if they are living a life like mine, a domestic tranquility that belies the threat so immediate outside our doors.

Once I almost ask Travis why he didn't come for me back at the village. I'm sitting across from him at the table and there's a break in the conversation and I want so badly to know the answers, to know what my life would have been without the breach. I am gathering my thoughts, the pain of the waiting fresh in my throat. But then he smiles at me and takes my hand, the pads of his palms rough against my skin, and I realize that it no longer matters. Because we're together now. And I don't want to mar the harmony that we have found.

We settle into rhythms. Argos spends his days napping in various locations. Travis keeps our house fortified and I keep our bodies fed. The outside world ends at our door and this includes our commitments to other people. Here, in our house, it's only us and our life together and for a while it's bliss.

Until one day when I find myself coming in from the porch on the roof and facing the trunks lining the other end of the room. For the first time I'm drawn to them and I pass my hand over the smooth wood, the smell of cedar invading my head.

Even though I know there can be no one behind me, since Travis can't climb the ladder that leads here, I turn to make sure I'm not being watched. And then carefully I lift the latch from one of the trunks sitting on top of the stack.

It's filled with clothes and I break into a smile, happy to have found a diversion for the afternoon. One by one I pull out dresses that are intricately beaded and decorated with fancy stitches, each one very carefully folded for storage. They are all different colors, some bright and some muted—some shades I have never seen before. The material is soft and gauzy; fine stiff netting is stitched into the skirts to give them more bounce, more thickness and spin.

I hold each against my body, wondering what it must be like to be covered in such beauty until I'm compelled to try them on. Initially I feel a rush, a giddiness at the foreign material against my bare skin.

But then I start to wonder what woman once wore these dresses and why. For days I've lived in this house and have forbidden myself from imagining its former occupants. Since I dropped the baby from the window I haven't allowed myself to speculate about the children who once ate at the table downstairs, the men who crafted the weapons, the women who preserved each fruit and vegetable, meticulously planning for a siege they would never live long enough to endure.

And now I am wearing her clothes and I'm assaulted by her memories. I know that she was taller than I am because her gowns sweep over my bare toes and trail on the dusty floor. I know that her breasts were larger than mine, perhaps from the children. I know that her arms were flabbier than mine because her sleeves swallow my wrists.

But I don't know what dreams she imagined as she twirled in this dress. What man put his warm hand against the small of her back, making her skin tingle and her eyelashes flutter.

Suddenly, I'm dizzy. All my thoughts collide inside me at

once and I must know these things. I run back to the platform, still wearing this woman's dress, and I kneel down and scout the Unconsecrated below. I examine each woman's arms, her waist, her hair, her wrists.

Which one of them slipped her head through this dress? Which one smoothed her hands over its fabric? Which one of them had the baby, raised the children, slept in the bed I sleep in now?

The Unconsecrated are almost impossible to differentiate in their unending hunger and drive, their slack skin and expressionless eyes.

None of the women below seems right and I run to the ladder, climb back down to the bedroom and look out each window. But it's too hard. They are massed too closely together; they crawl over each other, kicking up dust with their need to get into this house, to get to me and Travis.

Not even bothering to lift the skirt of my too-long dress I dart downstairs and grab one of the long-handled spears, startling Travis. I don't hear what he says as I stumble back up the stairs, the spear banging against the walls of the hallways. Its sharp rusty tip trails behind me, scraping against the scarred wooden floors as I race back to my window. I lean out over the edge of the ledge, straining against the seams of the dress and extending the spear out as far as possible. It's just long enough that I can reach into the fray from the second-story window and I prod apart the Unconsecrated, trying to get a better look at each woman's face.

It is like a hunger that I cannot satisfy, an unquenchable thirst: I have to know who lived in this house, whose life I have taken over. Which one is the wife and mother? I am almost convinced that I'll be able to tell just by looking into her eyes which one is banging on her own house, is seeking entrance back into her old life. The life I have stolen from her.

I'm in a frenzy, shoving my spear at the Unconsecrated with tears clouding my eyes, when Travis finally limps into the room, his breath heavy from the arduous climb up the stairs.

He puts his hand on my shoulder but I jerk away. Blindly I jab at each body, shouting, "Which one! Which one of you?"

Finally, he yanks the spear from my hands and pulls me away from the window. But by this time my mind has cycled on to other possibilities, other theories. "Maybe she got away," I tell him. "Maybe she couldn't get back to the house but she was able to get to the gates," I say. "Maybe she was like Gabrielle."

I bring my hands to my cheeks, everything coming into focus for one brief moment. Maybe she escaped, maybe they're all out there, alone and searching. Maybe I'm the one meant to find them, to remember them, to carry them forward. I begin to pace, my mind tripping over itself. "I can get to the gates," I say, my voice breathy and excited. "I can find her."

"Who?" Travis asks me, his tone loud and firm as he grasps both my shoulders. "Who are you looking for?"

"Her," I tell him, motioning to myself, to the dress I'm wearing.

"What are you talking about, Mary? You're not making any sense." His grip keeps me from continuing my pacing but my feet tap against the floorboards, my toes digging into the wood with desire to move, to act on my need.

"Don't you see? Someone right now could be in our village, could be in one of our houses. They could find my clothes and think that I'm one of them, that I'm Unconsecrated, but I'm not. I'm here and they would never know."

I pull my shoulders from his grasp and go back to pacing. I shove one hand into my hair and wave the other around as I think, trying to pull together the whirring thoughts in my head.

Who are we if not the stories we pass down? What happens when there's no one left to tell those stories? To hear them? Who will ever know that I existed? What if we are the only ones left—who will know our stories then? And what will happen to everyone else's stories? Who will remember those?

"There is no one at our village, Mary," he says to me. "And the woman who used to live here, why does she matter? She's no longer here. If she made it out alive, she didn't come down our path."

I snap my fingers. "You're right," I say, every thought in my head somehow clear. "She must have moved on. She must have gone down the other path, she must have continued away from here."

Travis shakes his head. "Mary." He takes my arm again to stop me from pacing. "Tell me why this matters to you so much. Tell me why now, all of a sudden this is so important?"

My feet fall still and I look into his eyes. His impossibly beautiful, calm eyes. "Because no one will ever know about her. And that means that no one will ever know about me." My voice is a whisper. "When they come to our village, who will know about me?"

"I know about you, Mary." He places a hand on my cheek, trails one finger along my jaw, and I'm forced to close my eyes so that he doesn't read in my expression the words that ring in my head but that I can't say aloud. That it is not enough.

That I am terrified he is not enough.

My throat burns with tears as he pulls me against his chest. "I know about you, Mary," he repeats, the vibrations of his voice trembling through my body. His lips are on my ear and as if he can read my mind he says, "Is life with me not enough, Mary?"

I am filled with emptiness as I nod my head because I cannot bear to tell him the truth. Even as he reads my mind, as he proves to me how well he knows me. Even though he already knows my answer. Because I'm still hoping that he can fill the emptiness and the longing and that tomorrow morning I can wake up in his arms and it will be enough.

# XXIV

I have taken to spending most of my time up on the porch
on the third floor, a place where Travis can't reach me because of his leg. I don't know what he does all day as I sit on
the edge of the wooden boards, my legs dangling out in the air
over the Unconsecrated below.

It's been a hot and dry summer, and every afternoon I
wait for the rain that never comes.

I'm back to wearing my own clothes, all the dresses of the
lady of this house folded neatly and packed into the trunk, the
lid secured. When I walk through the attic space to get to my
perch I try to avoid looking at those trunks stacked against
the wall, but I always sneak a peek. I always wonder what
other treasures are hidden inside.

I've promised Travis, if not out loud, that I won't take
such risks again. That I won't do anything to endanger us
both. That I'll try to be happy with our little life. And yet I
can't stop my curiosity. I can't stop wondering what else I
might find in those trunks.

And so one afternoon, when I can stand the boredom no longer, I slink through the attic and start to sift through their contents. The dresses I push aside, pausing only slightly to finger the softness of the fabric, the shininess of some of the buttons. There are more clothes—thick winter parkas, vests like the kind Gabrielle wore but in muted colors. I run my fingers over them and then force myself to set them aside as I begin to think about who must have worn these clothes.

I can't let myself think about the residents of this village and their lost stories.

At the bottom of one of the trunks I find a stack of books with cracked leather binding. I lift them out gently, flakes of leather crumbling as I maneuver them from their hiding place. I peel open the cover of the first book and run my fingers down the page. It's a photograph, yellowed around the edges, of a baby.

I've seen only one photograph in my life, the one that was lost to the fire in my village so many years ago, and I'm shocked again at how lifelike the image is. How the picture has captured an individual moment in life, frozen for all eternity. For strangers like me to wonder and ponder.

Carefully I turn the page to find more photos. Of a small room with the morning light slanting through the window. A young, unshaven man lounging on the bed, his hand hovering tenderly above the same baby from the picture before, now asleep in the covers.

Of a child sitting at a table, food smeared around her laughing face.

Of a child tentatively walking, her hand on a table, a faceless man behind her holding his hands out to catch her if she falls.

And then there are the photos taken outside. Of a child on a swing, a young woman watching from the side as the child flies high in the air. Of a child with pigtails, her cheeks puffed out, ready to blow on a cake studded with small thin candles.

Fascinated, I flip through the pages faster and faster, watching this child grow.

Until I come to one of a young girl with her long black hair wet around her shoulders. Her mother stands behind her, holding her in her arms. Around them the peaks of waves are eternally still, their soft whitecaps captured before the crash.

It is the ocean. Just like the picture of my many-greats-grandmother when she was a child. And for a moment my breath catches because the little girl in the picture looks just like me. And the mother resembles my mother.

Tears begin to choke off the air in my throat and my body shudders. Even as I see how this little girl could never be me: her limbs too long and gangly, the mother shorter and plumper than my own. But for a moment, for the heartbeat before my mind is able to discern these tiny differences, I'm lost in the idea of my mother and me and the ocean.

I flip through the rest of the book but the remaining pages are empty and bare. This is the last photo. A girl I have never met. Who existed before the Return. In the ocean safe with her mother.

Suddenly, the roof of the attic is too close. This house is not enough for me anymore. I know that this solitude will never settle through my bones and I realize that I still long for the ocean and it's not enough to just sit in this life and be safe.

My body aches with this realization and I shake my head as I try to convince myself that this cannot be true. That I am happy here with Travis. That this is what I have always wanted: safety and love.

The air is too thick around me, pressing me in and under, and I stumble to the door and out onto the ledge overlooking the others on their platform. I swipe at my eyes as the bright light nearly blinds me.

I spend the rest of the afternoon watching the others go about their day. Sometimes one of them will stop to wave at me and I will wave back, but more often they live their lives as if I am not there, hovering, examining it all.

Their house in the trees is cruder than the house Travis and I occupy, its walls made of rough logs, no glass in the windows. It sprawls over branches and it's difficult to tell -where the tree ends and the house begins. A large porch surrounds it all, with wooden platforms and walkways spreading out into the surrounding trees to other houses and other platforms that form a grid over the village. It seems they have plenty of provisions, as I've seen them eating and laughing.

And while they have plenty of space if they want to spread out, it appears as though they prefer to stick together. All living under the same roof.

A happy family. Like the family in the photographs.

Harry and Jed pulled a table out from inside one day and they now eat their meals outside and I watch them throw their heads back with laughter. I watch the way Harry's hand has started to linger at Cass's waist. How he spends more time with Jacob, as if he were his own son.

Even though I can hear nothing from their world over the din of the Unconsecrated, it seems so much brighter and louder and fuller than mine. It makes my own house feel silent and empty.

It's not that Travis and I don't speak, for we do. It's just that it seems words have become unnecessary between us. We know at a glance, at a thought what the other desires. And so our world seems to have fallen silent.

We are each trying to determine the best way out of this house, out of this life. Wondering how we can reach the others and flee this village. Already my toes curl at the thought of walking down the path, searching for the next gate, the next village, the ocean. Looking for the woman who once lived in this house and telling her that someone still remembers her.

That her life holds meaning.

▼    ▼    ▼

Late one morning I step out onto the porch, the boards already hot from the summer sun, and I see that Harry is standing at the end of his platform, the place closest to me. He waves to greet me and I wave back and then he spins his fingers in a circle as if to send me a message.

I raise my shoulders in a question, not understanding him. With his entire hand he draws a circle but still I'm lost. He continues the motions for a while and then gives up, his hands on his hips. Then he turns, his back to me, and looks over his shoulder. I do the same, keeping my eyes on him as I turn my back.

He shakes his head and I can see his shoulders lifting and falling as he laughs. Finally, he waves me away and goes back to join the others and I take my usual seat, feet dangling, and open a jar of fig preserves, spreading the sugary jam on fresh bread.

I kick my feet, letting the fresh air lift my skirt, and I contemplate the distance between our house and the fence. The distance between my porch and Harry's platform. The density of the Unconsecrated between us. And I look for ways to escape, my desire to continue searching for the ocean crawling at my skin as days slip past us.

I try not to think about the book full of photographs hidden in the trunk in the attic. I haven't mentioned them to Travis, afraid that he will think it's like the green dress all over again. That I'm somehow obsessed with the people who came before us and their stories.

I wonder if the girl in the picture knew what was coming. That the world would change so drastically. There's a part of me that wants to believe the photo was taken after the Return, that the mother and her daughter are still somehow safe enveloped in the waves of the ocean.

But there is no fear in their eyes. And no one lives after the Return without that fear. It's the fear of death always tugging at you. Always needing you, begging you.

To distract myself from such thoughts, I explore the village with my eyes. Wondering what it must be like to stroll along its streets, what it was like when it was full of life. Our house dominates the end of this street, with small but neat wooden dwellings stretching out from either side. Not too far away I can see the trade houses I noticed on our first day here, signs announcing wares for sale—clothing, food, services— swinging in the breeze, unharmed. It's an odd sight because in our village the Sisterhood provides everything and there's no need for trade.

But as much as I have searched I still cannot find any signs of God etched upon the buildings. Instead, Unconsecrated shuffle from houses, seep from shops. The whole scene is too surreal to comprehend, and so I look away, training my gaze back on Harry and Jed and Cass and Jacob.

When the sun is high enough to hit me full in the face I start to get thirsty and so I stand and turn to go inside. That's when I see it—the arrow protruding from the wood of my door. Wrapped tightly around the shaft and tied with a string is a small piece of paper.

I pull it from the arrow with my jam-sticky fingers and unfurl it. I immediately recognize Harry's small swervy letters. *Contact, Finally,* the note reads, and I can't help but giggle. The giggles turn into full-blown guffaws when I see the other arrows piercing the wood around the house, just out of my reach. Each one with a piece of paper tied around the shaft. There must be at least ten arrows in the side of the house.

And then I look over the railing of the porch and see that a few Unconsecrated are milling around in the dust with arrows sticking out of various body parts, each of these also with notes. I'm laughing so hard now that I have to rest my hands on my knees, my back heaving with the release of it all.

I turn back to look for Harry and he's at the end of the platform, waving like he always is, a large grin on his face. Now I understand his earlier motions, trying to get me to turn around and look behind me. I start to giggle again.

Even from here I can tell that he's proud of himself. Proud to have finally come up with a form of communication, no matter how many kinks the form contains.

I wave back and clutch the message to my chest. I wonder what the note on the first arrow said, if he had written longer missives that became shorter with each drift of the arrow as it careened past its mark. I wonder how many of the Unconsecrated below carry plans for escape.

It's my turn to write back and so I slip into the house and down the ladder and run down the stairs and into the kitchen, where I find Travis, who's in the pantry counting jars and making notes in a ledger.

"We've made contact!" I say, waving the sheet of paper in front of his face.

He frowns a little, perhaps lost because I'm so excited I can't explain myself very well. But then he smiles at my own grin and takes the note from my hand and reads it.

"It's from Harry," I say. "He tied it to an arrow and then shot it at our house. He had a few misses," I tell him. "Actually quite a few misses. Turns out I was betrothed to the worst shot in the village!"

I don't realize until after the word is out of my mouth: *betrothed*. It's as if the individual letters hang in the air like fat rising in water. Like a promise that still lingers. Our eyes meet and I think I see sorrow there. A realization that no matter what bubble surrounds us here, Harry and I have a history together. A bond.

"Travis," I say, not knowing what words I can utter next to reassure him. To make it better.

"What will you write back?" he says, filling the emptiness. He hands me the note and returns to counting jars.

"I don't know," I tell him. And it's true. There is a part of me that wants to write him everything. That remembers our friendship as children and our Binding night and how we were close once before. That remembers how close we were to becoming husband and wife before the breach occurred.

I'm surprised, suddenly, at how lonely I feel.

And this is a terrifying thought to have in front of Travis. Travis, who makes my heart beat and my fingers tingle just to think about. Travis, whose breath I measure as we sleep, whose heart is the cadence to my life.

I let the note drop to the floor and it drifts across the wood with a sigh. Travis turns as if to retrieve it and I stop him as he is halfway kneeling. I join him on the floor, eye to eye. I trace the contours of his face with my finger, trying to remember what it was like the first time I had such freedom with this boy.

I know the instant my nearness affects him. I know it in the sound of his breathing, in the way the air catches in his throat, the way his mouth opens ever so slightly. I know it in the way his eyelashes flutter, how he sees me now through a haze of desire.

He pulls my face toward him, his lips brushing mine, and then he places my head against his shoulder. His arms wrap tightly around me and I understand how he needs me. I curl against his body, let him twirl his fingers through my hair.

And I close my eyes because a part of me still feels lonely and lost. A part of me doesn't know what future we can hope for in all of this, what happiness we can wring from these days. What future can any of us have if we are the last humans? The ones with the burden of carrying ourselves on, of re-creating the world?

Responsibility crushes around me. Responsibility for Travis, for Argos, to the promises I have already made to Harry that still bind us somehow, even though we never completed the final ceremony. My chest begins to collapse with the weight of it all, the pure panic of the possibility of failure.

I slip from Travis's arms and do not look back to see the questions I know must be in his eyes. He says nothing to stop me.

Then I tear through the house for paper, my fingers shaking as I carry a small stack to one of the bedrooms upstairs.

As I stare at the blank page, I am at once awash in words but unable to find the ones I want to use. The words that can convey the turmoil broiling through me. And so I start by writing everything I wish I had ever said to Harry. And then to Travis. And to Jed and Cass. To my mother, my father, my future. I write it all, filling sheets of fine paper with cramped and hurried words that I don't care if I smudge.

When I'm done I take my stack of paper up to the attic and sit against the wall, a box of arrows by my feet. With trembling and ink-stained fingers I wrap each sheet around an arrow and tie it with string I found in a sewing basket.

Then I step out onto the porch and take aim. Growing up, all the children in our village are taught how to use weaponry, including a crossbow. The weapon feels familiar in my grasp as I run my finger down the shaft and load an arrow. For a brief moment I wonder how the paper and string will affect the trajectory, if it will still fly true.

I notch the arrow and then with a sharp thwang the bow-string snaps back into place, sending the arrow flying. I watch as it curves through the air before embedding itself in the skull of an Unconsecrated woman.

She falls and does not rise. I pick up another arrow with another letter and let that one fly as well. Again and again I embed my story into the skulls of the Unconsecrated that surround us and still they keep coming. Their hunger driving them on, not caring that they walk over the truly dead forms of their fallen legion.

By the end, when all my arrows but one are gone, I've dropped twenty Unconsecrated. And yet there's no rest. No dent. Nothing to mark my accomplishment.

I take the last arrow with the last note tucked around it and I let it loose. It flies straight and buries itself in the wood at Harry's feet, where he stands at the edge of the platform watching my little hunt.

He leans over and plucks the paper from the shaft, leaving the arrow where it lies. He unfurls the letter and reads it. I tell him we are well and ask him if they are doing okay. And then I ask him if they have pondered escape.

I wait for his answer.

# XXV

"They're starting to break through," Travis says to me when I come inside. He's sitting at the large empty table in the main room of the house, looking at the door. Argos sits next to him and Travis absently tickles his ears. We both hear the scraping of the Unconsecrated against the wood. It is unending.

"I thought you said it would hold," I say. I try not to sound accusatory but I cannot help but feel a certain sense of betrayal. As if Travis had promised to protect me and now he's giving up.

"We both knew it wouldn't last," he says and I wonder if he's not just talking about the door and our defenses.

"How do you know they're breaking through?" I ask, my voice soft as I walk to the door and place my hand over the wooden beams that separate me from the outside world. They feel strong under my fingers and yet I can sense the strain on each individual splinter, the constant stress these timbers are under.

"I can hear it. In the way the wood groans under their weight. When I'm down here alone that is all I hear."

My head drops to my chest under his accusing words.

"I've been trying to figure out ways to escape," I tell him. "But I haven't been able to come up with a plan that will work."

"Oh" is all he says.

I trace my finger along a wide crack in the wood. "To get one of us across. That isn't the hard part. It's . . ." I hesitate for just a moment too long.

"It's my leg," he finishes.

I nod. "And the dog," I add.

Travis almost laughs but it's more like a sigh as he pats Argos on the head. Argos leans against Travis's leg in response, his eyes closed with contentment. The loyal companion.

I turn to face the two, my hands behind me as I lean against the door. "I won't leave you," I tell him.

"I know," Travis says.

"You don't sound as if you believe me," I say.

"I know," he responds. "But I do."

"We will find a way out of this."

I am about to walk over and grasp his hands, needing him to believe me, when he says, "And then what? What will happen after that?"

"And then we will find a way out of this village and we can go down that path and we can find the outside world," I say to him in a rush of words. "It's like we always said—"

"It's like you always said," Travis cuts me off. He won't meet my eyes.

I swallow, the emptiness beginning to fill me again. My

heart flutters in my chest; my breath becomes shallow. I let myself fall back against the door.

"Travis, I don't understand. This is what we've talked about since the day on the hill. Since you were at the Cathedral and I told you about the ocean and . . ." I gesture to his leg and he places a hand over where his wound would be.

"Because I had hoped that it would make you happy," he says. "Up on that hill, when we finally kissed, I wanted you more than anything else in the world. More than the village or my brother's friendship or my betrothed." He cringes at the word as if it's bitter on his tongue.

"I still want you more than anything else in the world," he whispers. "I would still risk it all for you."

He places his elbows on the table and puts his head in his hands; his fingers dig in his hair. At his side Argos whines, upset at his new master's outburst, upset at the instant instability in the air.

"Then why didn't you come for me?" I say, my voice barely carrying any sound. I clench my fists, the heat and anger and shame of him never coming for me starting to roil in my body.

For a long while he does not speak. And then he asks, "Do you even know how I broke my leg?" I shake my head. He has never told me the story and I never asked, assuming he would tell me when the time was right.

He doesn't raise his head from his hands as he continues. "It was because of the tower. That old watchtower on the hill in the village. I used to climb it and look past the fence and into the Forest and wonder what else was out there in the world. I used to wonder how our little village could be all that was left of the once-great universe. How could we be all that was left? How could we be the ones God would entrust with the future of the human race?"

He looks up at me now. "We aren't Noah, we aren't Moses. We aren't prophets. Why us?

"And so I began to wonder why the Sisters would teach us that we were all that was left. That the fence marked the end of the world. And I would climb that tower and I would plan my escape."

His eyes get a faraway look as if he's imagining what it's like to be back in the village, up in that tower. As if he is seeing the old views, feeling the wind caress the tips of his ears.

"Did you know that when we were kids Cass used to tell me your stories? She used to laugh at you. Not in a mean way, but in the way that Cass used to laugh at everything before. . . ." He gestures around us at our world now.

I shake my head. "I thought Cass never liked my stories. Never remembered them."

"Oh yes, I would beg her to tell me if she had any new stories from you."

"Why didn't you ask me yourself?" I whisper.

"Because you were Harry's," he responds.

"Not always."

"Yes, always," he says. "Always in his eyes," he adds in a softer tone.

I begin to pace in front of the door, expanding my path until I'm striding along the room. "Why did you care about my stories?" I finally ask.

"Because you knew it too. You knew about the world out there. Past the fences."

"So what?"

"So I needed that belief. I needed that . . ." He shrugs. "I needed that faith."

"I still don't understand," I tell him.

He slaps his hands on the table, startling both Argos and me. "I climbed the tower that day to say good-bye to the Forest. To give up on those dreams and accept the life I had chosen. To forget about the world outside the fences. To forget about you."

I stop pacing. "What happened?"

"It was icy. I was careless. I thought of you and your stories of the ocean and how you always believed it so strongly." He lets a hand fall back onto Argos's head. He doesn't look up at me when he adds, "I slipped."

I fall into a chair with a thud. "I never knew."

He shakes his head, his gaze still on Argos. "At first, when I broke my leg, I was delirious with pain and I thought it was God's punishment for wanting more. For being unhappy with the choices I had made. For daring to imagine a life outside the Forest."

He looks up and meets my eyes. "I was ready to give it all up, then. To follow His path, whatever it was. But then you came into my room night after night and you told me about the ocean and pulled me through the pain and I didn't know what to believe anymore. I didn't know if I was being tempted or being shown the right path."

He wipes his hands over his face. "You must understand that Harry has always loved you. That he would do anything for you."

"I'm not sure that it's enough," I tell him.

The corner of his mouth twitches as if he is almost about to smile. "I'm not sure either of us will ever be enough for you, Mary," he says.

I know he's hoping that I will tell him he's wrong. I can see it in the way he holds his breath, waiting for me to correct him.

Instead, I look back at the door and the splinters and the cracks and the way it heaves under the weight of the Unconsecrated that will never stop pushing, trying to get into our world. That will never stop until we are all dead as well.

A shiver presses through my flesh and I pat my hand against my leg to call Argos to me for comfort. But he does not budge from Travis's side. Instead he lays his head on Travis's lap, his wide brown eyes staring up at me.

All I can remember is the waiting. With every breath and heartbeat, the waiting for him to come for me. "I wish I knew, Travis," I say. "I wish I understood."

"I know," he says. Because he does know. He knows my desires better than I do.

I wonder then about my mother. My mother, who grew up listening to stories about the ocean and then passed them on to me but never went to look for it herself. She believed in these stories. The passion with which she would pass them on, the tremor in her voice when she talked about the time before the Return. The way she would cradle that photograph of our ancestor in the waves.

And I never asked her why she didn't leave. Why she didn't go in search of the ocean. Why she only passed these stories down with no instructions of what to do with the enormity of the memories other than pass them down ourselves.

I wonder, now, if she didn't leave because of us. Because of Jed and me. But in my heart I know that's not the case. She didn't leave in search of the ocean because of my father. Because he was enough for her. Enough to keep her snug within the fences her entire life.

Until he was the one on the outside. Only then did she leave the village, only then did she take that risk. For the man she loved she was willing to wander the Forest in constant hunger.

But not for the ocean. Not for herself.

"What do we do now?" I whisper, afraid of the answer. The house shudders under the pressure of the Unconsecrated outside. I pace back over to the door and lean against it as if my added weight will keep them at bay.

"We find a way out," he says. "We keep going."

I nod my head and we're both silent for a while. Looking at each other but not really seeing each other. Both of us lost in our own thoughts, our own world.

"Do you think they know about us out there?" I finally ask. When I see the confusion on his face I continue. "Not out there where Harry and the others are. I mean out there. Beyond the fence. Down the path." I throw my hand out toward the shuttered windows.

Travis shrugs. "I guess I never thought about it that way. I spent so much time on that tower trying to figure out how to get out there that I never considered there would be people trying to get into our village."

I tap my fingers against the wood of the door, my hands still behind my back, as I ponder this. "Do you think Gabrielle was trying to find us? Do you think that she knew we were there? Or do you think she was just following the path like us, taking it wherever it would lead?"

"I don't know," he says. "She probably just escaped from this village when it was overrun, just as we escaped ours."

I tilt my head back until it rests on the door and I am looking at the ceiling. I think back to that night when I first found Gabrielle's footprints in the snow. "Before, I always imagined that she left her village by choice, that she had the fortitude I lacked. When I was in the Cathedral and it was silent at night I used to dream of following in her steps. Of slipping through the window and drifting down the path until I found her village."

I realize that I have tears in my eyes and I feel a little embarrassed as they run down my cheeks. "Everyone would welcome me with open arms and I would ask them about the ocean and they would lead me to it. I would be free from the Sisterhood and the Unconsecrated and all the rules and oaths and pledges and vows." Even now I can see it so clearly in my mind—I can feel their arms around me. I can taste the salt in the air.

"I would have escaped," I whisper. "But then when we got here I understood." I knock my head back against the door, the old resentment surfacing. "I realized she left because her own village was overrun. She was no hero, no explorer. She was like me—forced from her home and scared, without any options."

I bite my lip and then add, "It makes me wonder if I would have left if the fences had never been breached. Or if I would have stayed in the village waiting for you forever."

Travis sits, watching me. I'm waiting for him to protest, to tell me I'm wrong. But then I hear an odd noise. Travis hears it too; we both turn our heads and try to pinpoint the origin.

A creak growing so high-pitched that I can no longer hear it—then a pop and a splinter. Argos begins to bark and I feel the door shudder under my hands.

Travis is at my side. He pulls me to the stairs. Argos circles us, nudging us onward. Always at our backs, protecting us. We are halfway up the stairs when there is a crash so loud that I raise my hands over my ears. I hear the sound of Argos's toenails as he scrabbles up the stairs.

The moans echo behind him, reverberating off the walls of the house. There are more crashes and splinters, the sound of furniture scraping across wood.

Then the Unconsecrated are upon us.

# ▼ XXVI ▼

I push Travis up the rest of the stairs and look down to see the Unconsecrated swarming. The wood reinforcing the door is in splinters, half of it missing, and they seep through the hole like blood from a wound.

A thousand thoughts run through my head. How to stop them. How to fight them. Where to go. How to hide. How to survive. Travis's leg and Argos and the ladder and the attic.

Travis stumbles down the hallway, his gait unwieldy as he tries to run on his bad leg. "Sheets!" I tell him. "Grab sheets!"

He doesn't question but turns into one of the bedrooms. I rush into another bedroom and pull the mattress from the bed. It's heavy and bulky and I waste a few moments maneuvering it out the door. But then I'm back in the hall and I push it down the stairs, creating an obstacle to the Unconsecrated's advance on our position.

But they'll find a way past. They'll build up against it with a pressure that will finally spill over, their awkward bodies piling up the stairs until they reach the floor and come for us again.

I run back down the hall to Travis and take the sheets from his hands. I drape one over Argos who still growls and whines and shudders. Without bothering to console him, I pull the ends of the sheets together and knot them until I have Argos captured, a squirming mass of teeth and nails.

I sling the package over my shoulder and muscle my way up the ladder and into the attic where I dump the dog onto the floor. He spills out with his hackles raised and backs into a corner, his eyes wide and ears flat.

I look down to see Travis standing at the base of the ladder. It is as if time narrows and focuses on this point, my heartbeat the only indication that time still passes. I can hear the sound of the Unconsecrated as they pool around the mattress and slide down the hallway. Slowly wending their way toward Travis, toward the ladder.

He has one hand on a rung, his fingers loose around the wood. He glances over his shoulder as the Unconsecrated bear down on him.

I move to swing my legs around so that I can go back down to help him. He shakes his head once, a sharp no.

Not knowing what else to do, I scramble for the rows of weapons on the wall and grab a long-handled ax with a sharp double-edged blade. I drag it back to the trapdoor and lower it down to Travis.

He looks up at me, his hand no longer on the rung. I've forgotten how green his eyes can be. How the edges of his irises are rimmed with a light brown. How there is a scar hidden under his left eyebrow.

How he can look at me and make me feel whole.

Before he can stop me I jump from the trapdoor, not bothering with the ladder. I land with a thud next to him, going down on one knee from the force of the landing.

I wrench the ax from Travis and turn to face the Unconsecrated. I yell to Travis, "You had better find a way to make it up that ladder and quick!" When I sense him start to protest I lunge down the hallway, gripping the handle of the ax in both hands.

Never in my life have I killed a human being. It's one thing to sit on a porch and sling arrows at the Unconsecrated below. It's another to feel the slice of a blade cut through flesh. Because even though the conscious mind knows that the Unconsecrated are no longer living human beings, there's still a part of the mind that rebels against the truth. That insists the woman, man, child coming toward you must still have some semblance of humanity.

Especially for those Unconsecrated that are recently turned. That haven't lost limbs and flesh to time and the Forest. That haven't broken their fingers trying to reach through fences and doors. To see a pregnant woman, her body still large and firm, her eyes still clear, walk toward you and to know she's dead and must still be killed takes a force of will that is almost unfathomable.

And yet I swing. With all my strength I pull that ax across the hallway, severing heads from necks, decapitating them in order to end their desperate existence. I don't even realize that I am yelling until I have to suck in gulps of air. The ax lodges in the wall and I tug it free and swing again, blood slinging from the blade. Again and again I swing, cutting down the Unconsecrated that fill the hallway.

The ax lodges in the wall on the other side of the hall and as I pull on it again, the handle slick with blood, I am distracted.

A girl my age crests the top of the stairs. She wears a bright red vest just like Gabrielle's. My hand slacks; I lose focus and momentum.

And I hesitate a little too long.

Something tugs at my foot. I stumble back, kicking. My hands slip from the ax. Without that anchor my balance falters.

I fall.

A hand grasps my ankle.

I scream and kick and begin pulling myself back down the hall with the heels of my hands. More hands on my feet, my legs. Tugging relentlessly. Unconsecrated continue to swarm up the stairs, stumbling toward me. Tripping over the bodies of the true dead that I killed but coming for me nevertheless.

All I can see is a wave of Unconsecrated cresting over me and I feel helpless, at their mercy. Ready to be tossed in the tides of their will. In that moment I wonder if I'll feel pain. If there will be anything left of me to turn. And if the hunger for human flesh will be the same as my hunger for the ocean.

I want to close my eyes and let it come. Let the end take me and sweep me away, drown me in the sea of Unconsecrated. But I hear my name as the shock of a thousand bee stings travels up my legs. I refuse to look at the source of the pain, don't want to see the Unconsecrated teeth that might be piercing my flesh, sending the infection deep into my body. Instead, I look up and I see Travis on the ladder, his mouth open in a scream, his eyes wide.

He reaches a hand to me and I am stretching toward him,

desperate for the feel of his fingertips, when I see movement in the attic. Before I understand I'm engulfed in a frenzy of fur and fangs. I hear the sound of claws finding purchase on wood and then a ferocious growl reverberates down the hallway as Argos attacks the Unconsecrated at my feet.

He is nothing but action, tearing at the Unconsecrated flesh with his jaws, ripping them apart.

Suddenly free, I scrabble for the ladder, my hand connecting with Travis's. He is only halfway up and I take the rungs two at a time until I am directly underneath him. Then, with the strength of having faced death and survived, I throw my weight against him, almost catapulting him into the attic.

Beneath me I can still hear Argos battling the Unconsecrated, the moans growing more intense as their numbers multiply. I hear a yelp and I look down to see Argos backing toward me. Without thinking, I slide down the ladder and grab him by the scruff. Instantly he goes slack, as if knowing that struggling might make me drop him. Together we make it into the attic.

Travis slams the heavy trapdoor shut and then throws the thick bolts to secure it. Argos, covered in blood and shivering, begins to lick my legs and Travis must push him away to get to me.

He kneels in front of me and I sit with my knees bent, my weight back on my hands. I am afraid to meet his eyes. Instead, we both look at my feet and legs, which are covered in blood, my skirt in tatters.

"Were you bitten?" His voice cracks on the word. His fingers frantically prod my skin, trying to find the wounds.

"I don't know," I say.

"Were you bitten?" he screams at me and I yell back, "I don't know!"

He pauses, still looking at all the blood, some of it dripping onto the floor.

He cups my calves with his hands, his fingers wrapping themselves around the muscle. He closes his eyes as if somehow he can sense whether the infection of the Unconsecrated is even now eating away at my system. Killing me.

"I love you, Mary," he says and that is when I let the tears come. The great heaving sobs of terror and pain that shake my body until I can do nothing but grab on to Travis to anchor me to this spot.

He pulls me toward him and I curl around his body as I weep. I fall into darkness with his fingers trailing through my hair, my cheeks still wet and my body heaving.

In my dreams I feel hands pulling at me from every direction, tearing at the flesh that falls from my bones, and everywhere I look it's my mother clawing for me.

# XXVII

"Mary." Someone is tugging at my arm and I jerk awake, my dream still vivid deep in my mind.

"Mary, we don't have time now for sleep."

I dredge open my eyes to find Travis crouched by my side. I feel heavy and achy and then a memory sparks and I'm wide awake, tearing my skirt away from my legs.

They are wrapped in delicate fabrics, a few with spots of crimson betraying the wounds underneath. "Were there bite marks?" The words tumble from my mouth.

He stands and walks away from me to where the trunks are cast open, their contents spread across the floor. All the beautiful clothes I had tried on are now tossed aside, some of them ripped for my bandages.

"I couldn't tell," he says, one hand in his hair as if he's searching for something.

I watch his back, watch the way the muscles along his jaw contract when I see his face in profile. I wonder if I would know if I'd been bitten. I run my tongue over my teeth, wondering what death tastes like. Wondering what eternal hunger is like.

With trembling fingers I fiddle with the bandages, peeling their edges up. They stick to my skin for a moment before giving way with a sharp sting. Travis is right—it's impossible to tell if the wounds are bites.

But as I come fully awake I know. I know that every heartbeat isn't pushing the infection deeper into my body, killing me with every breath. I know that these wounds come from fingernails and broken bones, not teeth.

I know that I'm okay. That I have survived being tossed in a sea of Unconsecrated.

Travis kneels and digs through the clothes spread out near the trunks, inspecting each garment and then pitching some over his shoulder and others into a dark corner. Every now and then Argos will take an interest and chase the discarded fabrics as they flutter to the ground, growling and tearing at them with his powerful jaws.

Underneath me I can feel the vibrations of the Unconsecrated piling down the hallway, almost thrumming like a heartbeat. They will keep coming until there are so many they can reach the ceiling, reach the trapdoor by standing on the bodies of each other. I rub my hands over my legs at the thought.

I hear a thump as the book with the photographs skids across the ground. Travis is tearing through the trunks and tossing anything that isn't useful.

"What's happening, Travis? What are you doing?" I ask. I crawl to the books. Photos are scattered everywhere, the little girl's progression through life now a jumbled mass. He tosses another book, one I hadn't seen before, and paper explodes from it as it careens across the floor, yellowed pages fluttering down around us. I reach for one with the words *USA Today* written in large block letters across the top. Travis interrupts me before I have a chance to read more.

"We have to find a way to get out of here, Mary. We don't have much time."

I look back to the door to the porch. It's still closed.

"Have you spoken with Harry?" I ask.

"Just to let him know we're still alive," he says. I can tell that the fear is eating away at his patience.

I stand and walk to the door. When I open it I see that it's covered in arrows and a breeze blows through the attic, sending the papers into flight again. I look past the edge of the porch to where Harry and Jed stand and they wave frantically at me. They've watched as our house was breached. Watched and wondered what happened to me and Travis.

I turn back to Travis and an arrow whizzes past my head into the attic. I hear a sharp yelp and Travis storms out of the dark inside, his hand on his arm, blood seeping through his fingers.

He glares across the gap to where Harry still holds the crossbow. Harry shrugs with a sheepish look. "It's too bad that Argos is over here," Travis says, gritting his teeth. "I would feel much safer with him at the crossbow."

I try to pull his hand away and look at the wound. "Only a scratch," he says, batting me away. He goes back to sorting the clothes and I can't help but smile when he rips a strip of fabric from a frilly pink dress and wraps it around his arm to stanch the blood.

I pluck the arrow from the floor and unwind its note.

*What now?* it asks in shaky handwriting. I don't know the answer and so I cast the arrow aside and join Travis by the trunks. I kneel next to him, place my hand on his shoulder.

His sits back on his heels and rubs at his thigh as if it hurts. When he raises his head to meet my eyes I can see the weight of his sorrow there.

"We will make it," I reassure him. But we both know that we may not. That this attic may be our tomb.

Argos yelps as another arrow careens into the attic and sticks into the flooring. "I should have closed the door while Harry was still trying to send his messages," he says.

"They're worried," I say. "They want to help."

Travis plucks the arrow from the floor and tosses it into a dark corner without bothering to read the note. "We don't have time to deal with them. We must get ourselves out of here."

All at once he slumps against the trunks and I catch a glimpse of his profile, of the strain that he's been trying to keep from me.

"Mary." He looks down at his hands clenched into fists, the knuckles a bright white. "Can you tell anything? I mean . . ." I watch his throat convulse as he swallows. "Can you feel it?"

He is terrified of the question and it hangs in the air like a horrid smell.

"I'm not infected," I answer him, my voice firm and strong. He doesn't look convinced. "Don't you think I would know if I was infected? Don't you think the Infected can feel death eating at their veins?"

He thinks about what I've said and then seems to accept it. "Would you tell me if you were?" he asks, turning to look at me.

I am about to tell him that of course I would but I can't. "Not until close to the end," I say. Because I can't bear the thought of breaking his heart before I have to.

He opens his mouth to protest but then closes it and looks around at the clothing splayed across the floor. The thumping of the Unconsecrated pulses against the floor beneath us and his face falls into a hard tight expression of terror and purpose.

"Never mind about them," he tells me and I don't know whether he means the Unconsecrated or the others out on the platforms. "Help me tear these sheets and clothes and knot them. Braid them if it's not sturdy enough. We'll use them as rope."

I nod and take my place by a pile of clothing. I rip the sheets, tying them in sturdy knots. The first dress I pick up is the green one I wore so many weeks ago and I must tamp down thoughts of the woman who wore this dress as I pull it apart, the fabric protesting as it tears.

Travis goes back to the porch and begins pulling the thick ropes that dangle uselessly to the ground. They used to be part of a bridge and he kicks out the wooden slats with his good leg as he coils the rope into a rough heap.

"Will it reach them?" I call out.

"We'll make it reach, somehow or another," he answers, not looking up from his task, his fingers a blur as he knots the various pieces of rope into one.

I feel the floor shudder beneath me and I know that Argos feels it too because he growls low in his throat, his tail tucked between his legs. He comes and leans against me, his warm body positioned between me and the trapdoor. Like water filling a bucket the Unconsecrated flow into the space beneath us. I wonder how much time we have before they force their way up through the trapdoor and these thoughts make me even more diligent about my task.

When I have ripped apart every dress and knotted the strips together I rise from the floor and stretch, wincing at the pain in my legs, and join Travis on the porch. I ask him what more I can do and he grunts.

I stand there watching him, twisting my hands together and feeling useless. A wind blows around us, sweeping through the attic, pulling paper from the floor out to float toward the Unconsecrated below.

I try to catch them, to save them, but the paper crumbles in my hand, turning to dust. One page lands on my foot and I carefully pick it up. The edges are rough, as if it was torn from a larger page. Across the top *The New York Times* is written in large letters. Below that, in equally large letters, it says: INFECTION SWEEPS THROUGH CENTRAL STATES: CITIZENS URGED NORTH. Below is a picture of a massive horde of Unconsecrated, taken from above as if by a bird.

I hold the photograph closer, trying to ascertain the details in the graininess. It is more Unconsecrated than I have ever seen in my life. Stretching wide and deep and determined.

I stumble dazed back into the attic, scattering the other pages on the floor, looking for more pictures. The large black words scream at me from every page: GOVERNMENT MOVED TO SECRET LOCATION; CDC UNABLE TO DETERMINE CAUSE OF INFECTION; LAST STAND AT ROCKIES FAILS; OUTBREAKS REPORTED WORLDWIDE; PREVIOUSLY CLEARED AREAS ENDANGERED BY FAST-MOVING INFECTED.

My fingers shaking, I pick up one page that shouts NEW YORK CITY UNDER SIEGE with a picture of buildings taller than I could ever imagine. They are massive, stacked almost one atop another for as far as the eye can see. I feel dizzy just looking at them, remembering the stories my mother told me of buildings that used to touch the sky.

But I had never thought of anything like these, could never have dreamed of buildings such as these!

I swallow, my breath catching in my throat as I realize the implication of this photograph. It proves that my mother was right. That the stories she passed down are true.

That there is an ocean. And that it must be massive.

I scramble to my feet and run to Travis on the porch.

"You have to see this," I tell him, tugging on his sleeve.

He looks at me as if from far away, a furrow between his eyes as if he is deep in concentration.

"Are you ready?" He walks past me back into the attic. I follow him, holding out the brittle paper.

"Travis, look at this picture. Look at what it means."

He still looks at me from somewhere else, my words seeming to mean nothing to him. There is a loud thump and a crack of the boards under our feet. The floor tilts just enough that I stumble, throwing out my hands to catch myself.

The page crumbles between our hands as Travis reaches for me, steadies me.

"We must hurry, Mary," he shouts, grabbing the makeshift rope I had braided and taking it out to the porch.

My heart thunders in tune with the Unconsecrated writhing beneath us. My picture ruined, I drop to my knees, sifting through the rest of the pages for more proof. For another glimpse of those buildings. But everything vanishes as soon as I grasp it, falling apart, ripping into nothingness.

My eyes blur with frustrated tears. I no longer even see the words or the pictures, just blindly cast about for something to hold on to. For the memory. And then my fingers trace over something smooth, sturdier. It is a picture of a vast stretch of impossibly tall buildings—just like the picture I had destroyed only moments before. More buildings than I could have ever thought existed in the world, much less in one location.

Around the edge of the photo is a bright yellow border and the words *New York City* written in curvy letters.

I smile and stand, my foot kicking a small book that slides across the attic floor, coming to a rest by the door. I pick it up. Compared to the Scripture it is tiny, just slightly larger than the photo of New York City and only as thick as my thumb. I slip the picture inside and tuck the book into my shirt to keep it safe. On the porch Travis has tied one end of my makeshift rope to the thicker rope and the other end to an arrow. He notches the arrow, aims, holds his breath and then releases the bowstring.

The arrow soars through the air, its long tail of brightly colored fabric trailing behind it, before it digs into the edge of the platform at Harry's feet.

"Nice shot," I tell him.

His mouth curves up as he responds with a wink, "One of the many things at which I excel over my brother." I slide my hand into his; heat radiates up my neck and into my cheeks and we watch as Harry grabs the rope from the arrow and begins to pull. Travis holds our end up with his free hand so that it doesn't sag down to get tangled in the Unconsecrated.

Finally, my braided strips run out and the heavy rope begins to make its way across the divide between us. My body trembles in fear as I watch it span the gap and I constantly measure the amount left on the porch and how much space is left to cover.

I almost weep with relief when Harry grasps the thick rope and begins to wind it around a sturdy branch in their tree. Travis pulls his end taut and ties it off on a beam in the attic. The floor shudders beneath us with such force that I am forced to grab Travis to keep from losing my balance.

Glancing inside, I can see the trapdoor straining, Argos skittering around it, barking and growling. We're running out of time.

# XXVIII

Not wasting a moment, Travis dashes back into the attic. I hear crashing as he turns over and empties a large barrel once filled with flour, a cloud of fine powder shrouding him from view. He hauls the barrel out to the edge of the platform, his entire body now lightly dusted white. I want to laugh at his ghostly-pale appearance but his skin looks the color of death.

The color of the Unconsecrated.

I slip my hand over his and squeeze it. He tries to smile in return.

As I convince Argos to jump into the barrel Travis uses extra rope to make a sling around it, attaching it to the line spanning out to the platforms so that the barrel can travel from our porch to theirs. Argos whimpers, claws at the sides, and it's everything I can do to keep him from jumping out.

"You must go with him," Travis tells me.

"But what about you?"

"Please, Mary, don't argue. Please do this for me." Sweat beads in the flour dust on his face and I can see how rigid his muscles are. How scared he is. And so I nod my head and crawl into the barrel, holding the squirming Argos to my chest.

"Duck," Travis shouts to me and I pull my head into the barrel just before hearing a loud thunk. I inch my eyes over the rim and see an arrow sticking out of the barrel where my head had been moments before. Argos lets out a deep bark as if offended by Harry's terrible aim. Tied to the arrow is the rope I had braided and Travis tucks it into my palm, the other end stretched to the platform.

"Hold on tightly," he says and then he pushes the barrel off the porch and we are swinging in the air before I have a chance to scream or protest or kiss him good-bye. I have to fight against Argos as he kicks and whines and scrabbles against me. I almost lose my grasp as Harry tugs on the braided rope, pulling us across the divide.

When we get to the other side Harry lifts me from the barrel and Argos skitters around us, sending up puffs of flour with every step. I'm still coughing, great shudders that rack my entire body, when I hear Cass gasp as she looks at the house I just came from.

I turn to look. Travis is pulling himself onto the rope, awkward and ungainly.

He struggles to wrap his bad leg around it for support and then slips, both legs falling from it so that he's only holding on with his arms.

And then his fingers slip and he falls back to the porch. He wipes his palms on his pants, clouds of flour appearing.

"We need to send the barrel over," I say.

"There's no time," Jed says.

Even from here, on the edge of our platform, I can hear the insistency of the Unconsecrated as they bang through the walls of what used to be our sanctuary. I watch as Travis glances over his shoulder and I can see the color drain from his face and his whole body shudder.

My throat closes as he reaches a hand to the rope, as he wraps his fingers around it for a second time.

Harry grabs my shoulders, as if to comfort me or to protect me or to hold me up, and I want to shrug him away as an unnecessary distraction, as something that pulls me from the task at hand which is to focus all my attention on Travis as if I can will him across.

He stumbles and instantly he is dangling out over the space, his two legs kicking and spinning. Behind him the Unconsecrated emerge from the door of the attic, pushing their way out onto the porch. Travis bites his lip and I feel as if we are holding the same breath.

One of the Unconsecrated—a young woman with orange-red hair—reaches for Travis as he dangles like bait. She steps off the porch in her attempt to get to him and her hands slide down his legs and catch on his feet and suddenly Travis is holding on to the rope with only one hand.

The Unconsecrated woman pulls herself up, her face closer and closer to Travis's foot. Already I can see pricks of blood where her jagged fingernails sink into his flesh. Her mouth grows closer. His fingers slip, a few already dangling free.

I feel myself jolt and move to the rope. I want to scream but it's trapped in my throat, strangling me. Blood begins to drip over the Unconsecrated woman's hands, making her grip slick, causing her to double her efforts.

Another Unconsecrated lunges at Travis and he too falls from the porch, dislodging the woman who was already dangling from Travis's foot. With his newfound lightness Travis swings his body forward and wraps both legs around the rope. He lets his head drop back just a bit and I know that he faces the horde of Unconsecrated just a little more than an arm's length away.

"Move," I want to yell but again I'm silent. I can feel Jed and Harry noiselessly chant the same word.

With one hand and then another Travis eases his way toward us. The moaning of the Unconsecrated fills us, washes over us all as the rope dips from his weight, dropping him closer to the hordes beneath him.

I realize that the barrel carrying both Argos and me was too much weight. We must have loosened the knots or overstrained the fibers of the rope.

The world is too bright at that moment, the light of a dying day, the sun sharp in my eyes as I watch Travis make his way to our platform.

The rope dips lower, strains under his weight, and suddenly there's a new sound. A popping as the old rope begins to unravel.

I move forward but Harry's hands hold me back. "There is nothing we can do," he says but I shrug him off.

I slide to the edge of the platform, snaking forward on my stomach until I am as far out over the void as I dare.

"Travis," I call out. "Travis, you must hurry."

He shakes his head, his hands now frozen. One of the Unconsecrated stumbles out of the attic, onto the porch and lunges for him. As he falls he hits the rope, sending it swaying and causing even more popping sounds.

The rope dips even lower, impossibly low. The

Unconsecrated beneath Travis are in a frenzy now. Straining up, their fingers seeming to grow closer to him with each breath.

"Travis, you have to listen to me." He shakes his head again. I can feel the tears choking my words, closing my throat.

"The rope is snapping," Jed says to me, his voice soft so that Travis can't hear. "He won't make it."

"Mary, you shouldn't watch this." It's Harry, his voice low, a gentle murmur as he comes to stand over me.

"No, I will not leave him!" I stand and take the rope in my hands as if I can pull him back, lift him up away from the horde below.

The rope quivers under my grasp, vibrations from Travis's jumping muscles echoing through every strand. I want to close my eyes and push myself to Travis, to be there by his side and pull him back myself.

But I know that it would be useless for me to go after him. The rope would snap under our combined weight and we would both die.

I look out at him, trembling like bait cast out in the water. "Travis." My voice still thrums like a growl, not allowing any dissent. "Travis, you will listen to me! Forget about the Unconsecrated, forget about the rope. Forget about everything but my voice. Close your eyes and listen to my voice."

He doesn't do what I tell him to do and I snap at the line with my fingers. "Do it!" I yell louder than I have ever yelled in my life.

His eyes immediately close. "Now, I want you to reach out toward me and grab the rope." I watch as his hands slowly begin to move. Infinitesimally at first and then with more confidence.

"Yes, good job, keep coming," I reassure him as he moves his other hand closer to us. The rope begins to sway with his movement and under my own fingers I can feel it give just a little as more fibers unravel, as it loses more tension.

"Faster, Travis. Move a little faster." He's sweating now but he nods his head and soon he's pulling himself up the valley of the line.

The Unconsecrated are in a fervor beneath him as blood slides from his ankle, down his calf and drips from his knee. The moans are a physical force rolling over us all but still Travis moves closer.

Behind me I can feel the tension in Harry and Jed as they watch, as they chant Travis forward under their breaths, afraid of voicing their hope and breaking his concentration.

"Help him!" I say to them and they move as one to where the rope crests the platform and they are there when Travis comes within reach.

Finally, Travis is safe on our side of the chasm and I collapse from the lightness of it all.

# ▼ XXIX ▼

It's dark when I wake up. I am alone in a bed, piles of covers almost suffocating me. I start to fight my way through them when I feel fingers caress my cheek. I close my eyes against the familiar sensation.

"You made it," I whisper, raising my hand to cover his. I feel my body sink back into the bed with relief.

And then I remember. "Your leg," I say, struggling to sit up.

He pushes against my shoulder, his touch light but insistent, pushing me back into my warm nest of blankets. But I resist and stay seated. "It's fine," he assures me. "A few scratches." He chuckles under his breath. "She had nails, sharp nails."

In the dim light I watch as he shakes the memory out of his head. His face looks a little drawn, his eyes tight with a twinge of desperation.

"But you made it," I tell him.

"I did," he says.

For a moment we are silent. Listening to the world as it wakes up. To the moans of the Unconsecrated below.

"How long will we last here?" I finally ask.

He shrugs. He holds his hands limp in his lap now. "They've been talking about rigging the same system that we used to get here to get us to another path. To leave the village and escape these platforms." He stops, rises from the edge of the bed, looks out the window. "But there has to be someone on the other side for it to work."

He turns back to me. "One of us would have to get to the Forest. Would have to be there to tie off the rope."

"But how? How could any of us get there? It's too far to the fence, there are too many . . ."

The rest of the sentence hangs in the air between us. Travis doesn't nod or say anything but rather pulls a chair from the wall to the side of the bed, its legs scraping over the wood of the platforms. He sits, crosses one leg over the other. I notice that he has a strip of cloth wrapped around his left ankle that he tugs at absentmindedly.

"When?" I ask. "When will they try it?"

He still doesn't meet my gaze. Instead, his eyes seem to drift around the room, to see everything but me.

"Right now the idea is to wait until winter. Hope that it's a harsh one that will slow or freeze the Unconsecrated. Jed and Harry have taken stock of the supplies. So long as we have enough rain to fill the water barrels we should be able to last until then."

"Months," I say under my breath.

"Yes, it would be a long wait," he says. Again he tugs at the bandage around his ankle as if it's too tight and I reach out a hand to cover his. The muscles in his arm twitch at the touch.

"I wonder what that means for the two of us," I say. He doesn't answer. His flesh feels cold under mine, empty. He still isn't looking at me and I pull back from him, tugging the covers around my shoulders.

Something isn't right between Travis and me. Something has changed but I don't know what it is yet.

"Tell me," I whisper. Fearing the worst.

He shifts in his chair and I see him wince as he places his bandaged foot back on the floor. He stands, paces to the window and then back to the chair.

"Yesterday all I could think about was saving you. Saving us." He pauses as if trying to figure out what to say, how to order his thoughts into words.

"It was only yesterday?" I ask. He smiles, breaking the tension for a moment.

"Mary," he continues, "when I saw you in that hallway with the Unconsecrated pouring over you . . ." He shakes his head as if to dislodge the memory. "A part of me wanted to die at that moment. To switch places with you so that you would survive, so that you would make it."

He grasps the back of the chair and his knuckles begin to turn white.

"I realized something then, Mary." He loosens his grip, drums his fingers against the wood. He paces back to the window as if trying to postpone what he'll say next. I pull my knees to my chest, trying to prepare myself for anything.

"I haven't been fair to you," he finally says. My skin tingles; every sense sharpens. I can hear the way he breathes, the air entering his lungs, his heart pumping in his chest. I can still smell his fear.

"I should have told you earlier what Gabrielle told me. About the ocean." He looks at me now, his eyes pained and pleading. It's as though everything around me drops away until it's only Travis and me, together in this tiny room high up in the trees.

"What do you mean?" I ask and my voice feels small in my ears. My heart pounds ferociously now. "You told me she said nothing to you. That you didn't talk."

He taps one finger against the wood framing the open window. A morning breeze lifts his hair for a moment, circles the room and then slips away. He closes his eyes as if to savor the feel of fresh air on stale skin.

"Gabrielle had been to the ocean," he finally says.

I suck in my breath; the world seems to tilt for just a moment. "When?" I say as I exhale. "How?" In the silence it occurs to me that if she's traveled there then it must be close. It means that it exists and that I can go there as well.

I tear the covers away and my legs tangle in the fabric, causing me to wince as the delicate scabs from the attack yesterday break open. I stumble forward but Travis makes no move to catch me. When I have my balance I rush to him at the window, take his arms in my hands.

"Don't you know what this means?" I say to him. My body feels light. Suddenly, I'm the happiest I've been since my mother died.

"We can go there," I tell him. "If she went there then we can go there as well." I begin to pace, the energy boiling inside my veins.

"Did she tell you how far? Did she tell you how to get there?" I stop and walk over to face Travis, my chest barely brushing against his. "Did she tell you what it was like? About the waves? The smell?"

Travis grasps my arms, pulling me in on myself and almost lifting me from the rough wood of the platform.

"She told me it's dangerous, Mary!" I can see now that his chest is heaving, his breath fast, his face red and his jaw tight. He shakes me, just a little. "She told me it's dangerous," he repeats in a softer voice. As if I would only understand if he continues to tell it to me over and over again.

I feel my own face pinch in confusion. "Dangerous how?" I ask. I pull my arms from his grasp and cross them over my chest.

"She told me that the Unconsecrated rise from the waters and still walk the beaches. That there's no way to fence it off— no way to protect yourself. She said pirates ravage the shores and no one could ever really be safe there."

I want to protest, to tell him that he's wrong. But instead I look out the window to the trees, to the leaves undulating out in the Forest. The only ocean I've ever known.

"It can't be right," I whisper.

"It is," he tells me. "You know that it's true. The ocean your mother used to tell you about was before the Return. Everything has changed since then. Everything."

"But the ocean is too big for that," I protest. "Too vast, too deep. I don't understand how the Return can touch that too."

He waits for a moment before responding, "Nothing in this world is deep enough to withstand the Unconsecrated."

He looks me in the eyes, traces a finger along my jaw. "Not even us."

I almost believe him but then I shake my head, anger welling deep. "You are wrong, Travis. You are wrong." I ball my hands into fists and punch at his chest. "I don't know why you're telling me such stories but you are wrong."

He takes my hands in his own, curling his fingers around my fists. "She told me that if I allowed you to go to the ocean I would never see you again."

"Then she was wrong too!" I yell. I pull away from him, backing toward the door so that we're no longer touching. "If you are telling me the truth, then why didn't you tell me this before? Why did you give me such hope and then tear it away?"

"Because I thought I could protect you," he answers. "Because I was hoping I would be enough."

"No." I shake my head tightly. "I thought you wanted to see the ocean as well. I thought it was our dream. I thought . . ." I swallow and take a deep breath. "I thought you were coming for me."

He doesn't look at me as he shakes his head. It feels as if the world is falling away from me. The realization of what he's saying—what he's not saying—tunnels deep inside me. The words echo in my head: *he was never coming for me, he was never coming for me.*

Everything spins; everything becomes unbearably bright and then dim. My world tilts and I step backward until my knees hit the edge of the bed and I'm sitting.

My body hurts so bad I want to throw up. "You were never going to come for me, were you?" I ask.

"I'm sorry, Mary," he says and it's the same thing as a no.

Everything is breaking inside me, shattering. "I don't understand, why are you telling me all this now? Why are you doing this to me?" I put my hands over my head, curling into a ball.

"Because I . . ." He stops midsentence and is silent. A muscle ripples along his jaw. "Mary, I wanted you too much. And that day on the hill, it was everything. It showed me what life could be—what hope could be. I wanted to believe we could be together. I wanted to believe we could break our vows and that somehow everything would still be okay."

His gaze is distant and he shakes his head. "I was going to come for you, Mary. Even though I knew I could never be the type of husband that Harry could be. Even though I was a broken man I was going to come for you. I was going to let my passion overwhelm my common sense. But then seeing Gabrielle changed everything. I saw what happened to those who strayed from the Sisters' path. I saw what would happen to us—to you. And I couldn't bear it.

"All I could see was you in that red vest, you tearing against the fences. I couldn't let that happen." He drops his head to his chest.

Agony of what could have been chokes my words. "We could have made it," I say. "We could have escaped."

When he looks at me his eyes are wet with tears. "No, we couldn't have," he says softly. "We never could have escaped." He places a hand over his leg. "I'm too broken. They would have found us—we never could have gotten away."

He kneels in front of me, takes my hands and holds them in his. "Don't you see, Mary? Ever since Gabrielle I've done nothing but try to keep you safe because I was too afraid of losing you."

I shake my head, my thoughts swimming and swirling, tossing about wildly. "Why didn't you tell me all this before? Why are you saying these things now?"

"Because I have been protecting you for too long. Gabrielle said the ocean was dangerous and I thought I could keep you from it. But then when I saw you yesterday drowning under the Unconsecrated I realized that I can't do it anymore. I can't be the one to make these decisions for you.

"I realized yesterday that it doesn't matter about the ocean. Because even if we never find it you still no longer need me. Once I thought I could protect you. Could take care of you. But you're strong enough. I've never seen anything like what you did yesterday. I've never seen someone survive the way that you have. To fight the Unconsecrated and live!" He shakes his head, his eyes bright and wide. "I was in awe."

It's as though he's pulled a plug in my body and all the pain and anger is slipping out, leaving nothingness behind. "I will always need you," I whisper. "All this time I've waited for you. And you were never coming for me. Why did you let me wait for you?"

Travis sighs, flexes his fingers against the windowsill. "I think that even then I knew I wouldn't be enough for you, Mary. It's no longer about the ocean. It's about you and what you want and need. Maybe you'll be happy with me for a few years. . . ."

He pauses and I can see tears flooding his eyes again. "I can't be your second-choice dream."

I want to scream at what he's saying, to push him down and make him take back the words. Instead, I step past him and walk to the window. I lean out, my hips digging into the sill. For a moment I wonder if I would be able to smell the salt of the ocean from here. If I could close my eyes and concentrate hard enough, if I could discern the crash of the waves on the shore. If I could taste the air, taste the ocean.

Ever since that day on the hill, ever since he promised he would come for me, this was always supposed to be our dream, together. It was never supposed to be about having to choose one or the other.

"Mary," Travis says, walking up behind me. He puts a hand on my shoulder but I shrug it off. I don't want him to be right. I don't want to believe what he's saying, that I could be so cruel and selfish. His heat radiates against me, trying to fill the emptiness inside, but I wrap my arms tight around myself as a shield.

I turn away from him then and walk to the door. As I cross the threshold he asks, "Would you ever give up the ocean for me?"

I hesitate, place a hand on the doorjamb. I had once hoped that, as it did for my mother, love would keep all other dreams at bay. The realization that it will not washes over me and I walk through the door, leaving him without an answer.

# ▾ XXX ▾

I t's difficult to find solitude in the platforms in the trees and so I walk along the rope bridges until I am as far away from Travis and the rest as possible. I sit and let my legs dangle, the scabs from the Unconsecrated itching as they heal. I want to cry but I can't find the tears. I want to yell but I don't want to cause a scene. And so I sit and stare at the Forest and think about Travis's admission that he was never going to come for me.

That he was going to let me marry Harry.

I pull out the slim book with the photograph of New York City. In the full light of day the colors of the picture seem duller than they did in the attic, but I don't care as I trace my fingers over the buildings, wondering about them. Wondering about the number of people it would take to fill them all and wondering what happened to those people. Of all the stories that have been lost.

I set the photo aside and focus on the book. I've never

seen one this small—the only books in our village were the Scriptures and the genealogy tomes. Carefully I flip back the red leather cover and trace the elegant letters on the first page, not understanding their meaning: *Shakespeare's Sonnets*. The paper is thick and yellow and I can feel the edges crumble under my fingers.

Not able to resist, I flip through the book, page after page of carefully arranged text. And at the top of each page, a letter. My hands freeze, the wind flapping the paper in front of me. I swallow and turn back to the beginning of the book. There, over the first block of text is the letter *I*. On the next page, over the next block of text are the letters *II*.

I am shaking as I follow the pattern, everything suddenly making sense. The letters are numbers. I flash back to what Gabrielle wrote on her window and turn to the corresponding block of text, skimming it quickly. It talks of judgment and plagues and good and evil and truth and doom.

I remember the letters on the trunk near our village and turn the pages until I find *XVIII*, number eighteen. One line jumps from the page, making me catch my breath: "Nor shall death brag thou wander'st in his shade. . . ." I drop the book, too many letters and numbers and words swirling through my head.

It's so clear to me now that I can't understand how I didn't realize it earlier. The paths were marked with numbers. And there must be a pattern to them, an order we have yet to figure out.

I am so consumed by these thoughts that I don't register another person with me until he speaks. I tuck the photo in the book and push it under my skirt so that he doesn't see it.

"Mary, are you going to die like the rest of them?" Jacob

asks in his little-boy voice. "Are you going to turn and then come eat me?" He kicks his toe against the rough boards nailed to a thick branch.

I can't help but laugh as I say, "No, honey. I wasn't infected. What made you think that?"

He frowns and I realize that I shouldn't have laughed. "It was Aunt Cass," he answers. "Uncle Travis told her what happened before, when you were escaping. She said she wondered why you didn't just die when all those Unconsecrated were all over you in the house. She thinks you must be sick." With his slight lisp *Cass* becomes *Cath* and *Unconsecrated* becomes *Unconthecrated*.

"But Uncle Travis said you fought off the Unconsecrated and that you were real brave. Is that true, Aunt Mary? Did you really fight them?" He pauses for a moment and if possible his voice becomes even smaller. "Can you teach me how to fight them too? Because they scare me."

I tug at his hand, pulling him into my lap. His lip trembles and I wrap my arms around him and squeeze. "None of us wants to be like them," I say. "And I promise you that we will do everything we can to keep you safe."

"I don't mean to be afraid," he says. "But sometimes I can't help it."

"I know, sweetheart. We're all afraid," I tell him. And somehow holding him makes me less scared.

"You know," I tell him after a moment, "Argos is the one who really saved me. He's the one who rescued me when I fell."

He giggles. "I like Argos."

"Then he's yours."

He looks up at me with his large eyes. "Really?" I can hear the hope in his voice and it fills me with joy.

"Yes, really. You can have him—with him around you can be less scared."

He hugs me, his little fingers fierce around my neck.

I can feel the footsteps of someone approaching. "Jacob," Cass says, "your uncle Jed is looking for you to help him prepare dinner. Do you want to go help him?"

"Aunt Cass, guess what?" he shouts, jumping from my lap. "Aunt Mary said I could have Argos to protect me from the Unconsecrated!"

Cass smiles and ruffles his hair. "I hope you thanked her," she says and as his cheeks grow pink I say, "Of course he thanked me." I wink at him and he skips back down the platform and across the bridges calling out for Argos as if there isn't a world of death below us all.

"Thank you," she says when he's gone and I nod my head.

She comes to stand next to where I sit and leans against the railing as she scans the horizon. We haven't truly spoken since before the breach. Since she told me that I was to marry Harry.

"You know," she says, "it wouldn't be so hard if they didn't both love you so much. If it weren't always about you. Even growing up, it was always about Mary."

"That's not true," I say. But my words don't sound convincing for I am too empty to put up much protest.

"Oh, it is true," she says. Her tone is light, contemplative, not angry. "Growing up, Travis always wanted to hear your stories. He wanted to know what your mother told you and you passed on to me. Harry wanted to know what you liked and didn't like. Always it was about you. What you wanted. What you knew."

"I'm sorry," I tell her. Because I don't know what else to say.

She shrugs. "I don't say it to pick a fight," she says. "I just want you to understand me. Understand why I've changed. Why we've all changed. I guess I just want you to be my best friend again—but that can't happen if I'm angry at you and you pretend I don't exist."

"I've never pretended you don't exist," I answer.

She laughs, almost like breathing. "I don't blame you, but there was once a time when I would have come first with you, when I would have been more important to you than anything or anyone else. And when I no longer came first I got angry. Because not only had I lost Travis and Harry when they both fell in love with you, I lost you as well. Even before the breach. And it wasn't until I found Jacob that I understood. Because he comes first with me now."

I still don't know what to say to her.

"I guess I'm trying to forgive you. And I'm telling you that I no longer care about Harry and Travis and all of that. I only care about Jacob and making sure he has a full life. That he can grow up and find his way in this world. Jacob is like a son to me now and all I have ever wanted was a family." She shrugs. "Now that I have him everything with Harry and Travis seems meaningless. A useless waste of emotion."

I lie back against the platform, feeling the sun-warmed wood through my clothes. Large white puffy clouds slip through the blue sky, going along their way as if nothing has changed in the world underneath. As if the world is anything other than death and decay and pain.

"It's just that sometimes when there's not much hope in the world it seems time to put things right," she says.

"There's still hope left," I say. "They're working on a plan." I try to find shapes in the clouds but everything eludes me.

She laughs again. "You mean their plan to wait it out until winter and try to sneak to the fences? I don't put much faith in that. I think this will likely be the end of us, up here in the platforms."

The Cass I knew growing up was not so pragmatic. This world has changed us all, forced us to make terrible decisions when we weren't ready.

"I'm not willing to give up hope," I say eventually. "And I will not give up the ocean."

"I figured that would be the case," she says. "But I just wanted to make sure you know that if it comes between you and your dream of the ocean and keeping Jacob safe, I will choose Jacob."

"I know," I tell her. And then after a little while I add, "You make an excellent mother, Cass." I want to add that it's my hope we'll find a way out of here, find a safe place where she can get married and have a big family. But I don't. Instead, I ask her if she wants to join me in finding shapes in the clouds and we spend the afternoon side by side looking at the sky as if the world around us is not as it has always been.

# XXXI

"Fire!"

I'm startled awake and I throw my arms out to the side, hands reaching across the sheets for Travis or Harry—anyone. But I'm alone and each breath sears into my lungs as I struggle to remember what broke me from my dreams.

"Fire!"

I hear the word again and then it's my brother in the doorway, Jacob slung over his shoulder, and I realize that he's hazy, the world is hazy, and that's when I begin coughing.

"Mary, you have to come now," he says and then the doorway is empty, tendrils of smoke curling in his wake as if they too are disturbed by the nighttime commotion.

With a hand holding my shirt over my mouth I step from the bed and let my bare feet slip over the floor, looking for obstacles. Someone grabs me as I near the door and yanks me into the fresh air and before I have time to orient myself I'm pulled down to the platforms, where I see the others huddled.

At my back I can feel the blaze, the hungry flames that are consuming our refuge bite by bite. Tearing through the other houses in the trees, growing bright as they eat away at the supplies and race along branches.

We are all at the edge of the platform where I spent the afternoon cloud-gazing with Cass. She's now trying to hold Jacob, who is shuddering, sobbing and apologizing. Jed, Harry and Travis all stand with their sleeves rolled up, their foreheads glistening with sweat as they stare back at the flames.

The air is so dry it crackles, drowning out the moans of the Unconsecrated.

We are trapped, fatally so. Beyond us is nothing—the wide stretch of village below with puddles of Unconsecrated. Behind us is the fire, slowly eating its way down the long platforms.

Every now and again flames drop like liquid onto the Unconsecrated, which become walking furnaces lighting each other ablaze, spreading the inferno to the structures in the village.

"Maybe the flames will kill them all and then we can escape," Cass says, her chin resting on Jacob's convulsing body.

The men don't answer. Instead, they stand frozen, as if action would be too risky. I can already see blisters spreading across Jed's right arm.

Our world is filled with heat and light and finally Travis says so softly that his words are almost drowned, "One of us will have to get through them. One of us will have to go to the path to tie off the rope. We have to get off the platforms and onto that path."

Cass squeezes Jacob, slipping her hands over his ears as Jed and Harry nod.

"And it can't be you," Harry says to Travis, "because of your leg." I roll his words around in my head, searching for the accusation, but I don't find it.

"I could go," I whisper. I wait for their objections, pray for them, and after too many heartbeats they come. Simple, straightforward.

"No, you won't go," they say. "It will be one of us."

Jed and Harry don't look at each other as they contemplate which one of them will sacrifice himself for the rest of us.

"I can at least get the rope," Travis mumbles as he hobbles back down the platform, back toward the fire that grows ever closer.

Jed places his arm over Harry's shoulder and Harry places his arm around Jed's waist and they walk a distance away, bending their heads together.

They look as if they're in prayer and I wonder if this is all my fault because I stopped believing in God so many months ago. I wonder if I gave up my belief in the ocean, if I gave up Travis, if I gave up everything that stood in the way of me and God—if I could save us.

If I could save them.

Travis slips around Jed and Harry huddled together and kneels awkwardly at the edge of the platform closest to the Forest of Hands and Teeth and the path that could be our salvation.

I crawl over next to him and help him tie the knots.

"I don't understand how this will work," I tell him, my fingers shaking and fumbling.

"It will work the same way it worked to get us over here. But someone will have to be on the other side to tie off the rope," he says.

He places his hands over mine, the feeling so warm and familiar. "Those days back there, in the house. That is my world. That is my truth," he says. "That is my ocean."

In his eyes I can see the jumble of words that roll through his heart and when he opens his mouth he says only, "I wish I could have kept you safe."

He trails his finger across my lips and then stands to take the rope to Harry and Jed, to prepare them for the crossing.

My legs buckle until I'm no longer kneeling and before I understand what's happening a figure runs past me, his steps uneven, and launches from the edge of the platform, flying out over the ring of Unconsecrated below us and landing with a thud and a roll. In each hand he carries a blade, the firelight glancing off the metal.

He recovers, stands and then begins to stumble toward the Forest, toward the gate and the path, my brightly colored braided rope tied around his waist and trailing out behind him.

At first he's alone and the Unconsecrated don't notice his presence. But then they move toward him. They sense him, crave him.

"Noooo!" I yell as I crawl forward and grasp the edge of the platform, as if I can take the braid in my hands and yank him back to safety.

The sobs tear at my body but I don't let them out. Instead, prayers rush from my lips as I repeat over and over and over again, "Please, please, please, please."

He stumbles, he falls, he gets up but he can't keep up the pace of the sprint. His leg is too weak. His gait is too lopsided. His body is too broken.

"Please, please, please, please . . ."

The Unconsecrated reach for him, their fingers pulling at

him, their feet stumbling across the braided rope. He's constantly yanked back, brought to his knees as the rope is pulled tight.

"Please please please please . . ."

I can hear him yell when the first one reaches him. He lashes out at them but there are too many. He embeds a blade in one and before he can pull it free he's pushed back, stumbling. I can see the blood spread out against his shirt. My brother begins to tug at my shoulder, trying to pry me away from the sight, but all I know is that as long as I don't take my eyes off Travis he'll be okay and will make it to the fences unharmed, uninfected.

He stumbles again and the Unconsecrated begin to pile on top of him.

"Please, please, please." I fill every word with my life, willing to trade mine for his.

An arrow whizzes past my head and then another and another and another. Each piercing a different Unconsecrated. They begin to fall and finally Travis emerges from underneath the pile, stumbling toward the gate.

Harry stands behind me, his crossbow a blur of action, his cheeks pale and wet but his aim determined and true. Leaving me, Jed goes to his side, takes up a second crossbow, and together they begin to fell the mass of Unconsecrated.

Joy erupts inside me, belief and salvation so pure I feel as if light pours from every inch of my body.

For a moment, for one exquisite and blinding moment, I have complete and utter faith that Travis will make it to the fences unharmed. That we'll live and that I will see what's beyond the Forest. That I will see the ocean. I squeeze my eyes shut, hoping to contain the feeling.

And that's when Travis falls again. That's when his screams reach my ears and I crumble, my arms no longer strong enough to hold up my empty body.

"Please," I whisper one last time. Travis stands, staggers, reaches the fence and throws open the gate. A few Unconsecrated follow him through before he can get it closed but Harry and Jed dispatch them in short order, one arrow after another bringing them down.

Travis is finally alone and safe. Blood covers his clothes and even from here I see his chest heaving. And then he raises a hand and waves and I feel the shudder of the platform as Harry and Jed fall to their knees behind me.

"No," I whisper, unwilling to accept any of this.

It takes him ten tries before he's able to lob the end of his braided rope up and over the solid branch of a large tree growing beside the path.

We feel the flames growing stronger at our backs as he begins to pull the rope across the void.

As one we hold our breath. The heat sears us. Argos whimpers and Jacob shudders as the thick rope inches across until finally Travis pulls it tight and ties it off.

It sways back and forth. Our salvation. Travis collapses against the tree and before anyone can stop me I heave my legs over the rope, cross my ankles and begin to pull myself hand over hand away from the burning platforms. I hear Harry call my name, I feel him reach for my feet, but I lash out, refusing to be brought back.

"It's not safe yet!" Harry calls out. "You should let one of us go first, just in case!"

I shake my head. Concentrating on one hand and then the other. Ignoring the burning skin under my knees.

"You don't even have a safety rope!" he yells out.

I grasp the rope tighter and let my head fall back just a bit so that I can see Travis, my world upside down. He is leaning against the tree and slowly, as I watch, his head slumps to his chest.

"No!" I yell.

"You don't even have a weapon if he turns!" Harry shouts.

But I don't let their words distract me—I concentrate only on one hand in front of the other. The strain in my muscles. The rope splitting through my flesh. I focus on Travis and my need to touch him, to feel him, to heal him.

When I reach the other side I let my legs drop, blood beginning to pool back into my feet. I am facing the platform, Jed and Harry and Cass and Jacob highlighted by the flames.

I look down, my neck straining between my arms. To my left is the Forest of Hands and Teeth, where the Unconsecrated are beginning to gather, beginning to shamble toward us. To my right is the path leading into the darkness.

Directly below me is Travis, his body bloody, his arms upstretched, and I am suddenly paralyzed with fear. Fear of the way he stands, the way he reaches for me, the way the blood cakes on his skin, the way he waits below—as if to devour me.

# XXXII

My mouth opens to scream but no sound comes out. I am hanging by my hands, my body heavy, and it's hard to breathe. I feel my fingers begin to slip, the blood from the rope digging into my skin making my flesh slick. I try to regain my grip, to heave my legs back up, but my arms are too tired. My muscles shake with the effort of just hanging and I'm angry at my haste in not allowing Harry to wrap a harness around me.

Tears blur my eyes as I focus on Travis below. His fingers open and close. Finally, he lowers his arms until they hang limply at his sides, his effort expended.

With a whoosh I allow myself to drop and I crawl to him. He's leaning against the trunk of the tree just inside the gate. His body shakes. His breaths come ragged and sharp. But he is still alive.

"Travis!" I yell as I pull him close to me. I rock him like a small child. "You'll be okay," I tell him. "You're okay." My chin rests on his hair, his head tucked against my chest.

I can feel his blood seep into my own flesh.

"Why did you do this, Travis?" I ask. "Why?" My voice cracks and I can feel his lips moving but cannot hear any words.

His eyes roll back into his head.

I shake him now, almost violently. "You can't!" I shout in his face. "I won't let you!"

A smile twitches at the corner of his lips where a trickle of blood begins to trail down to his chin.

"We'll fix this," I tell him. "Maybe there's another village. Maybe there's a healer. Are you sure you were bitten? Are you sure they're not scratches like mine?"

His small chuckle stops time, pulls us into our own world back before this village and the breach. Before his broken leg.

Back when we were children. Before we knew of the world.

"It wouldn't have mattered if they were scratches or not," he says, his voice like liquid. "I was bitten during the escape from the house."

My limbs go weak, everything inside me folding in and collapsing on itself.

"I was already dead," he says, opening his eyes.

I can only mouth the word *Why*. I cannot find my voice, cannot force sound from my shuddering body. I swallow. I rub my hand over his forehead, his skin slick with sweat and blood. I bring my head down to touch his. My mouth hovers over his and all I can think about is the days we spent together in the Cathedral when I would tell him stories about the ocean.

"Let me pray for you," I whisper. My nose runs; my eyes are swollen with tears.

"You were never very good at praying," he says with a small laugh. "That was never what drove you. It was always the stories."

I shake my head, squeezing my eyes shut. "It was you," I say.

He laughs softly again, more like an exhale than laughter. "I wish it could have been," he says.

I pull him tighter into my lap, wanting to squeeze the infection from his body, to clean his blood with my love. "I'm sorry," I whisper. "I'm so, so sorry." The sobs roll over me now so that I can barely hear him tell me that he knows.

All I can think about is how I have wasted my last day with Travis being angry at him. That I should have spent this day memorizing his face. Counting the freckles on his shoulders.

I realize that I will never again see him when he smiles at me with the sun in his face, making him squint and bringing out the little wrinkles beside his eyes. I will never watch him walk, the rolling gait of his limp.

I will never feel the press of his palm against my cheek.

Suddenly, all I can think about are all the things I don't know about him. All the things I never had time to learn. I don't know if his feet are ticklish or how long his toes are. I don't know what nightmares he had as a child. I don't know which stars are his favorites, what shapes he sees in the clouds. I don't know what he is truly afraid of or what memories he holds closest.

And I don't have enough time now, never enough time. I want to be in the moment with him, feel his body against mine and think of nothing else, but my mind explodes with grief for all that I am missing. All that I will miss. All that I have wasted.

That we will not spend our lives together. That I do not

have enough time to memorize him and even now I am for-getting him.

That I am not ready for this, not ready for his death.

"Tell me about the ocean, Mary," he says. "Tell me about how it's the last place untouched by all of this."

I shake my head. "The ocean is nothing," I say. "It's just like the rest of the world."

He takes my chin in his hands, his grip surprisingly strong. "Promise me you'll go to the ocean," he says.

I shake my head. "But you said—"

"Forget what I said. Promise me you will taste the salt for me."

I want to pull back time, to grab it and stop it from unrav-eling. I want to gather it to me and hold it close and keep this moment from slipping away. But I can't. And Travis's hand falls from my face.

"No," I say, clutching at him, trying to keep him with me. "I choose you. I choose you over the ocean."

"Promise me, Mary," he says again. This time his voice is weak, his breath rattling.

"I love you," I tell him. But he does not answer. Because he is dead.

Then I'm being pulled away from him.

"No," I protest but the arms dragging me back are too strong. It's Harry and he drops me onto the other side of the path. I scramble back up.

"You must leave him," Harry says, pushing me back down.

"Get out of my way!" I shout back, digging my fingers into the dirt as I claw my way back to Travis.

Harry grabs my shoulders. "Don't you understand? Travis is infected. He's about to turn!"

Jed is standing behind me with a scythe. He's waiting, ready for Travis to turn. Ready to end it. I reach for the gleaming blade. He must think I'm trying to stop him, trying to keep him from Travis, because he struggles against me.

"Mary!" Harry tries to pull me back from Jed but I shove him with such force that he stumbles down the path, crashing into Cass and tumbling to the ground.

"Give it to me," I tell Jed.

"He has to be put dow—"

"Give it to me!"

"Mary, you should not be the one to—"

I lunge for the scythe, screaming, and this time I'm able to grasp its handle. I'm the one who loves him. I'm the one responsible for his infection. I'm the one he was trying to save, the one he sacrificed himself for.

"Mary, let me—"

"Release it." My voice is a growl.

His hand slips from the handle and in one motion I swing the scythe away from him and toward Travis.

I want nothing more than to close my eyes, to pretend that none of this is real. Everything just a nightmare. But as I swing the blade toward Travis, I see his eyes open.

Those impossibly green eyes.

He used to hunger for me with those eyes but never in such a vicious way as now.

I bury the scythe in his neck, shuddering as I feel it slice through his spinal cord. His eyes lose focus as if he sees through me. His body falls limp, every muscle releasing at once.

He is gone. Forever.

Blood slips down his chest and I am sobbing on the ground.

Jed takes the scythe and picks me up. I'm too weak to resist. I want to reach out and grab Travis's hand, to feel him one last time, to let his fingers lace through mine. But he is too far away.

Already I forget what he smells like, the smoke of the fire searing away everything.

Jed carries me from his body.

"No!" I yell. I scream. I beat against Jed. I can't even draw in enough air to sob. My memories of Travis are jumbling, rolling together, twisting, corroding.

"You did what needed to be done," he says. As if those words could be any comfort.

"I loved him," I whimper. "He was everything. Why couldn't I see that he was everything?" Regret eats away at me, stripping through my veins as if to replace my blood.

"I know," Jed says. I'm thrown over his shoulder and I can feel how his body shakes and I know that he is crying. For me, for Beth. And I wonder if there was ever a crueler world than this one that forces us to kill the people we love most.

# XXXIII

As the days pass we do nothing but walk, trying to put distance between us and the fire devouring its way toward us. We each deal with the loss of Travis in our own way.

Cass turns to Jacob and her love becomes fierce. It's as though he's her own child. As if this child has never belonged to another woman and she is the first. She clings to him. He's the only one who has pierced through her veil of silence.

Harry has taken for Cass. He is the one who ensures that she eats what meager rations we have, saved from the fire and dwindling with every step. He is the one who carries Jacob when Cass's arms become weak. When she stumbles under the weight of it all.

I drift down the path alone. A wanderer. Not noticing anything. Stumbling over the smallest roots, veering toward the fences and the Unconsecrated. I stare into nothing. Wondering how it can be that I have lost everything in my life but this journey. This hope that there is an end.

That this path will lead us there.

It's Jed who pulls me back to center. Who takes my hand in his when I drift toward the fences and who gently leads me onward. It's he who acknowledges the sorrow on my face. Who understands why the tears silently flow even now, three days after leaving Travis.

We have both lost our loves to the Unconsecrated. Both been forced to kill.

The fire still burns behind us, pushing us forward. Ash covers everything, turning the world around us gray and desolate. The air is thick, hard to breathe, which causes our steps to become slower and slower.

None of us speaks of Travis, or of the fire, or of our dwindling supplies pilfered from the platform along with weapons before it was consumed. None of us wonders aloud about how the fire is impacting the fences, if the metal is melting or becoming weak. If Unconsecrated are pouring slowly down the path behind us, slipping through breaches where the fences are falling to the heat.

We all release sighs of relief with each gate we come across and close behind us. But then the fire catches up when we sleep and we're forced to press on. Hot, tired, drained, hungry, thirsty.

One foot and then the next. Trying to keep our eyes on each other in the smoke. Trying not to smell how the air is tinged with burned, desiccated flesh. Only surviving. Existing. Not wanting to be the first in our group to give up.

Sometimes, when my feet refuse to move and my legs tremble with fatigue, I will wipe the sweat from my neck with a finger and write Travis's name in the ash coating my arms. I know that I can't let him down by stopping. He's dead because of me and I can't dishonor his sacrifice by refusing to move forward.

One night, when the dreams of Travis threaten to drown me with tears and rage, I walk away from the group craving air and solitude. The night glows orange on the horizon and my body shudders, knowing that the fire creeps steadily toward us and that tomorrow will be another long chase.

I hear sniffles in the dark and I look around until I see a small form huddled in a ball staring at the flames in the distance. It's Jacob. I go to him, sit down next to him and pull him, resisting, into my lap. Argos, who hasn't left Jacob's side since the fire, nudges his cold nose against my hand.

"I didn't mean to," he tells me, again. Since we escaped he has done nothing but apologize for starting the fire on the platforms and I shush him, my lips against his hair. "I'm sorry," he says through a sob and I hold him tighter. Regret washes over us both and I hate the thought of him carrying this guilt throughout his life.

"Can I tell you a secret?" I whisper.

His sobs quiet to sniffles and I feel his head nod.

"My mother used to tell me stories about the ocean, and about buildings taller than trees that touched the sky and how men used to walk on the moon."

He giggles. "You're making up stories, Aunt Mary," he says. But I can tell that he wants to believe me.

I lean in toward him and whisper, "It's true, and I have proof."

I take the small book with the photograph of New York City from my blouse and hand the picture to him. He holds it close to his face, squinting. There's just enough light in the air from the fire to show the outlines of the buildings. I hear his breath catch and hold. "What is it?" he asks. He runs his fingers over it tracing the letters.

"It's a picture of a place that existed before the Return. That may still exist."

"How do you know it's still there?"

I shrug. "Faith. Hope," I tell him. "And that's why I am giving it to you. So that you have stories to keep you going. Something to believe in other than this path." I smooth his hair off his forehead the way my mother used to do for me.

After a while I stand, tugging him to his feet, and lead him back to where the others sleep. For the first time I slip easily into my dreams and they don't cause me pain.

The next morning we continue to trudge down the path and I notice that Jacob holds his head a little higher, his shoulders a little straighter, and I smile for it.

But the days continue to be long and hard and unending. The meager supplies Harry and Jed rescued from the platforms are dwindling to nothing. And then finally, when I think I can go no farther, the first drop of rain slips across my forehead. Thunder echoes around us and lightning flashes. Thick drops of water begin to fall like pebbles, almost painful as they strike.

As we continue to trudge down the path I'm sure we all think the same thing: will this be the rain that quenches the fire? That allows us to slow our pace? That will allow us some rest, relief, reprieve?

I turn my face to the sky as the drops increase. I let the water slide down my face and mix with my tears and wash away my anger. Wash away the ash on my body, blurring where Travis's name was written on my arm until it's gone. I spread my arms wide, letting the water deluge me.

Cass and Harry scurry down the path, Jacob cradled between them, looking for shelter. Looking for a branch, a bush, anything to slow the sting of the punishing rain.

I allow myself to collapse, to fall to the ground while the water washes over me. Jed comes to kneel by me. He lays a hand on my cheek, asks me what I'm doing.

I grin, wide and strong. I tell him to leave me be.

He looks at me for a long moment, the water dripping from his hair and nose and chin.

And then he leaves me alone, for he understands my loss.

Water pools around me; I become part of the flow. I imagine myself in the ocean, every breath of air tinged with water. My lungs revolting as if I'm drowning.

The path beneath me softens into mud and I roll, allowing it to coat me, thrashing in the water and muck and tears.

I yell at the thunder. Shout at the lightning. I scream at the Unconsecrated, demanding to know why they have taken everything from me.

But the Unconsecrated only moan and paw at the fences.

I stand, race up and down the path, waving my fists. Baiting them. But they drop their hands. They wander away, shuffling down to taunt Harry and Jacob and Jed with their hunger.

Angry, I race to the fences, thrust my fingers through the links and shake with all my might. I bang against the metal.

But they leave me be. The Unconsecrated slip past me as if I'm not even there. The water and mud masking my scent.

Finally, Harry braves the rain again and comes to me where I'm slumped against the fence. He pulls me back just as Unconsecrated fingers slip through my hair like a fleeting memory.

With gentle movements he wipes the mud from my face. And then he pulls me to his chest and as the storm rages around us and the Unconsecrated beat at the fences he whispers in my ear, "I miss him too."

For a moment we are one in our grief, and then we hear the shouts.

I look up to see Jed skidding down the path, waving his scythe in the air above his head. When my eyes meet his he stops and motions us forward. I can't hear what he is shouting.

Harry and I stand, find our footing and follow.

We pass Cass and Jacob shivering under a wide bush. Argos begins to trail after me and I hesitate and then push him back toward Jacob. The little boy grasps at the dog's scruff, burying his head in the fur at his neck. Argos looks up at me and whimpers slightly. I flip one of his ears through my fingers, scratching the tip, and his eyes relax into contented slits as he slides to the ground against Jacob. Absently the little boy rests a hand on the dog's tummy, fingers drumming, causing Argos's left hind leg to twitch. Cass glances up and mouths "Thank you" and keeps her arms tight around Jacob, returning her lips to his ears as if recounting some secret story.

I run to catch up with Harry and Jed where they wait still and silent. Here the path is wide enough for us to stand shoulder to shoulder all in a row, Jed taking center position.

He lifts the scythe, pointing down the path, and then lets it drop as if the effort is too much.

I take a step closer, not sure of what I am seeing, not sure if my eyes betray me. I can hear Harry's breathing, ragged from running all the way down here.

I sink to my knees; the sharp sting of a rock digs into my flesh, causing a small trickle of blood to mix with the rain slipping down my shin.

It's the end of the fence. The end of the path. There's nothing beyond but Forest. Another dead end.

My shoulders slump, my fingers trailing in the mud.

"I'm sorry, Mary," Jed says. Because he knows that this was my hope.

"I guess we wait through the rain," Harry says. "Hope that it kills off the fire. And then retrace our steps, go back to where the path splits and take another route."

I shake my head, drops of water falling from the ends of my hair and my ears.

"This was the path," I say, my voice barely above a whisper.

"We will find another one," Harry says, trying to calm me. Trying to make me feel better. But it doesn't help.

I believed so strongly that this was the correct path. That this would lead me out of the Forest and to the ocean.

"Maybe . . . ," I say, standing and wincing as the pain from my knee slices up my leg. I take a step forward.

"Don't do anything stupid, Mary," Harry says. "This is just another dead end. We've encountered them before. No doubt we will again. This path wasn't anything special. None of them is."

I shake my head again. There is something about this path that's different—something about this dead end that looks different from the rest.

I trace my fingers around the edges of the fence until they brush against the metal bar. "It's a gate," I say as thunder booms overhead. I turn back to Harry and Jed, their figures obscured by the thick rain.

"It's a gate!" I shout. I feel for the metal bar to find the letters and turn it until I can read what it says: *I* for the number one. This is the first gate.

They glance at each other and then come to stand beside me.

"But the fences don't continue past the gate," Harry says. "It just opens into the Forest—why would there be a gate if this is the end of the path?"

My heart hammers hard in my chest, thumping so fiercely that my breath comes out in puffs at the same rhythm. If this is the first gate it has to be the beginning and the end.

"Because we're supposed to go out into the Forest," I say. With every beat of my heart I know this to be true.

But Harry just laughs. "How ridiculous," he says. And then he sees my face. Sees me calculating the Forest past the fences. He grabs me by the shoulders. "You don't honestly believe that, do you?"

My breaths come rapidly now and I nod my head.

Jed steps in at that moment. "Mary, you cannot be serious!" He pulls me away from Harry. "Why would anyone expect someone to go out into that?" he says, waving a hand at the deep dark Forest.

"I don't know," I tell him. "But it does not matter. This is the gate that will take us to the ocean. To the end of the Forest." I point to the metal bar. "It's marked with the number one. The letters correspond with numbers and this is the first gate. This has to be the way."

Hearing me, Harry throws his hands into the air and turns his back, his fingers massaging his temples as if that will help him control his apparent anger.

"Mary," he says. He turns back to me and places his hand against my cheek and it slips down my face in the slick rain.

He then takes my hand in his. I look at our twined fingers and it reminds me of the day down by the river when all of this first started.

Of the time we held hands under the water of the stream and he asked me to be his. All at once I realize all the pain I have caused him since then. The betrayal, the uncertainty.

"I'm sorry," I tell him. The rain drips into my mouth as I talk. "I am so sorry for everything."

He tilts his head. "Why would you be sorry?" he asks.

"You would have been a good husband to me," I tell him.

The truth dawns on him that I plan to go through the gate and leave him and his grip on my hand tightens. "I always cared for you, Mary."

I smile then, just a little. I wonder for a moment what my life would have been like if I had never held Harry's hand under the water that day. If I had finished the laundry on time, joined my mother on the hill while she looked for my father. Kept her from straying too close to the fences and getting infected.

I never would have joined the Sisters, I never would have fallen in love with Travis or met Gabrielle. I never would have learned their secrets and pined for a life outside the fences. I would have married Harry; our children would have grown up knowing Cass and Travis's children, Jed and Beth's.

I could have been content. Maybe even happy.

But fulfilled?

Harry drops my arm from his grasp. "But we both know you didn't want to be with me."

I open my mouth to protest but he shakes his head. "You never did," he adds.

I shake my head to clear it. "That world no longer exists,"

I tell him. "We have to find our own way now. And for me that means going through the gate." I glance over at Jed before continuing. "Please," I tell Harry. "Go back to Cass. Stay with her and Jacob now. You know she hates the thunder."

"But what if we're the last people?" he asks. "What if we are all that's left? If you leave us you aren't just damning us but all of humanity."

"If we are all that is left," I tell him, "then maybe we weren't meant to survive. Maybe we've only been postponing the inevitable by staying trapped in our village."

"Cass was right—you're only chasing stupid bedtime stories and it's selfish," he says as he throws his double-bladed ax to the ground and turns on his heel and walks away from me, back down the path into the damp darkness.

I pick up the ax, test its heft in my hand, the handle slippery with rain and mud.

"There's another way," Jed says as soon as Harry is out of earshot. "There are other paths, probably other villages. This can't be the only way to the ocean, if it even exists."

I watch the water trail down his cheeks and drip from his jaw. "No, this is the one."

Again I see Jed's irritation flash across his face. "But how can you know, Mary?" he shouts. His muscles seem tight with frustration.

I throw my hands in the air, equally frustrated. "Because I figured out the code and it works. Because according to the code this is the first gate," I shout back. "Because They wouldn't have put a gate here for no reason—"

"We don't even know who They are, Mary! How can we trust that They put a gate there for a reason? They've built these fences, these paths everywhere. Don't you think that if there was something important out there that They wanted us to find They would have just built a path there?"

"Jed, all I know is that—"

"You don't know anything! You asked us to take it on faith that we were following the right path and it led us to that village—"

"But it was the right path. And it was not on faith. I knew where we were going, I knew how to read the signs on the path. It led us to Gabrielle's village."

"It led us to a death trap, Mary."

"We had no other options, Jed!" I am panting now, my chest heaving and hands clenched into fists. "Why do you even care if I go through that gate?" I ask him. I can see that he's taken aback by the question. "You turned me away after our mother died!"

He steps back, his shoulders slumping a bit. He looks off into the Forest and for a moment we listen to the rain crash down around us. "Because you are all I have left of family," he says.

# XXXIV

"**M**ary, we can still go back," Jed says, rain flying from his fingers as he waves his hands. "We can let the rain douse the fire. Backtrack, take another path. The fire would have killed most of the Unconsecrated. We have a few weapons, we could get through it."

I can see how his eyes shine with the possibility.

"We might find another village, a healthy one. We could have a life. . . ." He lets his voice trail off. "It's what I have wanted." He speaks so softly I almost miss his words as they slip under the thunder. "Mary, why chase old dreams? What can the ocean give you that we cannot?"

I wonder if he's right. If my dreams of the ocean are only that: childhood dreams. Fancies. I wonder how I could have ever believed there was a place untouched by the Return. A world alive outside the Forest.

I think about turning back, of sliding back down the path and following its twists and turns, never knowing if we are going in the right direction.

"At least wait until morning before making a decision," Jed says, his voice gentle, sensing my hesitation. I can feel his hands around my wrist, tugging me back down the path. And a part of me wants to give in.

I hear a moan; I hear the familiar sound of bones breaking as Unconsecrated force their fingers and hands through the fence links.

"But tomorrow will be too late," I tell Jed, jerking my wrist free. "The Unconsecrated will surround us tomorrow. Will surround the gate."

Jed sweeps a hand at the fence, water flinging from his fingers. "They surround us now and you want to go out there?"

"But it's raining now, Jed. It will throw off my scent. This is the only time I can go."

I can already feel my limbs begin to shake in terror and so I place one fist on my hip, hoping he won't notice how the ax trembles in my free hand. I wonder if he thinks I don't have the courage to follow through. If I will go to the gate and hesitate. Lose my nerve, turn back.

"Mary, it won't work. I tried that with Beth in the rain but she was still attacked."

"She was attacked by Gabrielle," I counter. "And Gabrielle is gone." I think of her desiccated body the last time I saw her. I wonder if she has finally found peace or if she lives on, unable to move, staring into the sky.

Jed still shakes his head no but I stand straight, throw back my shoulders. I resist the urge to close my eyes as I place my hand on the latch holding the gate locked.

"I promised Travis that I wouldn't give up hope," I tell him. "I promised him that I wouldn't accept safe and calm. Not at the expense of my dreams."

"What are your dreams worth if you're dead?" he asks, his voice soft.

In response I turn the latch and slip through the opening. I'm already a few paces away when I hear Jed call out to me but I don't stop.

I am in the Forest of Hands and Teeth now. No longer protected by fences. There are no Unconsecrated by the gate and none that I can see or hear anywhere in the immediate darkness.

For the first time in my life I am the one on the other side of the fence.

I'm running, my arms pumping, gripping the ax tightly. The storm rages around me and I can hear the crash of trees, the sound of branches being tossed in the wind. I can't tell if the noises surrounding me belong to Unconsecrated. I keep my eyes glued on the ground in front of me, trying to look through the shiny darkness for anything that will cause me to fall. That will make me weak. Or a target.

I've gone fifty paces before I allow myself to breathe, to allow hope to squeeze fear out of my heart. I realize I'm actually going to make it. Then the crashes around me grow more intense and I realize that even though I'm covered in muck and mud the Unconsecrated still scent me. And then I remember my knee. Remember falling, the sharp pain, the blood.

They track me now, the tang of blood oozing through the rain-soaked night. I can hear their moans. Hear their echoes. My mind begins to scream at me to turn back while there is still time. To race back to the gate. To choose a life with Harry and return to our village.

But instead I push on. The moist air sears my throat and my lungs scream. The muscles in my legs burn and already I feel myself grow weak. The lack of food and racing from the fire over the last few days taking over.

I grow careless, my arms flailing around me, the ax handle slick in my hand. I feel broken fingers wrap around my wrist and I pull back and shriek. Everywhere I look now I see them coming out of the darkness.

I am surrounded by Unconsecrated.

I have to force myself not to panic. Instead, I grasp the ax with both hands and begin to swing, running through the clearing that my weapon creates. Flesh falls around me, the squelch of steel meeting putrefaction mixing with the sound of the rain beating the ground, of my feet slipping in the mud.

But it's not enough.

I stumble. Hands grasp at my feet. I roll onto my back. I swing. My arm muscles scream at the effort. I dig my feet in, trying to push myself back along the sodden ground. Everywhere, they are everywhere.

I am stuck in the mulch of leaves and limbs and sodden earth, my body pulled down by suction. I cannot escape. I am lost. Finally, the Forest, the inevitability of it all, has won.

And then I can hear the screams. Not of terror but of rage. I hear the voice telling me to run and suddenly the Unconsecrated are gone. A hand reaches down, drags me to my feet. Presses me onward.

It's Jed and he swings his blade alongside me.

A new sound emerges through the Forest: the sound of racing water.

"This way," I tug at Jed, pulling him toward me as we run in the direction of the sound. And suddenly, the ground slopes sharply away beneath us and we cling to each other as we tumble down a steep incline. I drop my ax and use both hands to halt my fall, scrabbling at the muddled earth. I dig my toes and elbows and knees into the ground, branches digging into the soft skin of the underside of my arms, pebbles scraping the flesh from my legs and a bramble pulling at my cheek. Finally, I come to a stop.

I take a deep breath, almost choking on the rain. My body throbs in too many places to count.

All I want to do is rest here, determine how badly I've been injured by the fall. But then I hear the moans and the water raging even nearer and I push myself to my knees.

I look up and see the horde of Unconsecrated at the top of the hill, watch as they tumble down after us. They slide around me, their arms out and mouths open.

With so many bodies it's impossible to find Jed. I begin to scream his name, terrified.

Finally, I see him. He's looking at me, standing where he slid to a stop. Just at that moment a large Unconsecrated man careens down the slick hill, colliding full-force with him.

I see Jed flip through the air and land on his back with a thud. I begin to sprint. The Unconsecrated man recovers his balance as my feet slip, getting stuck in the muck. I can't find my ax so I grab a branch to fend off the Unconsecrated that crawl around me.

"Jed!" I shout, "I'm coming, Jed, hold on!"

My eyes fill with useless tears, blinding me. I swipe at them with my arm but that only makes the problem worse as mud coats my eyelashes.

Jed isn't moving. The Unconsecrated man crawls closer. He's leaning over Jed as I approach. I'm screaming now, hoping to distract the Unconsecrated, hoping to keep him from biting my brother.

He bends his head down and I throw the heavy branch I'm holding at him. It careens off his head and he glances at me. For a moment I think I've won. I think that I've enticed him enough.

But then, with the ferocity of a feral animal, he hunches over Jed and lowers his head.

I trip then and fall to one knee, the knee I had hit earlier. Pain explodes behind my eyes.

I feel a hand scrabble at my back and I turn and punch a female Unconsecrated with all my might. She staggers back. Long enough for me to realize that I tripped over Jed's scythe.

I wrap my fingers around its smooth wooden handle, remembering the heft of it from when I used it to kill Travis, and swing. I take out the Unconsecrated woman and then I stumble toward Jed and swing at the Unconsecrated man.

It is a messy death and I have no idea if he's bitten Jed. Blood is everywhere, cuts on our arms, faces and legs from our fall down the hill. He is still not conscious but his chest rises and falls.

I tug at him, shake his shoulder. But a pair of Unconsecrated children advance on us. I leave Jed and approach them, my fingers loose around the hilt of the scythe. The Unconsecrated have no avarice, no skill in the hunt. Their only strength is numbers, wearing down the living. And so the two children shamble toward me and it is easy to swipe the blade at them. To watch as it cleaves through the skulls and they each drop, a pile of clothes surrounding desiccated flesh.

"Come on, Jed," I say. I get back to his side and begin to tug at his arms. "We have to move!"

He opens his eyes again but can't get his legs under his body. His movements are slow, uncoordinated. I keep pulling at his arms, bracing myself in the mud, slipping too much to get us anywhere.

More Unconsecrated advance on us and I leave him to

keep fighting. It's a never-ending stream of them. I look up to the top of the hill to see even more sliding down.

And I am certain that this is how I will die. That I have chosen wrong. That this was not the path I was supposed to take. The gate was nothing more than a gate. It was not an answer.

There are too many Unconsecrated bearing down on us. Too many for me to defend against.

# ▼ XXXV ▼

A hand grasps at my waist and I'm about to swing when I realize that it's Jed. The blade barely stops before it would have split his throat. He is hunched over, his face pinched with pain.

"This way," he says. I look back over my shoulder, see the horde bearing down on us. It's too dark to see how many but I know it's enough to overwhelm us. "There's a river nearby," he says. "We'll be safer there."

I nod and he leads the way, limping. I try to hold him up, to help him, but my own feet lose purchase and I constantly slip.

The roar of the water pounds in my ears and eventually Jed slows, sliding his feet out as if he's probing for something.

"We have to move faster," I tell him. "They're getting too close again."

He holds a hand up and I am quiet.

"Here," he says, and I'm about to walk past him to see what he's pointing out and he pulls me back at the last moment, just as I feel my right foot slipping into nothingness.

He kneels and I follow suit. Both of us scoot forward and then I feel the emptiness with my own hands. There's a canyon, cut by the river. Just up the river I can see a massive waterfall, churning and throwing debris into the darkness. The roar of the water is deafening now, fed by the storm. Waves glint below, the river frothy, foamy, hungry.

I'm terrified looking down on it, my fingers digging into the mud. Jed swings one foot over the edge of the cliff near the falls.

I grab his hand. "What are you doing?" I ask. My voice cracks from the strain.

"It's too high to jump," he tells me. "There might be rocks we can't see. We have to climb down."

I'm already shaking my head. "The ground is too soft, we'll never make it."

He grabs my hand, pulls me over the side and wraps my fingers around something firm and slick with rain. "Roots," he tells me. "We can use them like rope. Be careful of the rocks," he adds, "the rain may have loosened them."

I'm still unsure. I can't climb with the scythe and I'm unwilling to let it go. But then the Unconsecrated horde descends on us and Jed pulls me over the edge before the first one can get me and I drop the weapon into the darkness below as I clamber for purchase in the soft earth.

They begin to fall around us, bumping us, grabbing at us as they tumble down the side of the cliff.

"Hold on!" Jed yells. The stream of Unconsecrated bodies does not stop, their arms reaching for us as they slip past, forcing us to climb lower. We shuffle down until I find a little overhang that protects me from the falling bodies.

I don't hear them as they crash into the water but I don't dare look down.

Jed joins me on my tiny ledge and together we press ourselves into the side of the earth wall, digging our fingers into the mud, grasping at the roots and brush.

The rain still beats on our backs, the thunder mixing with the sound of the rapids and echoing around us. In the flashes of lightning I can see the Unconsecrated thrashing in the water so far below.

I realize that Jed has been talking to me and I have to strain to hear his voice.

"—sorry, Mary."

"What?" I yell at him.

"I said I'm sorry," he says. And this time I hear him.

"Why did you come through the gate?" I ask.

"Because I'm your big brother." He smiles, then laughs. "And I want to believe in hope." I cannot help but smile a little as well. At the two of us stuck here on the side of a cliff during a storm, unable to see anything around us but Unconsecrated that fall with the rain.

For a moment it's just the two of us, the way it used to be back before there was Beth or Harry or Travis. Before our father and mother turned and we turned on each other.

"Thank you," I say.

He's about to respond when an Unconsecrated bounces down the cliff, knocks into him and sends him tumbling away from me, out into the nothingness.

"Jed!" I scream. Over and over again I yell for him as I scrabble down the cliff grasping at roots and branches and rocks, sometimes losing my grip and skidding down until I can stop my fall.

Finally, I'm close enough to the water. It churns with branches and bodies. Whitecaps roiling over each other. No order, just chaos.

Sometimes a head will break the surface but never long enough for me to see the face. Arms flail but it's impossible to tell whether the arms belong to Jed or an Unconsecrated. Bodies continue to fall into the water, creating splashes that mix with the waves.

I realize that the current is impossibly fast in places and so I start to move sideways down the cliff, trying to make it downstream. Hoping that Jed was able to find something to grab on to, to pull himself out of the water.

As the night wears on my searches grow more frantic, more desperate. I find a tree that has fallen over the water and I inch my way out onto it, gripping the rough bark with my thighs. The rain continues to pound my back as I move forward, gusts of wind rip down the canyon, making me hug the tree so that I don't fall in.

When I'm out over the water I scan the surface below. The river clogs as a massive log jams into a narrow part of the canyon and the water begins to back up. Waves crash over my position.

I back down the tree, concentrating so hard that I don't see it coming. An arm reaches out of the water. Grabs me. Yanks me in. Pulls me under.

I kick and thrash and turn. Something tugs at my hair. My head breaks the surface and for a heartbeat I believe that my rescuer is Jed. That he's the one who has dragged me to the surface.

But then I see the face, the hunger, the teeth. I lash out, push against the water with all my might. The current slips past me as I fight it. Lightning splits the sky and I can see my surroundings clearly.

See the bodies like so much debris, a part of the swirling mess.

And then nothingness.

▼　▼　▼

In my dream I'm back in the clearing in the Forest, the one Sister Tabitha took me to through the tunnels under the Cathedral. The Forest is silent. No mosquitoes humming, no birds singing and I am alone. Suddenly, everything around me collapses. Sound clamors back and it's my mother screaming as she turned. I see the Unconsecrated rushing at me from the Forest, all of them fast, all of them wearing bright red vests. My mother is there and Jed and Cass and Harry and Jacob. Over and over and over I see the same faces coming at me, hungering for me.

Panic wells inside me until I remember the fences. I am protected by the fences. I scrabble to find the entrance to the tunnel but it's not there. The ground is smooth; I can't find a single stick to use as a weapon. The Unconsecrated hit the metal links of the fence and they push and pull. My head swells with their moans.

They're calling my name. "Mary . . . Mary . . . Mary," like a chant, like a prayer. Blood pools from their mouths. Every Unconsecrated is my mother, Harry, Jed, Cass or Jacob.

They raise their hands toward me, their fingers like claws, pointing at me. I can feel their accusations like a blow, like a ferocious wind pushing against me. And then the fence dissolves. There's nothing between us. They crawl toward me. Crawl like Gabrielle the last time I saw her. My only hope is that their strength will give out before they reach me. But I feel them on my legs, pulling me down. I'm surrounded, smothered. I can't breathe.

Their hands dig into me. It's as if they're all trying to crawl inside me at once.

I can't stop them and they keep coming and coming and coming until I drown under them.

# XXXVI

I wake to the sound of wind rushing through the trees. I'm on my back, water swirling around my toes. The earth feels different. Soggy. Soft. Smooth.

I try to open my eyes but the bright sun blinds me, sending sharp daggers of pain deep into my head. The rest of my body screams in pain as well and I let out a low moan.

For a while I just lie there. Breathing, remembering my dream and allowing the guilt of losing Jed to wash over me. I want to curl in on myself, to tear at my hair. But my body hurts too much and so I let the water tickle my feet, let the sun warm my cheek, let my body stop its throbbing. The air through the trees is calming, soothing, and I almost slip back into nothingness, grateful to forget about the Forest and Jed and hope and the Unconsecrated and my dream.

The sound of someone digging sifts through my head. The sound of a spade breaking through a root, burying itself into the soft earth, being pulled out again.

It's a familiar sound and makes me smile. Harvest season.

Time to celebrate the sun and spring. The sound grows closer and its repetition joins the rhythm of the air through the trees like a lullaby.

A shadow falls over my face and I open my eyes just in time to see a man standing over me with a shovel in his hands. He raises the blade above his head.

On instinct I roll to my right. The shovel misses my throat and buries itself in the sand where my neck used to be.

The man stands there slightly off balance, his blade buried very deep in the sand.

I fall back on my heels and as he yanks against the handle I raise my hands. "Wait, wait!" I shout at him, and he stops. His grip loosens and he looks at me with an odd and curious expression.

"You're . . ." He pauses. "You're not dead," he finally says.

"I would have been, had you had your way," I say. I keep my hands up and start to scoot away from him.

Something past his shoulder catches my eye—an Unconsecrated woman with stringy hair is lurching at his back. "Watch out!" I yell. He turns and decapitates her with a practiced stroke. She falls to the ground slowly.

He returns his gaze to me and starts to speak but his words don't penetrate my haze. I'm suddenly dizzy as I take in the world around me. At the expanse of water stretching out forever beside me.

"The ocean," I whisper. And then the night before breaks fresh into my mind again. "Jed," I gasp.

I stand, wobble and then start to run down the beach, examining the bodies washed ashore. Most of their heads have been severed, no doubt the handiwork of the man who's calling after me.

"What are you looking for?" he yells.

"My brother!" I shout. "He was with me and now . . ."

There are hundreds of Unconsecrated littering the beach and I am about to turn one over to see its face when the man catches up with me and pulls me back.

"Whoa there," he says. "Watch what you're doing. Some of these Mudo are still dangerous."

He pushes me aside and flips the body with his shovel. I clasp my hands in front of my face, peering around my fingers. But it isn't Jed. We repeat this with all the bodies on the beach. My stomach lurches every time and I pray that I haven't caused my brother's death. The man patiently leads me from body to body, turning them so that I can see and then swiftly cutting their heads as casually as he would dig into the earth.

We look at every body on the beach. We never find Jed.

"There's a lot of shoreline," the man says finally. "Maybe he washed up somewhere else. It's dangerous to leave this cove but I could take you if you wanted. Or he could still wash up here. Never know, usually after a storm like last night we'll have stuff comin' up for days."

I walk to the edge of the water and he follows.

"Why do you call them Mudo?" I ask him.

He seems taken aback by my question. Even blushes a little.

"I guess I like it better," he says, his voice a little mumbled. "It's what the pirates who hunt along the coast call them. It means speechless." He shrugs. "Seems to fit."

"Where am I?" I ask, keeping my gaze fixed on the line where the water meets the sky.

"This beach doesn't really have a name. Not since the Return, anyway. "

I dig my toes into the fine sand. Another wave crashes around my ankles, causing my feet to sink into the ground a little. A few cuts on my calves protest as the salty water probes the wounded flesh.

"I have never seen the ocean," I say. I wonder what Jed would have thought, taking in the expanse of water. If Travis would be proud that I finally made it. That I survived. I collapse onto my knees and the man jumps in alarm.

He turns to squat next to me and together we look out at the way the sun sets the water sparkling.

"It's usually not so full of debris," the man says. "Storms like the one last night will cause a lot of timber to pour out of the river, will churn things up a bit and make the water cloudy. But I've never seen so many Mudo before."

I like the sound of his voice. Its depth, its tone. It reminds me of Travis, melts into my memory of Travis's voice, of the way the words slipped from his lips.

"I live in the lighthouse up there," he says, pointing up the hill past the sand to a tall tower painted with slanted black stripes.

"My job after the storms is to come decapitate all the ones that wash up so they can't get into the town."

I look around me. At all the bodies of the Unconsecrated littering the beach. "So much carnage," I say.

He shrugs. "The tide will come in and wash them back out again," he says. "In about six hours you'd never know there was anything here other than sand and surf. The beach will be what it always is. Just a beach."

"But there will be more of them," I say. "There are always more."

He shrugs. "That's just the way life is. Some days you wake up and the beach is clear and you forget about everything that surrounds us. And some days you wake up and it looks like this. That's the nature of the tides."

He shifts his weight a little. "That doesn't mean it's not worth being here."

I sway toward the water and dip my fingers in. "Is it safe?" I ask. "Out in the water?"

He shrugs once more. "Safe enough," he says. "It's an outgoing tide; it won't be pulling up any more Mudo from the ocean."

I slip into the water. Waves push me and I fight them to go deeper. Until my feet lift from the ground.

The man stands on the beach and watches, the tip of his shovel buried in the sand in front of him, his hands folded over its handle. Waiting for me to return.

I kick my feet and fall back and allow the water to cradle me. I touch my lips with my fingers, licking the tang of salt from them.

For a while I let the water push and pull me, lift me, hold me as I fall. I watch the sky, the clouds, the sun, the birds darting overhead. I wait for peace and happiness but I can only think of Travis and Harry and Cass and Jacob. About how I have lost everything but this place. I try to think about Jed, shame holding me back from remembering how he came after me. How he died saving me. But a part of me also thinks he could be proud that I made it, that I survived. That he knew what he was doing when he stormed into that Forest after me.

I feel the burden of carrying his hope with me.

I raise my head from the water and realize that I have drifted down the beach. I pull myself against the current, let the waves push me to the sand. I walk back down the beach toward the man, my limbs feeling gangly and heavy out of the water. He smiles at me as I approach and I can't help but smile back.

"Do you mind if I ask where you came from?" he says as we watch the waves crash on the shore.

"From the Forest," I say. "The Forest of Hands and Teeth."

He looks at me out of the corner of his eye. "I've always wondered if there were folks in there," he says. "Though I've never heard it called by that name. Apt, though, I guess."

"What do you mean?" I ask.

"I mean, I grew up here. On the edge of that forest. And everyone always says there ain't nothin' but Mudo past that river, beyond the fences. That's why they took out all those fenced paths that led from the forest to the town when my grandpa was a child. Too many kids thought the path led somewhere special and got into trouble. The bridge is still there, over the top of the falls, but there's a gate at the end and nothing beyond."

I think of our gate, of how the rain masked the sound of the waterfall until we were right up on it. Of how dark the night was, how impossible it was to see past your own body. How we were so focused on the Unconsecrated and escape. I shudder to think that we were that close. That there had once been a path but that we had fallen off track in the slippery darkness.

"Folks don't like to talk about those things," he says. He holds a hand over his eyes as he looks out over the water, surveying the world around us.

"Maybe they're right," I tell him. I think about Cass and Harry and Jacob and how there must be a way to rescue them from the Forest of Hands and Teeth. I think about Argos and the way he dreamed of happier times, feet twitching and tail thumping in the morning, one ear flopped up. I think about Jed and the way he smiled at me the night before. The way his eyes shone as he talked about the possibility of life and a future.

And then I remember Travis pulling me against him and telling me about hope. His voice in my mind is soft, just out of reach like a spent echo. I wonder if these memories are worth holding on to. Are worth the burden. I wonder what purpose they serve.

Already the ocean is washing around the Unconsecrated on the beach, pulling them back into the water, reclaiming them. For a while I stand and watch, until the beach is clear and the man takes my hand and leads me to the lighthouse.

# ACKNOWLEDGMENTS

Many people say that writing is an isolating profession. I have been phenomenally lucky to have found wonderful support and friends through the process of writing, and I am grateful to everyone who has cheered me on, offered advice and listened to my meanderings.

I owe a very special thanks to my agent, the thoughtful and hilarious Jim McCarthy, for taking a chance on me and pulling *The Forest of Hands and Teeth* from the slush pile. Also to my genius editor, Krista Marino, whose enthusiasm and dedication are astounding. Many thanks to the fantastic team at Delacorte Press, who work tirelessly to make sure every detail is correct; to Vikki Sheatsley and Jonathan Barkat for their vision, and to Beverly Horowitz, Orly Henry, and Colleen Fellingham for all of their time spent with Mary.

Diana Peterfreund and Erica Ridley offered wonderful critiques, enthusiasm and motivation. The Davis family understood when my head was in the clouds, and Jason Davis and JP offered their wealth of biological and parasitological expertise to help me fine-tune the world of the book.

I am very proud of and honored by the support of my family. More thanks than I can express to my mother, Bobby Kidd, who always believed she'd be able to buy my book in a bookstore one day; to my father, Tony Ryan, who has always indulged me in long talks about world-building; and to my sisters, Jenny Sell and Chris Warnick, who have always been my biggest fans in whatever path I have chosen. Thank you and I love you!

Finally, to John Parke Davis, for somehow talking me into going to that first zombie movie, for holding my hand and warning me about the scary parts so that I could make it through and for spending countless hours afterward debating how to survive the zombie apocalypse. And above all, for telling me to write what I love, even if that meant writing about zombies. Without you, this book would not exist.

Visit the world of the Unconsecrated again in
The Dead-Tossed Waves, coming in 2010

# ABOUT THE AUTHOR

Born and raised in Greenville, South Carolina, Carrie Ryan is a graduate of Williams College and Duke University School of Law. She lives with her writer/lawyer fiancé, two fat cats and one dumb puppy in Charlotte, North Carolina. They are not at all prepared for the zombie apocalypse. To learn more, please visit Carrie at www.carrieryan.com.